A FAIRY TALE

She was reclining on the rock, stretching herself like a tawny cat, propped on her elbows, with eyes closed and gentle face turned skyward. The sunlight glinted off the burnished tendrils of hair that had escaped her heavy topknot and kissed the warm ivory of her skin.

The rose-colored calico stretched taut over her breasts as she arched her back and drew up her knees, and a pair of shapely calves emerged from beneath the dampened drape of petticoats. With a contented sigh, she eased herself upright and slipped her bare feet back into the waters. Morgan swallowed hard, unable to look away. She was the loveliest creature he'd ever encountered, and he wanted her all for his own.

For days now he had been making his plans, with but one end in mind — their future together.

"What are you thinking about?" she called to him.

"Did you know that you were sit   ngling your feet in the water just as you ar   first day I saw you?" he replied. "I   story of *The Lady of Llyn y*   'ale my mother used to   how a certain lad can   wife."

Lexi's eyes we   she frowned and reached down to   at him. "Now you're teasing me."

"I'm not," Morgan protested. "She swore that it was true."

"Will you tell it to me?" she entreated.

"Well," he began . . .

CAPTURE THE GLOW OF
ZEBRA'S *HEARTFIRES!*

CATHERINE WYATT
BENEATH A HARVEST MOON

ZEBRA BOOKS
KENSINGTON PUBLISHING CORP.

ZEBRA BOOKS

are published by

Kensington Publishing Corp.
475 Park Avenue South
New York, NY 10016

First Printing: March, 1993

Printed in the United States of America

*To my sister, Karen,
who's always yearned for a simple lifestyle
and a farm of her own.*

Chapter One

Buffalo, New York, 1865

By the time the summer's sun had risen high enough in the sky for its brilliant rays to slip between the louvered shutters of her bedroom window, Alexandra MacLennan Merritt was already dressed to begin the day. She made a habit of early rising, for as she'd reminded herself often enough, it was essential to the smooth running of a household that its mistress not lie abed.

Brushing back the thick tangle of her red-gold hair, Alexandra hurriedly fashioned a plait and wound it into a coil, which she pinned at the back of her head. But before leaving the vanity table, she paused to regard the reflection in her mirror.

Would Brendan find her much changed? she wondered. She had chosen this dress, a cheery summer frock of pale blue silk trimmed in French lace, especially for his homecoming. But as she studied the face that stared back at her from the glass, a strange melancholy washed over her. No matter what she wore, she wouldn't be the same young girl he'd left behind.

Just yesterday when she'd visited the bank to bring her father a packet of papers he'd forgotten, she'd overheard a remark made by one of the young clerks to his companion as she passed by the tellers' windows. "Don't you know? That's Mr. Merritt's daughter. I wouldn't waste my time on her, though. She's wholly devoted to her father and acts more the part of a dour old spinster every day."

Try as she might, Alexandra had not been able to forget that hurtful remark, and she could not help but notice now the frown that seemed to be permanently etched on her features. The truth was that she seldom smiled anymore. There was scarcely time for frivolity in her life. She'd been left in charge of domestic matters when her mother died some twelve years ago. Her father had an important position to maintain in the community, and organizing his social calendar and keeping the household running in an orderly fashion took all of her time and energy.

For the most part, Alexandra didn't mind what anyone else thought. She took pride in her accomplishments and was happy with her place, but now Brendan was coming home—after four long years—and she could not help but wonder if he, too, would be disappointed with the solemn young woman that she had become.

Alexandra pulled a deep breath and tossed her head as if to shake loose all her foolish notions. She hadn't the time for this, especially not today. The tempting aroma of fresh-brewed coffee and frying bacon was already wafting up from the kitchen, and so she swept out of the room and hurried downstairs.

Along the way, she paused to remind one of the upstairs maids about some mending that needed her attention and stopped in the dining room to give instructions and a shopping list to the young kitchen maid, who was busy setting plates upon the table.

When Alexandra finally reached the kitchen, she found the cook bent over the stove, keeping a close eye on the bubbling pot of porridge while she poked a long fork at the bacon sizzling on the griddle. At first glance, Clara Fraser seemed a stern character, tall and broad-shouldered in her starched white apron with her iron gray hair pulled back into a tight knot—but Alexandra knew differently. The stern exterior was meant to gain her respect from the other servants. In truth, the woman was as softhearted as could be.

"Oh my, Miss Alexandra. Don't you look pretty?" she remarked, turning her attentions on her mistress. "Is that a new dress?"

"It is, indeed," Alexandra replied. "I have some calls to pay this morning. I must thank Mrs. Ashworth for inviting Papa and me to her dinner party last Saturday, and afterwards I thought I'd take Mrs. Truesdale a lemon cake and a jar of your strawberry rhubarb jam. Her rheumatism has flared up again, and she hasn't been able to leave her bed in weeks."

Alexandra did not make mention of the fact that she would also be going to the station to meet the two o'clock train. No one else seemed to understand her special friendship with Brendan O'Neill. Papa was far too busy to give it much thought, but Mrs. Fraser, who'd been with their family for years, considered herself obliged to offer Alexandra motherly advice.

9

And on this subject, the advice had always been that a young lady whose father was the president of the Merchants' Bank of Buffalo ought to find herself a young man more suitable to spend her time with.

Alexandra was not in the mood to be scolded this morning, and so she promptly changed the subject. "Has Papa come down yet?"

"Daisy took up his hot water nearly fifteen minutes ago. He ought to be down directly."

Alexandra wandered to the table where the serving tray was set and perused its contents. "If he's not down soon, I shall have to go up and fetch him myself," she said, lifting the napkin from the basket of biscuits and pinching a crumb from one as a sample. "He's expected in his office at the bank for an appointment at half past eight."

After she had finished examining the breakfast tray, Alexandra spied a bowl nearby, brimming with dark red raspberries. "What's this?" she asked.

"I'll be making my special tarts for dinner tonight," Mrs. Fraser explained, sounding particularly pleased with herself.

At this, Alexandra's brows rose slightly. She'd always planned the weekly menu herself. Mrs. Fraser had never varied from it before. "I thought I'd decided on baked custard," she said to remind her.

"The mister requested them himself," Mrs. Fraser explained. "Seems as how his lady friend took a liking to them last time she was here, and he wants things to be extra special tonight—"

"His lady friend?" Alexandra echoed, apprehension threading through the words. "You don't mean

10

to tell me that he's invited that widow, Mrs. Palmer, to dinner *again?*"

"Perhaps I oughtn't to have spoken," Mrs. Fraser replied to this. "He did say something or another about a surprise."

Alexandra's pale brows knit together as she approached the bowl of fruit, then carefully chose the plumpest raspberry she could find and popped it into her mouth. That's one less for Mrs. Palmer, she told herself, pleased with her small act of defiance.

"I thought he'd decided not to see her anymore," she said, "after all the rumors—"

Mrs. Fraser pretended not to be interested, and instead concentrated all her attentions on the stove, but Alexandra continued regardless. "She has a house in Canada, you know, but they say she isn't accepted by polite society there, so she's come across the river, hoping to escape the gossip."

Despite the indifferent stance she'd taken at first, Mrs. Fraser was now beset by curiosity, as evidenced by the knitting together of her brows and the frenzied tapping of one foot upon the slate floor. "Whatever is the poor woman accused of?" she asked when she finally could stand it no more.

Alexandra drew nearer to the stove and lowered her voice. "She pretends to be a lady of refinement, but they say that the truth is that she was no more than a common opera dancer when Colonel Palmer found her in Paris. She charmed him into marriage, and when he was assigned to a command in Canada, he brought her out with him. They say that all the while he was lying on his deathbed, she was carrying on with another man."

11

Mrs. Fraser digested this with a deep frown, then pointed her fork accusingly at Alexandra. "You shouldn't be listening to such talk, miss," she chided. "You can't put stock in such malicious gossip."

"No, but anyone with two eyes can see that this Mrs. Palmer is an 'accomplished' woman," Alexandra argued, "and Papa is so trusting. I'm only afraid he'll be hurt in the end."

But Mrs. Fraser did not agree. "He's a grown man, miss, and if you ask me, this Mrs. Palmer has done him a world of good. He's not spending nearly so much time locked up in his office lately. Why, I haven't seen such a smile on his face since—"

Mrs. Fraser left the uncompleted thought hanging in the air, but Alexandra knew well enough what she meant. Papa hadn't looked so happy since before Mama died, and quite probably she was right. But in spite of that, Alexandra was uneasy.

At breakfast, though, she did not mention Mrs. Palmer to her father at all. Let him believe Mrs. Fraser had kept his little secret. For now, Alexandra needed time to work on a strategy for revealing the Frenchwoman's true character, and so she made only polite conversation, reminded her father of his appointments, straightened his necktie, and then sent him down the front walk to his carriage with his portfolio tucked up under his arm.

After she had shown him the truth about his lady friend, he'd see how foolish it would be to go on seeing her. Miss Alexandra MacLennan Merritt was not about to allow herself to be supplanted by a French opera dancer. And one way or another, she would make certain that this woman would not have an opportunity to take advantage of her father as she had the hapless Colonel Palmer.

The train was late. Alexandra had been pacing the length of the platform for a quarter of an hour now, her anxiety increasing the more she contemplated the reunion that was about to take place.

Brendan O'Neill had been an important part of her life ever since she was a child. When her mother died, her father—in his grief—had buried himself in his work. There had been no one for Alexandra to turn to then, no one but Brendan. To her, he became the brother she'd never had, a trusted friend and confidant, and when she was with him, his joyful enthusiasm infused her.

All those years ago, before Alexandra's father had attained his present position at the bank, he had been a simple clerk, and they'd lived in a shabby but snug little flat near Main Street. The O'Neills lived in the flat downstairs, and it was thus that Alexandra first made the acquaintance of young Brendan: a boisterous lad, the same age as she was, but with a gift for squeezing every last drop out of life.

Surprisingly, she and Brendan had managed to continue their friendship even after Daniel Merritt moved his family up in the world, to the big brownstone with its two parlors and formal garden and carriage barn and staff of servants. Not that the O'Neills hadn't prospered. Brendan's father, Eamon, a hardheaded Irishman, eventually saved enough to rent a small storefront, where he sold dry goods, and by the time of Eamon's death, his family was secure—O'Neill's had grown into a thriving establishment.

13

Alexandra had been a fresh-faced girl when Brendan went away. When President Lincoln called for volunteers to put down the Confederate rebellion, Brendan and his brother Sean had signed up that very first day. "You needn't worry about me," he'd told her when he came to say good-bye. "I'll only be gone a few months."

But now Alexandra was twenty-six, practically an old maid, as she'd so recently heard herself described. President Lincoln had fallen victim to an assassin's bullet, and poor Sean was dead, only one of the many casualties of a bloody war that had dragged on far too long. And Brendan? Brendan was coming home at last, but who could say how these past four years had changed him?

The train pulled into the station at last, amid billowing clouds of steam and the metallic squeal of brakes. The platform was soon crowded with people: those waiting to greet the disembarking passengers, and vendors whose repeated cries carried over the hiss and chug of the locomotive engine, and porters already busily transporting baggage and stacking it upon the platform.

Alexandra retied the ribbons of her straw bonnet so the wind could not carry it off, then wrung her gloved hands tightly together as she scanned the crowd for a familiar face. At least half a dozen uniformed men caught her eye, but when she saw the brawny soldier with the tousled auburn hair, wearing a sadly tattered uniform that was faced with the bright green of the Irish Brigade, she began to wave excitedly.

"Brendan!" she called out. "Brendan, over here!"

He waved an arm over his head in reply, then began

to thread his way through the crowd. When he reached her at last, he tossed his bag down on the platform and lifted her into his arms.

"Lexi, darlin'," he said, his voice no more than a choked whisper. He squeezed her so tight she could scarcely breathe. "There was times I feared I'd never see this day."

"*I* never doubted it for a moment," Alexandra replied, conjuring up a cheerful smile for him, though her own voice threatened to break as emotion welled in her.

She drew back to meet his eyes, her own now brimming with tears. It was apparent at once that he was not the same boastful, vibrant young man he had been when they'd said good-bye on this same platform. There was a weariness about him, and the expression on the broad, boyish face was subdued.

"Why, Brendan, you've grown a mustache!" Alexandra remarked. Eager to lighten the mood, she reached out to run a gloved finger along its bristly length. This particular change amused her, and she found herself giggling like a schoolgirl.

"Mind your manners now," he ordered, "and stand back and let me have a look at you."

She did as he asked, turning around slowly. She couldn't miss the gleam in his amber eyes.

"A mite rounder than when I saw you last," he commented after a long silence. "I'd guess you've been allowin' yourself second helpings of Mrs. Fraser's peach cobbler. Or could it be that apple cheesecake you like so well?"

Now this was the Brendan she remembered. And it was good to have him back. Life had been far too solemn without him. It was fair to say that Miss Alexandra Merritt commanded a cool respect from all those about her—but respect was one thing she'd never get from Brendan O'Neill.

He still insisted on calling her "Lexi," the pet name her family had used for her when she was only a child, and he told her—when she'd asked—that Alexandra was still far too grand a name for the likes of her. He'd always teased her unmercifully, it was true, but he made her laugh, and she was grateful to him for that.

"Brendan O'Neill, you ought to be ashamed of yourself for saying such things—"

He laughed aloud then and pointed to the gold chevrons on his sleeve. *"Sergeant* O'Neill, if you don't mind, missy."

"Well, Sergeant O'Neill, four years of army life hasn't served to improve your manners at all. I've half a mind to enlighten your mother as to just what sort of rogue her son has become."

"Now, Lexi, you know 'twas all meant in fun," he defended. "Truth is, I haven't seen a woman to compare with the likes of you in all the time I've been away."

"It's too late now for your flattery," she told him with a mock frown.

"Not even if I tell you that I've spent my nights dreamin' of those eyes of yours, Lexi? Those eyes as green as the Irish hills. . . ."

There was a note in his voice that Alexandra had never heard before. It was a wistfulness, a painful longing, and she was hesitant to admit that the sound made her uncomfortable.

Slipping her arm through his, she cleared her throat and promptly changed the subject. "Come along now. The carriage is waiting, and your whole family will be anxious to learn that their prodigal son has returned home at last. I still cannot understand why you wouldn't let me tell them that you were coming."

Alexandra could not read his expression as he bent down to retrieve his bag. "I wanted it to be a surprise."

"It will be that," she agreed.

"And besides, I wanted to spend some time alone with you."

Again Alexandra felt a prickling of uneasiness. Once they were settled side by side on the seat of the open carriage, she gave instructions to the driver, then tried to induce Brendan to tell her something of his wartime experiences. "I worried about you, you know. Your letters were so brief," she said, hoping to prompt him.

"I'm not one for letter-writin' and that's the truth of it," he replied, still revealing nothing. "But I'd much rather hear your sweet voice, Lexi darlin', than listen to me own tales. Tell me all of what's happened since I've been away."

"*My* letters to you were long and detailed, Brendan," she reminded him. "I believe I kept you well advised on all that was happening here."

"Aye, but 'tisn't the local news and gossip I've been wantin' to hear. What I'm askin' you, Miss Alexandra MacLennan Merritt, is what you've done with your own life these past four years. You never wrote much o' that. You haven't gone and married one of them

17

fancy-dressed bank clerks who work for your father—but haven't yet found a way to break the news to your old friend?"

"Married? No. No, of course not. Who would take care of the house . . . and Papa? He'd be lost without me there to manage things."

"Well, I am glad to hear it," he replied, edging near enough beside her on the seat so that he could whisper in her ear. "Ain't a one of them puffed-up popinjays worthy of such a fine-lookin' lass as yourself."

The carriage jolted to a halt just then, and Alexandra was able to hide her blush by turning her attention to the storefront with O'NEILL'S painted on a signboard in large black letters. Through the window, she could see Brendan's mother, Maeve. She was standing behind the counter, chatting with a customer. The twins, Rose and Mary, who were sixteen now and already catching many a young man's eye, were busy arranging bolts of yard goods on the shelves.

Outside on the plank walk stood young Ned, broom in hand. He had on a long white apron that had been folded up to fit, and a mass of unruly red curls tumbled across his brow as he concentrated on his sweeping. As he heard the carriage approach, Ned looked up.

"Good afternoon to you, Miss Merritt," he called out respectfully, but only cast a curious eye at the man sitting beside her.

"Good afternoon, Ned," Alexandra replied.

"Ned? Can this be our Ned, then?" Brendan cried out as he jumped down and struck a pose before the bewildered lad, with chest puffed out and arms

18

akimbo. "Ah, but I don't believe it. Why, he was no more than a babe when I left. Don't you know me, lad? 'Tis your own brother, Brendan, come home at last."

Ned's gaze swept slowly upward, taking in the man who stood before him — from the shoes, scuffed and worn, to the poorly mended trousers, to the blue wool coat with its long row of brass buttons — and finally settling on the broad face, lit up by a friendly smile. "Brendan?"

The broom clattered onto the boards of the plank walk as the boy dropped it and rushing forward, wrapped his arms around his brother's middle.

Brendan's eyes were rheumy when he finally released the lad and reached up for Alexandra's hand. "Come along now," he told her. "Let's go inside."

Little Ned had already run ahead and was calling excitedly for his mother. "Ma! Ma! Come quick!"

Alexandra kept her place on the carriage seat. "No, Brendan, I have to go," she replied. "I've some errands to run, and there's so much to do at home. Papa has a guest coming for dinner tonight."

"Aw now, Lexi," he entreated.

The look in his amber eyes was hard to resist. But Brendan knew as well as she that their families did not understand their unusual friendship, and though Maeve O'Neill had always been polite enough to Alexandra, it was more than clear that she would prefer to see her son devote his full attentions to making a marriage with a nice Catholic girl, instead of contenting himself in a friendship with the high-toned daughter of a bank president, who was sprung from a long line of Protestant Scots. But was it only friendship he wanted? Alexandra asked herself now.

Brendan caught her eyes with his, which were glimmering with a warm, golden light. "We need to talk, you and I," he said, serious now.

"And we will," she promised. "There'll be plenty of time. But for now, you go on and enjoy this reunion with your family."

Before Alexandra knew what he was about, Brendan had climbed back into the carriage, taken her face in his two strong hands, and kissed her full on the lips.

"It's been four years," he said with a grin. "I don't intend to wait much longer."

Gathering up his bag, he jumped back down onto the plank walk and, without looking back, strode to the entrance of the dry-goods store, where his family had already begun to gather.

"Go on, then," Alexandra called to the driver, the irritation in her voice masking a whirl of confusion.

As the horses stepped up and the carriage rocked into motion, she pressed a gloved hand against her lips, still tingling from Brendan's startling kiss.

She had been trying to avoid the truth since he'd taken her in his arms on the railway platform, but she could not deny it now. Their relationship had changed with a suddenness that left her feeling unbalanced. Brendan had demonstrated quite vividly that he wanted there to be more, much more, between them. But Alexandra had never even imagined such a possibility.

This changed everything, and all at once she was angry. She felt as if she had been robbed of her childhood friend. She'd never needed to confide in anyone

20

else; and now there was no one else who'd understand. Oh, what was she going to do?

Sitting in her place at the foot of the table, Alexandra feigned an interest in her raspberry tart, flaking away the crust with the tines of her fork. Actually she had lost her appetite some time ago, but it was too early yet to excuse herself, and so she endeavored to slowly dissect her dessert and keep her eyes fixed on her plate, hoping to avoid being dragged into the conversation that her father was having with his lady friend at the opposite end of the table.

For the most part, the pair seemed content to engage in a cozy little chat between the two of them, but every now and again a question or comment would be directed Alexandra's way, requiring her to address the scheming Mrs. Palmer with much more civility than she would have liked.

"How thoughtful of you, *chère,*" the woman said to her then, and flashed a generous smile, "to arrange for the cook to prepare my favorite dessert."

Alexandra lifted her head to stare upon her adversary. This evening the widow Mrs. Palmer had chosen a low-cut dinner dress of deep sapphire blue, a color that was particularly flattering to her. Her lustrous chestnut hair was drawn back into a caul, weaved of matching silk thread and set with seed pearls, and her face was carefully painted to lend her a youthful appéarance, though Alexandra had it on good authority that she was well over forty. It was not hard to see why her father found the woman captivating. But once she'd found some way to make him see the truth about her, Alexandra told herself, he'd give her up soon enough.

"Actually it was Papa who gave Mrs. Fraser the instructions," she replied coolly.

"Not that Alexandra hasn't done a fine job managing things," Mr. Merritt put in. It was apparent that he'd been made more than a trifle nervous by the tension that had been hanging like a pall on the air all evening.

"But running an entire household is so much of a burden to put upon a young girl, Daniel," Mrs. Palmer replied to this. "When does she have time for her friends? A girl of her age ought to be spending her time at parties and picnics and other such things."

"Friends—? Why, I didn't think that she—" her father stammered, "that is to say, well, Alexandra seems content with things the way they are."

"I *am* content, Papa," Alexandra insisted firmly, "and I wish that the two of you would not discuss me as if I were not in the room. I am not a child, and I know well enough what I want out of life."

That final statement had slipped out so easily, but as soon as she'd spoken, Alexandra began to wonder if it were true.

"Pardonnez-moi, chère," Mrs. Palmer said sweetly. "I did not mean to interfere. It's only that when you are young and beautiful, the whole world can be yours."

For a brief instant, Alexandra met the Frenchwoman's dark eyes. She hadn't expected to see such sincerity there; it left her baffled . . . and silent. But she could not be deceived for long; surely the canny Mrs. Palmer was only trying to cloud the issue.

Alexandra endeavored then to turn her thoughts away from what might be missing in her own life and address the problem at hand: how to convince her father that his lady friend was no more than a fortune hunter who was using her considerable wiles to deceive him.

"I suppose that it's high time I give you the news, Alexandra," Mr. Merritt said then, and casting his eyes upon Mrs. Palmer with a secretive smile, he took up her hand.

Alexandra regarded him cautiously as trepidation flooded through her. "Papa?"

Daniel Merritt had always been a quiet man, absorbed in his work, peering out at the world over the tops of his spectacles only when occasion demanded it. It was Alexandra who'd insisted that a man of his position must maintain a social presence within the community. It was she who'd accepted invitations for them both and arranged dinner parties and receptions, which included the privileged elite of Buffalo society. And so, she realized ruefully, it was entirely her fault that her father had ever met this woman in the first place.

"Mrs. Palmer and I are engaged to be married," he announced, beaming with pride. "The wedding will take place in five months' time, at Christmas."

Alexandra felt the heavy thud of her heart in her breast as her worst fears were realized. "But, you can't!" she cried. "Papa, don't you see that she . . . that I—"

Clutching at her skirts with two tight fists, Alexandra rose up from her chair and cleared her throat in order to steady her voice. "If you will excuse me," she announced weakly, but with her chin still held high, "I think I shall go to my room."

Before anyone could object, she had rushed out of the dining room and padded up the stairs, her taffeta skirts rustling behind her. She flung the door back onto its frame with a slam that shook the walls, but resisted the impulse to throw herself down onto the bed and dissolve in tears. That would accomplish nothing.

Standing there in the darkness, with her arms clamped across her breast, Alexandra hugged herself tightly and began to pace the narrow stretch of carpet before her windows. This was *her* house, *her* life, *her* father, and there was no way that she was going to allow some scheming French opera dancer to take it all away. There had to be some way to stop this marriage.

She didn't have much time to consider the question, however, for she was soon interrupted by a sharp knock at her door and then her father entered. He seemed surprised to find his daughter standing silently in the darkened room, her stiff form silhouetted against the window.

"Has *she* gone?" Alexandra inquired.

"I've sent her home in our carriage," Mr. Merritt replied, and proceeded to light the lamp on the bureau. By the time he turned back to her, its yellowish glow had illuminated every corner of the room. There was nowhere for Alexandra to hide from the confrontation that was surely to come. "I must say that I'm disappointed in you, Alexandra," he began. "You're behaving like a child."

"You don't understand, Papa," she said, none-too-anxious to have this conversation at all. "You don't know what sort of woman she is."

"I know that she is kind and gentle-spirited," Mr. Merritt said. Drawing nearer, he absently ran a hand through his thinning brown hair. ". . . that she has had more than her share of misfortune, and I know, as well, that you have not allowed her even the slightest opportunity to prove her affection for you."

"You've been blinded, Papa," Alexandra shot back. "You believe precisely what she would have you believe."

She was deeply wounded by the adamancy with which her father defended the woman, even in spite of her objections. It was obvious to her that he had made his choice between them, and she struck back instinctively. "Your Mrs. Palmer may play at being the mild-tempered widow, Papa, but everyone knows the truth. She is no more than a scheming adventuress, who has already married once to improve her lot and then had the poor taste to take a lover to her bed before her husband was even in his grave."

In a reflexive response that was wholly alien to his nature, Daniel Merritt's arm shot out, and he slapped his daughter's face. He was just as shocked as she by the action, but he stood his ground and regarded her sternly.

"I thought I'd raised a sensible daughter, one who knew better than to give credit to malicious drawing-room gossip," he said, the hollow tone of his voice reflecting his disappointment. Shaking his head, he turned away, strode out of the room, and shut the door behind him.

Alexandra stood frozen, a trembling hand pressed

against her cheek where her father had struck her. In the course of one day, her comfortable world had been turned upside down, she had lost her childhood friend, and her father had become a stranger. What was she going to do?

Chapter Two

At sunrise the following morning, Alexandra slipped quietly out of the house. She carried with her a single carpetbag, packed with the basic necessities, and two dried-up biscuits left over from last night's supper, which she had filched from the larder, hastily wrapped into a handkerchief, and shoved into her pocket.

The streets in the residential section of the city were still quiet at this hour, but Buffalo was a busy manufacturing center with a population of eighty thousand, and for many the day had already begun. She passed more than one delivery wagon and a number of pedestrians, but thankfully no one who would recognize her and question her reasons for venturing out at such an hour.

When she reached the O'Neills' two-storied frame house at last, Alexandra felt some measure of relief. She hadn't been able to sleep at all last night after her father had left her. But she'd put the time to good use — in contemplation of her future. She had decided upon a course of action, and this morning she had already taken the first step.

Standing beside the fragrant hedge of honey-suckle that grew beneath Brendan's window, Alexandra bent down, picked up a few pebbles, and tossed them upward, where they clattered against the panes of glass. There was no response, and so a few seconds later she tried it again. This time the shade went up, and Brendan appeared, wearing a puzzled frown. When he noticed her standing below, he threw up the sash and stuck out his head.

"Well, good mornin' to you, Lexi," he called down. "Now ain't this a fine surprise? Go on into the kitchen; the girls are already up and about. They'll have the coffee on shortly."

"I can't, Brendan," Alexandra replied, keeping her voice low. "I haven't the time. I've only come to say good-bye."

"Good-bye?" he echoed.

With that, he motioned for her to wait and disappeared. In less than a minute, he'd come out of the back door. He was barefooted, but had slipped on a shirt and trousers and was dragging his suspenders up over his shoulders. He beckoned to her to join him on the back porch.

She did as he bade, and they sat down side by side on the wooden steps.

"Now what is all this nonsense about sayin' good-bye?" he demanded. "And what the devil do you think you doin' carryin' about that carpetbag?"

"I'm going across the river, Brendan. We don't have long to talk. I have to catch the ferry."

Brendan's expression grew solemn as he realized that she was serious. "What's happened?" he asked.

"I just can't stay here. Everything's changed. Papa's become engaged . . . to a widow, a scheming Frenchwoman. I've heard some awful things about her. I'm afraid he's been taken in this time, and there's nothing I can do. So I've left him a note telling him I've gone to stay with Gran for a while."

"You don't mean to say you're runnin' out? That you're plannin' to go off and hide at your grandma's farm 'cause you're feelin' a wee bit helpless. Why, that's not at all the plucky girl I remember—"

"I am not running," Alexandra insisted. "Papa's fiancée, Mrs. Palmer, lived in Canada before she came here. Once I settle in at Gran's, I shall go up to Hamilton and visit some of her old haunts—to see if I can learn the truth about her. It's clear that Papa will only listen to reason if I'm able to bring him some kind of proof."

Brendan leaned over and took up her hand. "Why don't you forget about all that, Lexi?" he suggested. "You won't need a place in your papa's house, not if you marry me."

Alexandra was shocked by this sudden proposal, but still managed a thin smile and squeezed his fingers tightly in reply. Brendan himself was the second reason for her leaving, though she could not rightly tell him so.

She had given a good deal of thought to the change in him in the course of the sleepless night she'd just passed, and she'd reached a conclusion.

During the war, Brendan must have called upon the memory of their friendship to sustain him, but in those times of fear and loneliness, he had imagined a deeper bond between them than had truly existed.

To Brendan, Alexandra was no longer just a childhood friend, but some idealized woman with whom he fancied himself in love. She knew that, in the end, she would only disappoint him, for she could never live up to his ideal, and she had no wish to hurt him. Brendan only needed time to settle into his old routine, and then he'd see the truth of things. And it would be so much easier for him to adjust, Alexandra told herself, if she went away for a while.

"I *have* to go, Brendan. You know how important our friendship is to me, but . . . marriage? Please understand, it's just not right for us."

Brendan was silent. He dropped his head, then slowly reached up to comb his fingers through his tangled auburn locks. He looked so utterly crestfallen that Alexandra felt she had to do something. "At least, not now," she amended.

It was wrong to buoy his hopes, she knew, but this small concession seemed to satisfy him, for a smile tugged at the corners of his mouth. "You'll change your mind, Lexi, just wait and see if you don't. Maybe you do need this chance to get away for a while—to think things over. And mind, I'll be waitin' right here for you when you get back."

Across the Niagara River lay the Niagara

Peninsula, which was part of the British province of Upper Canada. It was a rustic wilderness when compared with the burgeoning metropolis of Buffalo. There were a few country towns just over the border, and scattered throughout the surrounding lands were small farmsteads, one of which belonged to Anna MacLennan, Alexandra's maternal grandmother.

Alexandra took the ferry across the river to Fort Erie, then boarded a westbound train at the depot for the town of Ridgeway. From there, her grandmother's farm was some six miles to the northwest, not far from the village of Stevensville. If she had sent word she was coming, Gran would have sent Jacob down with the wagon, but there'd been no time to write. Alexandra told herself, though, that she didn't mind the walk. The road, a dusty wagon track, was wide and hard-packed, and although the summer's heat was intense, the tall pines that girded the route provided cooling shade.

When the sun was at its zenith, she stopped to rest for a while, settling herself upon a fallen log half-hidden in the tall grass by the roadside. She'd had no breakfast this morning. Her stomach was grumbling a noisy protest, and so reaching into her pocket, she drew out the handkerchief and unwrapped the two dry biscuits.

The soft breeze that had been blowing died away now, and the still air was stifling. Alexandra removed her gloves and began to fan herself with them. Her gray foulard traveling suit and the chic straw hat perched atop her head with its ribbons

31

and gauze veil might have been appropriate enough for the streets of Buffalo, but here in the wilds of Upper Canada, such stylish garb was wholly inappropriate. She'd been away too long, she told herself; she'd forgotten what life here was like.

Once she'd finished her meager lunch, Alexandra picked herself up and set out again, more eager than ever now to reach her destination. The last time she'd seen her grandmother was when she'd come to Buffalo for a visit last spring. They exchanged letters, but neither one of them seemed able to find the time to get away.

Alexandra hadn't been out to the MacLennan farm at all in the past eight years. When her mother was alive, they would go every summer and stay for an entire month. Of course, Papa had remained behind in the city; he couldn't leave his work. Even so, he did manage to visit once or twice on weekends, and she carried the fond memories of those childhood days with her still.

She had been walking for hours. By now her feet had begun to blister and ache, but even so she quickened her step, for the landmarks were becoming more familiar to her. Turning off the main road at last, she headed west along a less-traveled path that was bordered by fragrant, towering pines.

Ahead was a white clapboard farmhouse, sheltered by a stand of tall trees, and a gambrel-roofed barn which stood out in bold silhouette against the azure afternoon sky. Alexandra began to run. She was nearly out of breath when at last she reached the whitewashed fence that surrounded the house. "Gran!" she called out, gasping for air as she lifted the gate latch and stumbled into the yard. "Gran, it's me! It's Lexi!"

She hadn't referred to herself by her childhood name in a long while, but here — in this place — it sounded right. Here she could feel like a child again, and she found herself anticipating spending carefree summer days with her grandmother, just as she had all those years ago. And she decided that for now at least, she would leave sensible, capable Alexandra and all of her troubles across the river. Here she was simply Lexi.

Before Lexi could reach the house, her grandmother had come out onto the porch, wiping her hands on her apron. Gran never changed. She looked the same standing there now as she had in years past when Lexi had spent her summers here. Her dress was a faded blue cotton that matched the color of her eyes, and her thick gray hair was neatly plaited and wound into a coil pinned to the back of her head.

At first glance she seemed a frail woman, with her fair skin and slender frame, but Lexi knew how deceiving appearances could be, especially in Gran's case. Grandpa MacLennan had brought her here from Scotland as a young bride, and forty-five years of farm life in Upper Canada had toughened her up considerably. Through those years, she'd acquired a disposition that was hard as flint.

"So it *is* you, lass," she said, in a surprisingly

matter-of-fact tone. "I was beginnin' tae think myself daft, hearin' voices in the wind."

Lexi rushed to embrace her. "It *is* me, Gran," she assured her, smiling at the melodic ring of her grandmother's Scottish burr. "Aren't you surprised?"

Before her granddaughter could draw back to regard her, Anna MacLennan hurriedly reached to brush a tear from her eye. "Aye, that I am, but ye ought tae be ashamed o' yourself, frightenin' a puir auld woman like that."

"I'd have sent you a letter to let you know I was coming, but . . . but I—"

Lexi found herself stammering as she attempted to explain, but Gran didn't seem to be listening anyway. She was far more interested in inspecting her granddaughter from head to toe. "D'ye mean tae tell me that ye walked all this way frae the train depot?" she questioned. "And wearin' them fancy city shoes? I hope ye brought better than them in that carpetbag you're carryin', lass."

"I'm afraid I left home in rather a rush," Lexi admitted.

Gran eyed her suspiciously but didn't ask for details. There'd be plenty of time for talk later. "Well, then, 'tis just lucky that I've kept some o' your mother's things upstairs in her room. I'm sure you'll find somethin' tae fit."

"Where's Jacob?" Lexi inquired next. "I didn't see him out in the fields."

"I sent him tae Stevensville for supplies. He ought tae be back by this evenin'. Off wi' ye now and get out of them dusty travelin' clothes. I'll fetch some wash water directly."

Lexi did as her grandmother bade her, hurrying up the stairs to the attic bedroom which had once been her mother's. She was eager to see if Gran had made any changes there. To her delight, she found everything just as it had been. Somehow, though, the room seemed even smaller than she remembered.

A battered chest of drawers, washstand, and narrow bedstead filled up the space, and there was scarcely room at the foot of the bed for the worn leather trunk in which Gran kept some of the things that had belonged to Lexi's mother before she'd married.

The sloping walls were papered with a pattern of cheery yellow daisies, and while the blooms had faded somewhat over the years, they still brightened the room. With a pensive smile, Lexi recalled how, as a child, she'd slept beside her mother on the narrow bed, and how on bright summer mornings those daisies would be the first thing she'd see when she opened her eyes.

Removing her bonnet, Lexi set it on the chest and began to pull the pins from her hair. When she'd removed them all, she shook her head vigorously and combed out the heavy mane of burnished gold curls with her fingers. It was a great relief when finally she'd shed her traveling suit and petticoats. A breeze was stirring the curtains on the tiny window up over the bed, and the weather seemed much more congenial now as she stood there, clad in her muslin chemise and drawers.

With a sigh, Lexi eased herself down into the wooden chair beside the bed, unlaced her shoes, and gingerly removed them. She rolled down her stockings, pulled them off, and groaned when she saw the effects this morning's walk had had on her feet. There were blisters on her toes and heels and still other places where the skin had been rubbed raw.

"First of all," she remarked aloud, as she kneaded one foot and then the other between her hands, "I think I shall go and dangle these poor blistered feet of mine in the stream, down where the water rushes over the rocks—"

"Aye, an' while you're there, ye maun pick a basketful o' them blackberries frae the patch," Gran replied as she came in carrying a kettle of hot water, which she promptly emptied into the washstand pitcher. "No need in makin' a useless trip. We'll have ourselves a pie for supper. Jacob loves blackberry pie."

"Yes, ma'am," Lexi replied, pretending to be chastened by her grandmother's remark as she went to kneel down before her mother's trunk. She lifted the lid. "No need in making a useless trip."

Within the trunk was a tray in which was neatly arranged a number of hair ribbons, a worn pair of gloves, several handkerchiefs, and a book of poems. Taking the book in hand, Lexi opened the cover. The name *Grace MacLennan* was inscribed on the flyleaf, and though Lexi ought to have expected it, the sight of her mother's name, written in her own neat hand, unsettled her somehow.

Her mother been dead twelve years now, but here in this house where she had spent her youth, Lexi suddenly felt the pain of her passing as if it had only happened yesterday. She could not seem to look away from the page. Tears had begun to pool in her eyes, but she blinked them back fiercely and clapped the book shut, tossing it back in the trunk.

Once she had recovered her composure, Lexi lifted the tray and rummaged hurriedly through the contents beneath, at last drawing out a worn dress of pale green sprigged muslin. She chose a matching ribbon to tie in her hair, then got to her feet, and holding up the dress, she stood before the washstand mirror. The style was years out-of-date, and although the cuffs were frayed and the skirt a trifle short, she decided that it would serve her well enough until she could send for some of her own things.

When Lexi had put on the dress, Gran came to stand behind her and stared at her reflection in the mirror as she helped fasten her hair with the ribbon. "Ye do favor your mother," she told her, and for the first time the voice sounded wistful. "In that dress, wi' your hair all loose . . ."

Lexi studied herself in the mirror, wishing that she, too, could see the resemblance, but a long time ago she had accepted the fact that she would never be more than a pale shadow of her mother.

Grace MacLennan Merritt had been a vibrant woman, spirited and carefree, a natural beauty with glorious red hair. Lexi had always considered herself, by comparison, a plain sort: her own features were soft and bland, her blonde hair possessing no more than a glint of fire, and while it was true that some of her mother's traits were evident in her, they were tempered by the sober, responsible nature she'd inherited from her father.

Still, as Lexi's gaze turned to her grandmother's rheumy-eyed reflection, she could not help but wonder what the old woman saw that reminded her of her daughter. Maybe there was more of her mother in her than Lexi had imagined. The thought filled her with unexpected pleasure, and she turned around and clasped her arms tightly about her grandmother's shoulders. "Oh, Gran," she told her. "I'm so glad I've come."

Morgan Glendower wiped the sheen of sweat from his brow with the back of his hand, cast his line into the water once more, and settled down on the bank, propping himself against the nearby trunk of a tall tree as he drew up his long legs. Even with the heat, it was a splendid afternoon, and he would have been satisfied to do no more than bask in the summer sun, listening to the soothing sound of the water as it rushed over the rocks downstream. Thus far, however, he hadn't been allowed to relax, for the fish in these waters — perverse creatures that they were — struck at his line each time he cast it.

Morgan remained here, fishing rod in hand, even after he'd caught more than his share. He wanted to fill his mind and his senses with this rustic setting, for he knew that too soon he'd be obliged to leave it all behind. He hated the thought of abandoning this refuge, even for a few days, but his godfather, Arthur Sinclair, had invited him to Hamilton for a visit, and he simply couldn't put the man off any longer.

It wasn't that he was avoiding Sinclair, for in fact it was his affection for his godfather that had induced Morgan to emigrate to Canada. But he'd not been to Hamilton in almost two years, not since he'd broken with Celeste, and the city held nothing but bad memories for him. Still, he had to go.

Unbidden thoughts flooded his mind, and Morgan found himself unable to stem the tide. His jaw clenched as he prepared to meet his past, knuckles whitening as unconsciously he gripped the fishing rod tighter. Two years ago he'd been certain of his future—certain that he and Celeste would be together. He had told himself since that time that he ought to have tried harder to convince her to come away with him, but he supposed that he'd known even then that she didn't love him, not the same way that he'd loved her.

The merest remembrances of her still had the ability to torture him. He could still see those black eyes that mirrored the melancholy deep within her, the thick waves of dark hair spilling over her soft shoulders. . . .

Morgan shut his eyes tightly as if it could block out the memories; there was no good in dwelling on the past. Drawing a deep, cleansing breath, he concentrated upon the melodic trilling of a bird somewhere in the branches above him and the warmth of the sun on his face. He was thankful for the peace he'd found here in the wilderness.

With composure restored, Morgan turned his attentions downstream and was surprised when he caught a glimpse of a comely young girl emerging from the thicket. He visited this spot often, but he had never before encountered another human being here.

Studying her as she approached, he noticed that she was barefoot and clad in a simple dress that was the pale green color of new-mown hay. Tendrils of burnished gold hair that had escaped from the ribbon tied at the nape of her slender neck formed a bright halo of wispy curls about the soft oval of her face. Lingering by the bank of the stream, she reached into the basket on her arm, which was heaped with dark berries, chose several for herself, then slipped them one by one into her mouth. Mesmerized, he watched her slowly lick the juice from her fingertips.

Still unaware of his presence, the young woman set down her basket and proceeded to tuck the hem of her skirt up in her waistband, revealing to him the lacy fringe of her petticoat and a pair of shapely calves. Then, using the rocks that were scattered across the water like stepping-stones, she cautiously made her way to a smooth boulder that rested midstream. Settling herself upon it, she dangled her bare feet in the frothy foam of the churning waters and threw back her head, baring the arch of a smooth, white throat as she drank in the summer's breeze.

Watching her, Morgan was reminded of the tales he'd been told when he was a boy in Wales about *Y Tylwyth Teg,* the fairy folk. This one certainly had the look of a water nymph about her, he mused, and he told himself that he'd not be at all surprised if, before another minute had passed, she left her rocky perch, stepped down into the waters, and disappeared.

But she did not disappear after all. She lingered on the rocks for a long time, a satisfied smile curling on her full lips as she cooled her feet in the swirling waters. Morgan watched her in shameless fascination. He wondered if she might be no more than a vision that his mind had conjured to distract him from his memories of Celeste, for this creature was her opposite in every way.

All at once, the fishing line went taut, and instinctively Morgan clambered to his feet, pulling up on the rod as he began to reel it in. With that, a large trout leapt out of the water, writhing in the air for a moment before striking the water again with a splash. It was not long before he had reeled in his prize, and as he removed the hook from the mouth of the flailing fish and added it to his string, he remembered the young woman he'd been watching nearby and turned to see if she was still there.

The commotion had alerted her to the fact that she was not alone. Wearing a startled expression now, she met Morgan's eyes for an instant, then got to her feet and began to scurry back over the rocks toward the bank. In her haste, she misstepped, lost her balance and landed with a splash—bottom-first—in the shallows.

Morgan set aside his fishing rod and rushed to her aid, but by the time he reached her, she was already on her feet, wringing the ice-cold water out of her skirts. As she sought to regain her footing on the slippery rocks, though, she promptly went down again—landing in the same unladylike position. Standing on the edge of the bank, Morgan put out his hand to her.

"Are you all right, miss?" he inquired.

And then he laughed. He could not help himself; she looked rather like a helpless, half-drowned kitten as she stood up and shook her fair head, scattering silver droplets everywhere.

At this, a rosy blush stained the young woman's face. She formed her full, red mouth into a pout and glared at him. Refusing his help, she dragged her sodden skirts through the shallows and helped herself up the bank.

"You don't belong here, you know," she said sharply. She began to wring the water out of her skirts once more, and tossing back her head, she turned on him. "And you oughtn't to be fishing in this stream. You're trespassing. This land belongs to my grandmother, and we don't take kindly to poachers."

Morgan was left speechless by the fiery-tempered reply and by those eyes of hers, which were spitting emerald sparks. He struggled to gather his thoughts, but she did not even allow him the opportunity to defend himself. Hesitating only long enough to retrieve her basket from where she'd left it on the bank, she swept off, leaving him standing in stunned silence on the bank, his mouth agape.

Chapter Three

"Well, I can see you've nae lost your knack for gettin' into mischief, lass," Gran said, stifling a grin as she scraped a long peel off the potato with her paring knife and let it drop into the bowl in her lap. "I send ye off for blackberries, an' ye come home soaked tae the skin. A body would think ye'd know by now that ye dunna hae tae dive for 'em. I wonder ye didna drown."

"The water wasn't even a foot deep where I fell in," Lexi protested, and then finished kneading the pie dough in chagrined silence.

She sprinkled a bit more flour across the wooden board upon which she was working, reached for the rolling pin, then shook her head and sighed. Standing here before the woodstove, her dress had dried in no time at all, but even so it seemed she would not be allowed to forget this afternoon's misfortune. It was embarrassing enough to have had her clumsiness witnessed by a stranger, but now she had to put up with Gran's ribbing, good-natured though it may have been.

"Good afternoon!" a deep, masculine voice called out from the yard.

Gran got up at once, set aside her bowl, and went outside. Lexi absently swiped the wisps of hair from her eyes with a floured hand, leaving a dusty, white smudge across the bridge of her nose, and then followed her grandmother out to see who'd arrived. Wiping her hands on her apron, she drew up at the edge of the porch and felt the color drain slowly from her face when she saw that their visitor was the fisherman whom she had encountered earlier this afternoon down by the stream.

She studied the man more closely. Yes, it was indeed him. He was wearing the same striped cotton shirt, with dark trousers tucked into high boots of polished black leather that seemed to be molded to his calves. They were expensive boots, Lexi observed now. She'd been so flustered when she'd encountered him earlier that she hadn't noticed how tall he was, nor that his eyes were such a clear shade of blue. As he crossed the yard and drew nearer, Lexi fancied that she could almost see herself reflected in them.

"It's been pointed out to me that I've been fishing on your property without permission, Mrs. MacLennan," he began, and for the first time Lexi was aware of a deep voice with a cultured accent, "I suppose the only honorable thing for me to do is to offer you the catch."

He set down his rod, drew a crowded string of

fish from out of the covered basket he had slung across his shoulder, and offered them up.

Gran turned a suspicious eye on her grand-daughter. Although Lexi hadn't mentioned the presence of this fisherman when she'd related the story of her tumble in the stream, it did not take long for the old woman to deduce at least part of what had happened. She met the stranger with a pleasant air. "And a fine catch it is, Mr. Glendower," she told him, "but ye needn't ask my permission. We're neighbors. You're welcome tae fish on my land whene'er ye like."

Lexi was now more embarrassed than ever as she realized that this man was no stranger at all, but an acquaintance of her grandmother's. She shrank back against the wall of the house, wishing she could squeeze between the clapboards and disappear.

"Still, this is more than a meal for one man," he insisted. "I should be obliged to you if you'd accept them."

Gran weighed the offer. "Aye, I might do that, but only if you'll agree tae join us for supper." She paused, giving him a chance to consider. "Well? What say ye? Have we a bargain?"

Morgan considered her offer. Two years living in the wilds, and he'd only had the briefest contact with his neighbors. That was the way he'd wanted it; that was why he'd come here in the first place—for the solitude. He wanted to believe that it was only curiosity that had drawn him

46

here today, but there was more to it than that.

"We have, indeed, ma'am," he replied at last, and punctuated the statement with a brisk nod of his head.

With that, Mrs. MacLennan cast a glance over her shoulder now at her errant relation. "I'd venture tae guess that you've already met my granddaughter, Lexi," she said to him. "Splash a wee bit o' water on her, an' she forgets her manners entirely."

Morgan found himself grinning as he swiped a careless hand through his thick black hair. "I'm afraid we've not been *formally* introduced," he admitted.

He hadn't been sure at first about this decision—but now, as he watched the lovely young girl with the flour-smudged nose nervously shifting her weight from one bare foot to the other, he was glad that he had. "You mustn't judge her too harshly, Mrs. MacLennan," he told the old woman. "I do confess that I provoked her."

There was a twinkle in the old woman's eye. "Well, now, I wouldna be at all surprised if ye had."

Morgan Glendower favored Gran with a sly wink, and she smiled in return. For her part, Lexi was genuinely surprised by the air of familiarity between the two. She had learned long ago that her grandmother was not a woman easily charmed.

"I'll just take these fish out to the barn and clean them," he told them.

47

"We're much obliged tae ye, Mr. Glendower."

The man nodded to them both to acknowledge the thanks. Lexi pretended to pay him no mind, but still she could feel his gaze lingering over her before he turned on his heel finally and headed up the path to the barn.

Lexi strode promptly back into the kitchen, intent on finishing the preparations for her pie—and avoiding her grandmother's questioning stare. With her attentions fixed firmly on the worktable, Lexi fitted the dough into the pan and then proceeded to pour the berries into the shell. Her cheeks were flushed, but she told herself that it had nothing whatever to do with the encounter with Morgan Glendower; it was only the effect of the summer's heat and the fact that she was standing too close to the stove.

For a long while, the two women worked side by side in silence. "Mr. Glendower's cabin is just up the road," Gran said at last, as she leaned over the stove, lifting the lid to stir the vegetables bubbling in the pot. "He's a curious sort, that one. Been in these parts nigh on two years now, but we dunna see much o' him."

Lexi stopped fussing with the pie dough. Her brows lifted slightly, her interest piqued by this information. "In all that time, no one's learned who he is or where he comes from?"

"We may be curious, but we dunna pry into a man's business."

"But, Gran, he could be a thief or a murderer,

hiding out here in the woods, and you've invited him to supper—"

Gran scowled at her. "He's a gentleman," she insisted, " 'tis plain tae see that. You've spent too much time in the city, lass, tae think such things."

Lexi dropped her head, chastened. It was clear that her earlier childish display of temper and this distrust of Morgan Glendower had earned her her grandmother's disapproval. "I'm sorry, Gran, for being so suspicious. And I oughtn't to have lost my temper with your neighbor."

" 'Tisna like ye at all, Lexi, tae be impudent with a stranger," Gran noted. "But I imagine you're upset about whate'er it is that's made ye leave home in such haste."

At first Lexi ignored the unspoken question in her grandmother's words, concentrating instead upon the task before her: rolling out the remainder of the pie dough, then fitting it over the blackberries which she'd already arranged in the pan. But when she could stand it no longer, she let go a weary sigh.

"Papa's decided to marry."

"Well, God bless him," Gran replied, and shut her eyes as if to say a silent prayer. Surely the news had caused her thoughts to turn to her daughter, Lexi's mother, but after only a brief silence, Gran shook off the pensive mood. "There's no denyin' that a man needs a wife for himself."

Lexi was disappointed by her grandmother's complacent reaction. Somehow she thought they'd

49

be allies in this. "I've managed the household well enough on my own for all these years," she said, a bitter edge to her words now. "I remind Papa of his appointments and see that his meals are served and his shirts are pressed. . . . We don't need this Mrs. Palmer interfering in our lives."

"Och, come now, Lexi," Gran soothed. "Surely ye maun be old enough tae understand that a man of your father's age still needs . . . companionship."

"But *you* don't understand," Lexi protested, her agitation increasing. "She's a Frenchwoman and little better than a fortune-hunter. Papa doesn't need a woman like her. If she comes into our house, she'll turn everything upside down. She'll want to do things her own way. There'll be no place there for me."

Gran frowned at her. "Your father ne'er expected ye tae earn your keep," she replied. "Maybe this marriage will prove a good thing. I've always said that you took on too much responsibility when your mother died. 'Tis time ye learned tae enjoy bein' young."

With that, Gran laid a firm hand on Lexi's shoulder. It seemed meant as a reassuring gesture, but it told Lexi quite plainly that her grandmother would brook no further argument.

"It looks as if your pie is ready for the oven," Gran said to her next. "I'll take care o' that, and in the meanwhile, ye can fetch some water for Mr. Glendower and bring him out a towel and a cake of my good soap. He'll be wantin' tae wash afore supper."

Lexi obeyed her grandmother's instructions without question; she couldn't seem to muster the strength to continue to argue her case against her father's marriage just now anyway, and in spite of her grandmother's scolding, she was still curious about Morgan Glendower. If he was not a fugitive from justice, then why would such a handsome British gentleman hide himself away here in the country?

She collected the soap and a towel and trod up the dusty path to the barn, taking time to gather her thoughts as she stopped to fill the pail with water from the pump, for she was determined that this time she'd not make a fool of herself.

Just inside the open doors, Morgan Glendower had placed a wide length of board across the top of a barrel, and his dark head was bent over the makeshift table as he deftly scaled and filleted his catch. Lexi came to stand before him, set down the pail, and drew a wary breath. The air here was full of a pungent mixture of sweet grass and manure.

"Let's begin anew, shall we?" she entreated, putting out her hand. "I'm Lexi Merritt."

"Morgan Glendower," he replied, and knelt down to rinse his hands in the pail of water before he rose again to take the one she proffered. "I'm pleased to make your acquaintance, Miss Merritt."

The expression he met her with was sober and

51

earnest, but there was the faintest glimmer of amusement in his blue eyes and a smile playing at the corner of his mouth that told Lexi he had not entirely forgotten their earlier encounter. He caught her gaze in his and hesitated for a long moment before releasing her hand. "Lexi, is it? That's a rather unusual name."

"It's only a nickname, really, but I've been told it suits me," Lexi explained, an unexpected breathlessness in her voice as she reached to hand him the soap and towel she'd brought. "Gran thought you'd like to wash up before dinner."

"Thank you."

Beneath the fan of his dark lashes, those deep-set eyes of his continued to peruse her with a leisured thoroughness, and Lexi shifted her weight nervously from one foot to the other as she endured his scrutiny. She turned to leave him then, but to her surprise, he called to her. "Perhaps, Miss Merritt, if your grandmother can spare you from the kitchen, you might keep me company while I finish up here."

Lexi regarded him with a cautious air. She had decided that Morgan Glendower possessed a dangerous amount of charm. But despite her earlier suspicions about his character, there seemed to be nothing untoward in his manner. And she had to admit that she was curious about him. "I'll stay if you like," she said.

She settled herself upon a stack of fresh hay, which had been piled into the stall nearest the doors, and watched as Mr. Glendower went back to cleaning his catch. He worked with a swift precision, and she noticed now how long and slender his fingers were. There was no dirt beneath his nails. Likely Gran was right. Likely he *was* a gentleman. But what had driven him here, to this rough life? she wondered.

"So you've come to visit your grandmother," he began, without looking up from his work. "How long do you plan to stay?"

"I haven't decided yet."

"No doubt she's happy to have you. It's beautiful country, but it can get awfully lonely out here."

"Gran's an independent sort . . . sees her neighbors at church on Sundays, and that's often enough for her, or so she says. I've told her time and again that Papa wouldn't mind if she and Jacob came across the river to live with us—we've plenty of room—but she refuses to give up the farm. She's every inch a fiery Scotswoman and stubborn as a mule."

At this, Morgan stifled a grin. He had already learned, from his recent encounter with her, that Miss Merritt possessed more than a little of her grandmother's temperament. But he could not deny that she was a breath of sweet, fresh air that had swept into the stale sameness of his life.

"Jacob?" Morgan said, repeating the name he'd heard her mention.

"Jacob MacLennan," she told him, "He's my

uncle, although I never refer to him as such. You see, he's no more than a few years older than I am—"

"I believe I may have encountered him on the road once or twice," Morgan replied. "He's rather a quiet sort, isn't he? When we meet, he smiles but never speaks."

"Jacob has always been uneasy around strangers," she explained. "He manages well enough here, working in the fields and tending the animals but . . . to be honest with you, he is, well, different. He may seem normal enough to look at, but his mind is that of a child. There was some difficulty with his birth, as I understand it."

Morgan nodded sagely. He felt a pang of guilt for letting the girl believe he had no knowledge whatever of Jacob MacLennan. Even though he did not socialize much with the folk in these parts, he had managed to learn a little more about them each time he went into Stevensville for supplies. He'd heard of the young man living here, but never by name—he was always referred to by those with need to mention him as "Anna Mac-Lennan's poor idiot son." By feigning ignorance on the matter, though, Morgan had gotten a surprisingly frank assessment of Jacob from the girl. Clearly, the MacLennan family was not ashamed of their lesser member.

"Jacob is the reason Gran won't be moved from this place," Miss Merritt informed him then. "It's the only home he's ever known, the only place he feels comfortable. I suppose he'd never be happy living across the river with Papa and me."

"You seem very much attached to him."

She favored him with a sweet smile. "I spent my summers here when I was a child. Jacob and I were playmates. When I was old enough to understand, my mother explained that he'd never be truly grown-up and that we had to be patient with him."

Morgan watched as she resettled herself on the haystack, drawing up her legs and adjusting her sprigged cotton skirts so that only her bare toes peeped out from under the hem. He wondered now about this free-spirited, gypsylike creature with a decided aversion to wearing shoes. Where did she come from and what sort of life had she led?

"Tell me something of yourself, Miss Merritt," he prompted.

"There isn't much to tell. My life is rather commonplace."

"Somehow I cannot believe that. You strike me as the sort of woman liable to cause excitement wherever she goes. I already know that you live across the river in the States with your father. Is he a farmer, too?"

With this question, Miss Merritt bit down on her lip and developed an odd, faraway look in her eyes. "No, he . . . that is, I . . . Let's talk of something else, shall we?"

The pleasant note in her voice sounded forced,

and rising from her place, she walked beyond reach of the waning sunlight, and with her back to him, she began to pace before the empty stalls in the shadowy recesses of the barn.

Morgan finished filleting the fish, set down his knife, and knelt to wash his hands, all the while contemplating Miss Merritt's odd reaction to his harmless inquiry. He could only surmise that her home life had not been a happy one.

For herself, Lexi was wondering how things had gotten turned around. She'd come out here fully intending to learn more of the mysterious Morgan Glendower, but somehow he'd managed to steer the conversation so that she was the one doing all the talking.

"Enough about me," she said as she emerged from the shadows to meet him face to face. "You've a very distinctive accent, Mr. Glendower. Is it English?"

"Welsh," Morgan replied.

Before he could say more, he was distracted by a flash of movement outside. He turned in time to see a black streak cut across the barnyard and hear the deep, ominous snarl of a wild animal as it bounded full-speed toward them and leapt up, intending to spring upon the unsuspecting Miss Merritt.

In one swift move, Morgan caught her around the waist, flung her onto the hay-covered floor of the empty stall, and threw himself over her, shielding her body with his.

She let out a sharp cry of surprise, and then there was only the labored rasp of their breathing, and the low growl of the huge, black beast, which had regained its footing and drawn up a few feet away, its yellow eyes trained on them, fangs bared.

Chapter Four

Morgan found himself unable—nay, unwilling—to move, for in spite of the possible danger, a surfeit of pleasant sensations engulfed him now. Her breath was sweet and warm against his cheek, her heart beating an insistent rhythm against his own. He inhaled deeply, filling his senses with the heady mix of violets and new-mown hay, and the soft, slight body beneath him stilled for a moment as if she, too, was experiencing some distraction.

For the moment at least, the snarling beast held its ground. When it became apparent that it did not intend to attack them outright, Morgan regretfully eased himself up, then fumbled for the knife at his belt—remembering too late that the sheath was empty. The knife still lay upon the makeshift table where he'd been using it to fillet the fish.

Lexi gulped a breath of air as the weight of his body lifted suddenly. Rising up on her knees, she scrambled backward to the farthest corner of the stall. There was no denying that she was frantic

58

and trembling, but she told herself it was only out of fear. Even though Glendower had put himself between her and the huge, black beast, she could still hear the low, warning rumble that vibrated deep within its barrel chest.

"What is it?" she asked him, her voice scarcely a whisper. "Some kind of wolf?"

Her companion did not shift his attention; he was occupied with staring down the animal. "A wild dog, more likely," he replied. "Go out the other door and get back to the house. I'll try and keep it busy. But don't move too quickly—we can't be sure how it will react."

Lexi slowly got to her feet. She had no intention of leaving Morgan Glendower to face the wild dog alone and unarmed, though. He would need a weapon, but there was only the knife and it was too far out of reach. In another moment he would likely insist that she leave him. With her anxiety increasing, Lexi scanned the corners of the darkened stall until at last she spied the hayfork. With a sigh of relief, she reached for it.

Morgan was still considering his options as a shrill whistle pierced the air. At the sound, the growling dog fell silent. It lifted its head and turned, sprinting across the yard toward a burly young man with a thick thatch of red hair and generous sprinkling of freckles across his broad face. He'd drawn up his wagon in the yard at the bottom of the hill and was now striding vigorously up the path.

The air left Morgan's lungs in a rush as the danger evaporated. Behind him, Miss Merritt dropped the hayfork she'd been clutching, and as it clattered to the ground, she cried out, "Jacob!"

Heedless now of the great black beast gamboling at the young man's feet like a playful puppy, she swept past Morgan and ran headlong down the path to throw herself into Jacob's arms.

"Lexi?" the young man replied in an animated fashion. "Lexi? Is it you?"

The girl seemed only able to bob her head in reply to his question as, taking up his arm, she led him toward the barn. It took a while longer before she could manage to find her voice, and when she did, it was choked with emotion. "Is this monstrous beast who's pawing at my skirts another one of your strays?" she asked him, frowning in mock-irritation.

"Aw, now don't be . . . m-mad at him, Lexi. Hawkeye's a good dog. I . . . f-found him out by the south pasture last winter. He was hungry and he . . . f-followed me home." Morgan listened with interest. It was the first time he'd heard Jacob speak. But for the stammer and slow speech, the young man seemed fairly bright. Somehow he'd expected worse.

"I ought to have known," Miss Merritt said, turning a grateful smile on Jacob as he pointed a finger and the great beast promptly sank down on its haunches. "I've come for a visit, Jacob," she said to him next. "What do you think of that?"

"I'm glad, truly," the young man responded, reaching to swipe away the tears that had begun to pool in his wide, gray eyes. "You've . . . n-nae come tae see us in a long while."

Morgan's attention was fixed on Miss Merritt as she cast her own rheumy eyes downward, and her pale cheeks flushed with color. In fact, he couldn't seem to look away. It was as if she'd bewitched him. The memory of her scent and her soft body pinned helpless beneath his returned to him in a sudden rush. He hadn't felt this alive in months.

"I know," he heard her say. "I know, and I'm sorry. Lately it seems that I've been so busy taking care of Papa." Reaching up, she smoothed Jacob's ruddy, wind-ruffled hair. "You aren't angry with me for staying away so long, are you?"

"I couldna be angry wi' ye, Lexi."

Again Jacob reached to embrace her, but this time the act was accompanied by a garbled chirp which caused him to draw back in startled surprise. "The bird! I'd . . . f-forgotten."

The pair drew up only a few feet from the place where Morgan stood, and he watched curiously as Jacob MacLennan reached to withdraw a fluttering brown bird from his pocket and gingerly cupped it in his two hands. "I . . . f-found her in the woods. She's hurt. She canna . . . f-fly."

Miss Merritt drew nearer to examine the wounded bird. She lightly stroked its feathers with the tip of one finger, but it only shivered in reply, too weak to protest. Her gentle expression was

61

marred by distress as she noticed something. "Oh, Jacob! It's her wing. I think it's broken."

Lexi could scarcely believe that she'd forgotten about Morgan Glendower, but as he approached them now and reached out to take the poor, frightened creature from Jacob's hands, she was, in fact, surprised to see him there. His heavy brows drew together, and he studied the bird in cautious silence before commenting.

"She's a fragile thing," he said at last, "but we can try and set the break, if you like."

Jacob had worn a puzzling frown when first he regarded Mr. Glendower, but now a broad smile spread across his face. "I know you. You're the . . . m-man from the cabin down the road."

"This is our neighbor, Morgan Glendower," Lexi explained to him.

"Pleased tae meet ye . . . M-Mister Glendower," he replied.

"And I'm pleased to meet you, Jacob. But if we're going to be friends, you must call me Morgan," Glendower instructed with a friendly smile. "Now how would you like to help me set the broken wing?"

Jacob nodded; he was brimming with enthusiasm. "D'ye think I can?"

"I'd welcome the help. Now, you do understand that she'll be in your care. You'll have to spoon-feed her for a while—that's if she'll take it—and there's only a chance—and a slight chance, mind you—that she'll come through all right."

Jacob nodded, his features taking on a sober air. "I understand . . . M-Morgan."

"Come along into the barn, then, and we'll work on it together."

They left Lexi standing there, dumbstruck. She had to admit that at first she'd been worried about how Mr. Glendower would react to Jacob. Most people were uneasy and shied away from him, unsure of what to say and how to act. But Morgan Glendower had easily made a friend of him within minutes. And this made Lexi more curious about him than ever.

In honor of their guest, Gran covered the kitchen table with a linen tablecloth and instructed Lexi to set our her prized blue willow dishes. When they all sat down at last, Lexi found herself directly opposite Mr. Glendower. She thought briefly that it might be uncomfortable to have his eyes on her for the duration of the meal, but she needn't have worried, for as soon as Gran had offered the blessing, his attention turned full on his plate.

Morgan Glendower was no small man, but still Lexi was surprised by his appetite. It was a compliment, she supposed, to all the work she and Gran had put into the meal: fish fillets, breaded and fried, summer squash, greens, biscuits — and blackberry pie. But as Glendower reached for a third biscuit, she wondered if he'd underestimated himself when he'd told Gran that he couldn't possibly have eaten all the fish he'd caught. Needless to say, the dinner conversation was nonexistent.

"Jacob's brought home a wounded bird," Lexi told Gran, hoping to fill up the awkward silence. "Mr. Glendower helped him to mend the wing."

"What kind of bird is it?" Gran proceeded to ask Jacob.

"A wee one," he replied, "w-with brown speckles."

" 'Twas kind of ye tae offer your help, sir," Gran said to their guest. "I hope my son hasna been too much trouble."

Mr. Glendower looked up. The question in his eyes made it plain that he hadn't been listening as closely as he should have been. "Forgive me, Mrs. MacLennan," he said, chastened. "But you set such a fine table, I find myself overwhelmed. The meal is . . . superb. I've been cooking so long for myself that I've all but forgotten what food tastes like that hasn't been burnt first."

"When then we maun invite ye more often," Gran replied. "I wouldna like tae see such a fine brawny man waste away tae nothin'. We'd welcome the company, too. We dunna get much news of the world except when we go into Stevensville."

"I have the newspapers sent down from Hamilton," Mr. Glendower told her then, "but most of what I read in them we can well do without. Occasionally there are interesting items, though.

"People are worrying again about the Americans," he went on to explain. "Now that they're done with their war with the Southern states, it's supposed they'll begin to look our way, instead of keeping their noses on their own side of the border where they belong."

Lexi bit down on her tongue and let his disparaging comments about Americans pass without remark. He was a guest, and she knew how Gran would react if she were to take him to task at the table. Besides, she was finally beginning to learn something of the man.

"Aye, there's always talk," Gran said to him in reply.

"There'd be a quick enough end to such talk if the provinces would quit squabbling amongst themselves and band together for the common good. United we'd be strong enough to—"

With this, he stopped himself mid-sentence and adopted a contrite air. "I must beg your forgiveness again, ladies," he said. "It was inexcusable of me to speak so vehemently. I've been removed from polite society for too long. I'm afraid I'm no longer a fit dinner companion."

Lexi waited for Gran to respond, but Gran was looking at Jacob now. He'd taken the stub of a pencil out of his pocket (it was a prized possession of his, for Jacob loved to draw), and he'd begun to make a picture upon the tablecloth before his plate.

"Jacob?" Gran cried out in dismay, "Aw, Jacob,

what are ye up to—scribblin' on my best white tablecloth?"

" 'Tis the bird," he explained, pointing at the sketch he'd rendered. "I've . . . m-made it with my pencil, so ye could see."

Gran softened as she met his eyes, then craned her neck to see his drawing. "Aye. Aye, lad. 'Tis a fine bird."

"You're quite an artist, Jacob," Mr. Glendower added, trying to smooth things over.

After that bit of excitement, the conversation settled into the usual discussion of the weather and what the neighbors might be up to. Once supper had been eaten, Jacob went out to the barn to see to his bird. Mr. Glendower offered to help with the dishes, but Gran shooed him out onto the porch to finish his coffee and sent Lexi out shortly thereafter to keep him company. Lexi obeyed this particular order without question. It was, she decided, her chance to indulge her curiosity and finally discover precisely who this man was and where he'd come from.

"Gran sent me out here to entertain you," she announced as she stepped outside and crossed the porch to rest her hands on the rail.

Mr. Glendower, who'd been sitting on the steps, set down his mug. Drawing up his long legs, he stretched out his arms and then, lacing the fingers of his hands together behind his neck, he leaned back against the support post. As he gave her his full attention, he grinned shamelessly, his blue eyes sparkling with mischief. "Ah, entertainment! And just what did you have in mind, Miss Merritt?"

At this, Lexi felt her face flush with color, and she cast her eyes downward. He was certainly not a shy man. "Well," she drawled, scuffing a bare toe on the weathered boards of the porch floor. "I'm afraid I'm not much good at singing or dancing . . ."

"That *is* a shame," he remarked, looking solemn enough but for the wry smile that twisted on his lips. "How about a dramatic recitation, then?"

Lexi wasn't certain if he was making fun of her or only aiming to amuse them both. She decided to give him the benefit of the doubt, though, and sank down on the porch steps beside him, regarding him closely before she gazed off toward the horizon where the waning sun cast a ruddy glow.

" 'Calm security and a life that will not cheat you, rich in its own rewards, are here.' " Although she began softly, her voice gathered strength as she continued: " 'The broad ease of the farmlands, caves, living lakes, and coombes that are cool even at midsummer, mooing of herds, and slumber mild in the trees' shade . . . Then let the country charm me, the rivers that channel its valleys, then may I love its forest and stream, and let fame go hang.' "

She'd hoped that this particular quote might prompt him into revealing something of himself, but he met her with such an incredulous look that she felt compelled to explain. "It's a favorite of

67

mine," she said, "from Virgil's *Georgica* . . . translated from the Latin."

"Yes," he told her. "I recognized that, but however did a simple American girl—"

Lexi had listened in polite silence at dinner as he'd voiced his dislike for Americans, and in truth she hadn't taken it personally. But it was the word "simple" that vexed her now.

She got to her feet and stepped out into the yard, expending her energy by pacing back and forth in the dust as she scowled at him. "We're not all barbarians across the river, Mr. Glendower, despite what you might think. We Americans have books and some of us can even read."

With that, she turned her back on him and pushed through the dooryard gate, heading for the orchard. What was the use in this? No matter how she tried to draw him out, this man always seemed to find a way of turning the conversation back to her. She'd never find out about him, and at this point she wondered why she even cared at all.

"That wasn't what I meant," he explained anxiously, as he hurried after her. "Please, Miss Merritt . . . Lexi. I am sorry if I've offended you. What can I do to apologize?"

Lexi stopped suddenly, pretending to admire the wisps of clouds that had spread across the crimson sky as she reconsidered her chances of learning his secrets. A soft breeze was rustling the leaves in the apple trees overhead and carried on it the sweet scent of ripening fruit. Settling herself on an overturned stump, she met him with a sly smile. "Well, Mr. Glendower . . . let's say you entertain *me* for a while."

When he saw that her anger had dissipated, he flashed her that brilliant smile of his and crossed his arms over his chest as he leaned back against a nearby tree trunk. "What a shame that I can't sing or dance," he said, borrowing her excuse.

"Oh, I won't let you off that easily," she retorted. "Tell me a story, then."

His handsome face was solemn as he considered. "I'm afraid I don't know any interesting stories—"

"How about the story of a young gentleman who leaves his home and family and crosses an ocean to settle in the midst of the Canadian wilderness . . ."

As soon as he realized what she was about, his expression turned grim. Even his voice had lost its vibrance. "You don't want to hear that story. There's an unhappy ending."

But Lexi was not about to be put off again. "If you ask me, I'd say the ending's not been written yet," she protested.

"As well as, Miss Merritt," came his terse reply.

If Lexi had been curious about this man before, she was doubly so now, but he sought to escape her by hiding himself deeper in the growing shadows of the orchard. Undaunted, Lexi scurried after him, closing the distance between them and hovering just behind his left shoulder as she spoke. "You can't really believe that, Mr. Glendower . . . Morgan. We all control our own destinies."

Lexi could not see his face, but she heard the harsh bark of his laughter. It was not a pleasant sound; in fact, it did not sound like him at all. "You're so young. You don't even know what you're talking about."

The remark stung, but Lexi bit back a sharp retort. She knew he was responding instinctively, and his vehemence told her that something—or someone—had hurt him badly. She could not deny that she'd been a little afraid of him at first, afraid of the secrets he might be hiding, but now she only wanted to help him, to somehow ease the pain she'd seen in his eyes. She reached up to lay a comforting hand on his shoulder and felt his muscles tighten beneath it. "Then tell me so that I can understand."

In an instant, all Morgan's thoughts fled and he was aware only of the pressure of her slight hand on his shoulder and of the heat that seeped through the fabric of his shirt, warming the skin beneath. He tried to draw a breath, but his lungs would not obey. He'd not been this close to a woman in two years, he'd never wanted to be again, and yet—

Turning, he took a bold step nearer to her, until he was so close that he could hear her surprised intake of breath and see a blush of color spread from her collar to the roots of her hair. She cast her eyes downward, and he found himself unable

70

to read anything at all in them, veiled as they were by the golden fan of her lashes.

Some rebellious part of him made him reach out for a tail of her hair ribbon and tug until it slipped free. He watched in fascination as the fading light of day caught the reddish highlights in her golden hair, seeming to set it ablaze as it washed over her shoulders. For so long, Morgan had felt frozen inside, chilled with the loneliness. This woman seemed to have all the fire and warmth that his wounded spirit had been yearning for.

At last he managed a long, quavering breath. The air was thick with the scent of summer grass and damp earth and ripening fruit . . . and violets.

"I don't want to talk anymore," he said, his voice so deep with need that he scarcely recognized it himself.

She turned her face up to him, and a question flashed in those deep green eyes of hers, but Morgan paid no heed. This was madness, he knew, but his purpose was fixed, his concentration centered on the soft fullness of her parted lips. Before she knew what he intended, he'd slipped one hand into the silken mass of her unbound hair to cup her head, and gently catching her chin between his thumb and forefinger, he claimed a kiss.

Lexi's eyelids were heavy. They drifted shut as his lips coaxed hers to response. The hand he'd entwined in her hair slipped lower now and his long fingers began playing upon the tender skin at the nape of her neck. Delicious waves of heat radiated from the spot, warming her to the tips of her toes. Odd, she thought with surprising clarity, this was her second kiss in as many days, but she hadn't felt this way when Brendan kissed her. Somehow now there was warm molasses running in her veins. The marvelous sensation muddled her thinking and kept her from fighting him.

In a far-off corner of her mind, Miss Alexandra MacLennan Merritt was shocked to the core of her Protestant upbringing. Oh, but Lexi was enjoying this; Lexi wondered why she'd never realized before how delicious a kiss could be. Still, she had not lost her senses completely. She knew she must stop this at once. It was hardly proper. She was behaving like . . . like a common barmaid from one of the dockside taverns back home.

When finally she managed to gather the strength to raise her palms to his chest and push him away, she was left to contend with the startling rebelliousness of her own body. Her heart was hammering a frantic pace, her head spinning like a child's top, and her wobbly legs threatened to give way at any moment. All this because of a kiss, and a stranger's kiss at that. She still knew nothing at all of this man. Just how far would Morgan Glendower go to keep her from learning his secrets? she wondered. How far would she let him go?

Lexi did not want to hurt him. She knew, with

an uncanny certainty, that his heart had already been gravely wounded. But he was looking at her in that way again, with lids half-closed and purpose glittering in the icy blue depths of his eyes. She knew that she had to say something to distract him.

"Whatever it is that's haunting you," she began, her voice soft and quivering. "I'd like to help, if only you'd let me. If only you'd tell me . . ."

His long arm shot out in a fluid arc and hooked her waist. He drew her against him, whispering urgently against her ear. "Don't make me remember, Lexi. Help me to forget."

In an instant, his lips were on hers again. Lexi felt her strength draining away. She, who was so accustomed to taking charge, could not control this situation, and she was truly frightened.

When she stiffened in his arms, he drew back to look into her eyes, but he did not release her. Instead, he took another tack, whispering soothing words against her hair while his strong hands slipped to the small of her back, urging her nearer still to him.

"But I—I can't—I don't even know who you are," she protested, drawing a ragged breath as she lifted her fingers to her lips, still burning from his kiss. "I need to know."

With that, Morgan released her, stumbling back awkwardly.

Damnation! Why did there have to be questions? Was the girl so naive that she couldn't see it there in his eyes? Did he have to spell it out for her? He was a fake, a failure, a fool of the highest degree. Surely everyone could see it.

"Here's your story, then," he said with a harsh growl, "the one you've been so bloody anxious to hear. 'Tis the tale of a young man, sick to death of war, who seeks a new life for himself in Canada. But what he finds there is love . . . with another man's wife."

Lexi felt the color drain away from her face. She was shocked, but determined not to show it. After all, she'd asked him for this, hadn't she? It was her infernal curiosity that spurred her on, making her ask questions whose answers she did not want to hear. "Was she very beautiful?"

"Yes. God, yes." His voice was deep with aching need. "The most beautiful woman he'd ever seen. A tall, dark-eyed Venus with chestnut hair, and every bit as graceful and well-mannered as she was beautiful."

Lexi felt an inexplicable ache in her breast. "A paragon," she muttered softly.

"Precisely," he replied, the word honed razor sharp.

Lexi had a sudden, vivid flash of memory—of their meeting this afternoon, when she'd slipped and fallen in the stream and then railed at him for laughing at her, as if her clumsiness were his fault. She wondered if he had not itemized his lady's charms only in order to point out to her her own failings, for Lexi was this beauty's opposite in every way.

"The husband dies," he continued, without emotion. "A happy circumstance for our young gentleman, you say? But as I've already told you, there is no happy ending to this tale. Everyone suspects that the young man is responsible for the death, although there is no proof. Even the beautiful wife begins to watch him askance . . . wondering if he's guilty."

"And . . . is he?"

Glendower stiffened and then turned away, looking off toward the sunset so she could not meet his eyes. "What? Would you have me be a murderer?"

"I've asked you to tell me a story, that's all," she replied as calmly as she was able. "We've not once mentioned any names."

"Lexi? Lexi? Where've ye gone off to, lass?"

At the sound of Gran's voice, the mood was broken. It would not do for Gran to come out here looking for her, and so Lexi called out promptly in reply. "Coming. . . ."

When he turned back to her, his feelings were well hidden behind a mask: heavy, black brows drawn over eyes so cold they sent a chill through her, even from this distance, and a mouth that was set in a hard line. Every feature from the broad, square forehead to the deep cleft of his chin seemed set in stone.

He cleared his throat and formed an apology.

"I'm sorry for everything that's happened tonight. Your family has offered me kindness, and in return, I've taken unpardonable liberties. So, you see what sort of man I am."

He turned to walk away, then hesitated, his eyes trained on the ground before him. "Thank your grandmother for the meal for me. Goodnight, Miss Merritt."

Chapter Five

Lexi oughtn't to have been surprised to find how swiftly the weeks passed. But she'd forgotten that the routine of farm life left little time for idling: up at five, breakfast by six, wash the dishes afterward, gather eggs and feed the chickens, and back to the kitchen to prepare the noon meal. And at this time of year, in addition to the daily chores, there was weeding to be done in the kitchen garden, and pickling and preserving that required hours spent laboring over the hot stove. On more than one occasion as she sank exhausted into her bed at night, Lexi found herself wondering how Gran and Jacob had managed for all these years on their own.

With her every waking hour occupied, she had been able to put aside the troubles she'd left across the river, but somehow she hadn't been able to forget her charged encounter with the mysterious Welshman, Morgan Glendower. Although he had not crossed her path at all since that night he'd come for supper, the memory of a stolen kiss in the orchard and the unmistakable pain she'd read in his eyes returned to her often and fueled her curiosity about the man. If she'd been honest with herself, she might have admitted that she was only waiting for an opportunity to see him again. . . .

There was no denying that Jacob MacLennan had an affinity with animals. One had only to observe how the black hound Hawkeye trailed at his heels like an obedient puppy or the way in which the speckled brown bird would poke its tiny beak between the willow bars of its cage whenever he came near in anticipation of the breadcrusts he would offer. But when, after a few weeks of captivity, his bird took to fussing and fretting, Jacob had no idea what to do.

"She's . . . d-dyin', Lexi," he remarked frantically one morning after breakfast as they stood together on the porch.

The bird had just refused his offering of toast scraps with a wild squawk and awkward fluttering of her bandaged wing.

Lexi gently touched his arm. "Oh, no, I don't think so," she replied, although in truth she had no idea what was amiss.

"But she . . . w-won't eat anythin', and she flaps her wings at me like she's angry. I dinna . . . w-want her tae die."

" 'Tis in the Lord's hands," Gran called out from the kitchen. "Dinna fash yerself about it, lad."

Although Gran might not have considered it a

serious matter, the crestfallen look on Jacob's broad, freckled face was more than Lexi could bear. "Mr. Glendower did such a fine job bandaging her wing," she reminded him. "Do you think he might be able to tell us what's wrong?"

Jacob considered the idea and brightened at once. "Aye. Aye, he might."

Lifting the cage by its crudely fashioned handle, he pushed it toward her. "But I've chores to . . . d-do. Will you take her to him for me?"

Lexi could hardly refuse him, but then she had not intended to. This was precisely the opportunity for which she'd been waiting. And so she snatched a sunbonnet from the kitchen peg, informed Gran of where she was bound, and with cage in hand, she started off down the road.

Along the way, Lexi considered what it was about the Welshman that intrigued her so. He seemed to have so many secrets. She had learned some of them, and what he'd already revealed to her was by no means flattering. What she did not know about him could prove worse still. She ought to keep her distance, she told herself. Idle curiosity was a dangerous thing. But there was more than curiosity involved here, Lexi felt sure of that. Was the truth that she felt she might help him with his troubles somehow, or did she only hope to experience again the thrill she'd felt when he'd touched his lips to hers?

The thought made her blush, and the pleasant warmth that flooded through her was not caused wholly by the heat of the sun on her back. She promptly put away such thoughts, concentrating her attentions instead upon a hawk circling in the cloudless sky high above the green, fringed tops of the pine trees. At the sound of its cry overhead, the speckled brown bird fluttered anxiously against the bars of the cage in her hand.

The day was clear and still, the air scented with a fragrant mixture of sweet grass and pine. Lexi allowed herself to be swept up in the beauty of the late summer day and the rustic scenery as she followed the gentle slope of the road, humming snatches of a half-remembered tune from her childhood. When she reached the crest of the hill, she paused to admire the picturesque wooded valley below and the clearing where Morgan Glendower's cabin stood.

The cabin was fashioned entirely of rough-hewn logs. It was larger than Lexi had imagined it to be, though, and had a deep porch that ran along its entire length, with a low table at one end and a battered wooden rocking chair standing beside the door. Some yards away from the main structure was an outbuilding that she guessed served as the barn.

As she studied the scene, Lexi noticed that Glendower was nearby, hard at work. His dark head was bent and his back was to her, but she knew him just the same. The sun glinted off the curved blade of his scythe as he cut a wide swath through the tall grass in the dooryard, and she found herself following the graceful swing of his movements in silent fascination.

The fabric of his blue chambray shirt was dampened with sweat and pulled taut across his broad muscled back with each powerful stroke. He'd rolled his sleeves to the elbow for comfort, revealing a pair of forearms that were tanned to a warm bronze. Lexi studied him appreciatively. It was a powerful image, indeed: the tall, broad-shouldered man intent on his work.

Lexi hesitated, reflecting on her own appearance. Her face was no doubt streaked with dust and sweat from her walk, and beneath the broad-brimmed sunbonnet, much of her hair had already slipped free of its topknot. She could feel strands of it plastered against her temples. The dress she wore was a faded rose-colored calico that had once been her mother's. She'd not yet found the courage to write to her father asking him to send some of her own things, and for the first time, she regretted that weakness.

How she'd have liked to saunter down the hill, looking cool and refined, in her new blue silk with her lace gloves and the white chip bonnet trimmed in pink roses and morning glories. Surely that would capture the attention of even such a stone-faced Welshman. It was a silly, girlish notion, wholly out of character, and surprised at herself, Lexi banished it at once.

Lifting her arm over her head, she waved and called out in greeting. "Hello? Mr. Glendower?"

He gave off working when the sound of her voice reached him, and he turned to beckon to her. All the while as Lexi made her way down the path, her eyes were trained on Morgan Glendower. He'd laid down his scythe and in a few long strides had crossed to the far corner of the porch, where he stripped away his sweat-stained work shirt and the balbriggan one beneath and proceeded to wash up in the tin basin that was set on the low table there.

He may have thought himself out of sight, but while Lexi was still some distance away, she could see him well enough as he stood, working a bar of soap between his two hands. With quick, vigorous strokes, he spread lather first up one long arm, then the other and across the well-formed planes of his chest. Bending over the basin, he dunked his head, took up the enameled water pitcher, and doused himself. And when he straightened up, he stretched his arms high over his head as if to ease the pull of his strained muscles, then ran his fingers carelessly through the thatch of his thick black hair as he reached for the towel that hung over the porch rail.

Droplets of water glistened on his skin and clung to the mat of dark hair that shaded his chest. Lexi felt the color flood her cheeks as she stared at him, but she could not seem to make herself look away.

Thankfully, by the time she reached the cabin, he'd gone inside. She lingered on the footpath, several yards away from the door and tried to pretend that she had not been spying on him all the while. When he came out again, he had pulled his suspenders up over his shoulders and was buttoning a clean shirt.

"Good morning, Mr. Glendower," she said.

The greeting sounded vague, for Lexi was still more than a little flustered.

"Ah, Miss Merritt," he returned, with a cool but cordial air. "And what brings you out so far into the wilderness on this fine morning?"

"I've come to ask your help."

Until now, Lexi had kept both hands tucked shyly behind her skirts, but now she extended to him the one in which she held the willow cage. "It's Jacob's bird. She won't eat, and she keeps thrashing against the bars of the cage. He thinks she's dying. You seem to know something of animals, and I thought — well, that is, Jacob wanted me to ask you . . ."

He hesitated for a long moment before putting out his hand. "Here, then, let me have a look at her."

Lexi gave over the cage, and Morgan sat down on the steps and set it beside him. At first he only observed the captive bird, but then he gently poked a finger between the bars, prodding her into a flurry of movement. Finally, he unfastened the latch, reached in and, despite a loud squawk of protest from the patient, he drew her out, gingerly cupped between his two strong hands.

"Come hold her for me, will you?" he entreated.

Lexi was unsure of herself, but felt compelled to obey his command. She came to sit beside him on the steps and awkwardly put out her two hands. Morgan settled the bird into them, and for a moment as his callused fingers brushed over her skin, Lexi was aware of a tingling surge of blood through her veins, but when he drew back, there was only the faint, frantic pulse of the bird's heart beating against her fingers.

She watched in hushed admiration as Morgan removed the splint on the bird's wing and ran his fingers deftly over the mend. "She's not dying," he explained patiently. "In fact, she's nearly healed. But she's had enough of being caged. Would Jacob mind very much, do you think, if we set her free?"

When he fixed those clear blue eyes of his on her, Lexi found herself hopelessly tongue-tied and so endeavored to focus all her attention on the frail creature she held in her hand. "I—I think he'd understand," she replied at last.

With that, Morgan took the bird from Lexi. Extending his arms, he swept his hands in an upward motion, urging her to fly. She took off well enough, then fluttered at an awkward angle until she'd settled in the dust of the footpath only a few feet away.

Lexi pulled a sharp breath and got to her feet, but soon felt the calming pressure of Morgan's hand on her shoulder. "Give her a minute more," he advised, and sure enough, after a few tentative flaps of her newly healed wing, the speckled bird took to the air once more, this time gaining height, soaring gracefully up over the treetops in a fluid arc until at last she disappeared from sight.

Lexi's eyes followed the bird's ascent, but Morgan's were fixed on the girl beside him, her lovely face half hidden by the brim of her sunbonnet, her hands clutching tightly at her well-worn calico skirts.

"Oh!" she exclaimed. "You've done it, haven't you? You've mended her wing!"

There was a childlike wonder in her voice that Morgan found hard to resist, and when she turned to him, her wide green eyes sparkling with excitement, he could not help but smile. It only took a moment, though, for him to recover himself. Clearing his throat, he resumed his solemn air, and regretfully, he removed his hand from her slight, soft shoulder.

"I only set the break," he corrected. " 'Twas a higher power did the mending."

"Nevertheless," she insisted, "thank you for all you've done, Mr. Glendower."

Morgan turned away from her, his gaze seeming to follow the path that the bird had taken. He had been surprised when he'd looked up to see Lexi standing there at the top of the hill, surprised but not displeased. He thought now that she reminded him of the first wildflowers of spring, thrusting their brightly colored heads carelessly up through the melting snows. Had she been sent here to bring warmth and light back into his life, to melt the ice that flowed in his veins? Was that what he wanted of her? No, he told himself. No, it was far too late for that. And she deserved better than he could give.

Lexi could sense the turmoil in him, although she could not discern its cause. There was so much about this man that she did not understand. But if he meant to keep her at arm's length, then he'd made a grave mistake that night in the orchard. Lexi's heart had responded at once when he'd asked for her help, and she knew that even now beneath the stoical facade, he was hurting. And she had already decided that she would help him if she could.

"This is a fine cabin," she said, wanting to fill up the uncomfortable silence. "Gran tells me you've lived out here by yourself for two years."

Morgan kept his eyes trained on the sky, as if he expected the bird he'd freed to return. "I bought the place from a British officer," he told her. "He'd planned to retire here, but found he couldn't adapt himself to the rustic life."

"You seem to have adjusted," she observed. "What is it about this place that you find so appealing?"

With his back still to her, Morgan shrugged his shoulders. "It suits my needs."

"I don't imagine you have many visitors out here."

"You're the first."

Thrust and parry, thrust and parry. It seemed ever thus with Morgan Glendower. Lexi felt as though she were making no headway at all. She would not give up easily, though. "It's so restful and quiet here. Gran says that a man could lose himself in those tall pines, just step into the thick of them and never be seen again. Is that what you've intended? To lose yourself out here?"

She watched his back stiffen and knew she'd struck a nerve. When he faced her at last, his eyes had turned to pale blue ice. "If so, then I've done a damned poor job of it, haven't I, Miss Merritt? You found me easily enough."

He spoke with measured calm, but each word was as sharp as a knife's edge. Lexi winced. Pinned beneath his unforgiving glare, her confidence fled. "I—I'm sorry," she stammered. "I shouldn't have come."

With that, she hurriedly gathered her skirts in two tight fists and withdrew.

As he watched the slender figure retreat up the hill, Morgan let out a low, painful breath. He had to strive mightily to quell the urge to run after her. But it was better this way, he assured himself. Lexi Merritt was a kind and generous soul, a fresh, unspoilt beauty—and far too valuable a prize to be wasted on a man who'd already proven himself unworthy.

Chapter Six

The city of Hamilton, located at the head of Lake Ontario, was a bustling port and major commercial center with a population of nearly twenty thousand—a stark contrast to the lush wilderness and isolated farmlands of the Niagara Peninsula to which Morgan had become so accustomed.

A growing discomfort welled in him as he watched the shops and factories, homes and offices, roll by the open window of the cab he'd hired at the depot. Slipping a finger between his collar and his throat, he tugged at the knot that threatened to strangle him and ruined the fold of his gray-striped cravat in the process.

His godfather, Arthur Sinclair, had built himself a spacious, two-storied home made of blocks of the local limestone and located on the fringes of the city. It was a suitable neighborhood for a prosperous physician, near the base of the Mountain, which was the common name for the three-hundred-foot-high Niagara Escarpment that rose up just south of the city. The late summer weather was pleasantly warm, the scenery picturesque. On another occasion, Morgan might have looked forward to this long-put-off reunion with his godfather, but ever since he'd stepped off the train, he'd been plagued by the intrusive presence of old ghosts.

He'd stiffened unconsciously at the sight of redcoated British regulars when the cab passed the military compound, and turned his head away from the long row of shops on King Street, uncomfortable with the familiarity of the scene. Even now, as he paid off the driver, picked up his valise, and headed for the broad front steps of his godfather's house, his eyes drifted past the neatly trimmed yew hedge to the formal gardens that spread out behind the building. On a summer's night a lifetime ago, he'd walked there with Celeste. . . . What a lovesick young idiot he'd been!

Morgan reached for the iron ring of the door knocker and beat it against the plate with more vigor than he had intended. The doors opened only a few seconds later, and he scarcely had time to collect himself before he was greeted by the cheery smile of the housekeeper, Mrs. Edmunds, a white-haired, plump, pink cherub of a woman who'd been with his godfather for years.

"Come in, Doctor Glendower, come in," she bade him, stepping aside. "It's been a long time since we've seen you here, a long time indeed. Doctor Sinclair will be pleased to know you've arrived safe and sound. I daresay you're looking well."

Morgan followed her in, smiling at her chatter as he set down his valise on the handsome slate floor of the foyer. "Why, thank you, Mrs. Edmunds, and may I say that you're looking as fetching as ever."

Her furrowed brow reminded him that she was immune to his flattery. "You oughtn't to have stayed away so long," she chided, wagging a finger at him. "He's been worrying more than ever over you lately and him with his weak heart and all."

"Weak heart?" Morgan exclaimed in mock-surprise. "Now I hope you're not letting the old reprobate pull the wool over your eyes. He's been making that claim for years, but I can assure you, Arthur Sinclair has the constitution of an ox."

"Just the same, he's been worried."

Mrs. Edmunds did not regard him again. Shaking her head, she turned and led the way down the hall to his godfather's study, and all the while, Morgan heard her muttering under her breath. "No respect for his elders . . . running off to live in the woods and with scarcely a word to anyone . . . ungrateful young fool."

In spite of the disquiet he felt at this homecoming, Morgan found his mood lightened considerably by this hardheaded assessment of his character. His mouth flexed into an amused smile. Young? At thirty-eight, he could scarcely be considered that anymore—and ungrateful? Never. He would always be thankful to Arthur Sinclair for all that the man had done for him. But in calling him a fool, Mrs. Edmunds had hit the nail squarely on the head.

Dinner had always been a formal affair in this house. And even though the two gentlemen dined tonight with only each other for company, habit made them arrive at the table in their black cutaways and trousers with starched shirts, white ties, and waistcoats.

Morgan had had only a brief interview with his godfather earlier in the afternoon before being sent up to his room to settle in. Dr. Sinclair was, of course, pleased to see his errant relation at long last, and he'd said as much when he'd welcomed him. But even though their conversation had not gone beyond vague niceties, Morgan knew, with an undeniable certainty, that he had not been summoned here merely for a pleasant reunion. He was due a thorough dressing-down. And while he could not dispute the fact that he deserved it, he did not look forward to the event.

The meal was superb, for Dr. Sinclair had a gourmand's palate, as his ample girth attested. Soup *à la jardinère,* salmon with parsley and butter, roast lamb, assorted vegetables, and iced pudding for dessert; and all this set before a man who, for the past two years, had lived on whatever rude combination of meat, beans, and biscuits he'd been able to devise for himself. Morgan made a conscious effort not to indulge too freely, in spite of the temptation.

It wasn't until some time later, after they'd moved into the study and his godfather was holding out a glass of brandy to him, that the older man noticed the thick layer of calluses on Morgan's hand. With a deep sigh, Dr. Sinclair swept his fingers through his thinning gray hair and prepared to broach the subject they'd both been avoiding.

"It's a sorry shame, that's what it is, to see you come to this. What would your father think if he were here?"

Morgan pulled a steadying breath before forming his retort. "My father never saw the good in anything I did. He was your friend for years. Have you forgotten him so soon? He wanted a warrior for a son — a combination of steel and sinew who'd follow him out on his campaigns to uphold the rule of the almighty British Empire. Once I'd shown him I wouldn't be that man, he didn't give a damn about me."

Sinclair regarded the stern set of his godson's jaw and swallowed the denial he'd intended to make. There'd been too many years of bad blood between father and son for Morgan to believe it now anyway.

"Think of yourself, then," Sinclair said instead. "You're a skilled surgeon, lad. When you were studying at Edinburgh, Dr. Branleigh wrote to tell me that he'd never encountered a doctor with more promise. How can you simply throw all that away?"

Morgan considered the words, but kept his attention focused on his brandy, swirling the amber liquid along the curve of the glass. "You know it's not that simple, sir."

"I know you let a pack of vicious rumormongers drive you away from here," Sinclair replied as he set down the decanter on his desk and began to pace before the mantelpiece, "that you've lived like a hermit for the past two years in some tumbledown shack in the middle of the wilderness. No woman is worth it, I tell you."

Settling himself into one of a pair of leather wing chairs that faced the hearth, Morgan swiftly downed his brandy and felt his throat burn and constrict in its wake. "It wasn't the woman," he responded, surprising himself by the abrupt admission. "Oh, I'll admit I might have been addlepated about Celeste for a time. What young man hasn't made a fool of himself over a woman? But she's not the reason I resigned my commission.

"After the war, I was sick. You knew that. I came all this way, hoping to escape it. And I managed well enough for a few years; in time I thought I'd forgotten, but living at the compound there were always reminders—the bugler's call, the tramp of marching feet, and the uniforms. Do you have any idea how many uniforms passed under my hands at Scutari—burned, shredded, soaked with blood?"

Arthur Sinclair sank down into the opposite chair and endeavored in vain to find a comfortable position. This reunion was not going at all as he'd planned. As he considered now, he realized that he'd never spoken to his godson about the war. He knew well enough what Morgan had suffered. Hadn't he come here in a state of nervous exhaustion? But they'd never discussed the worst of it. Better that the boy should bury the memories, he'd thought, but it was apparent now that Morgan had not been able to do that.

"Forget about the army, then," he advised, and carefully directed the conversation to the subject he'd been wanting to address. "Come back and take up practice with me. I've been wanting to cut down my workload. You know you'd be a great help to me, Morgan."

"I'm not so sure of that. I can't even heal my own wounds; how can I be expected to heal anyone else's?"

Morgan rose and went to fetch the decanter, and as he poured himself another drink, Dr. Sinclair did not miss the fact that his godson's hand was shaking. "I've found some measure of peace in the wilderness, sir," he went on. "You can't ask me to give that up."

"No," Dr. Sinclair agreed grudgingly, "no, I suppose not. But one day, after I'm gone, all of this will be yours, you know. I want you to give me your promise that . . . when the time comes, you'll come and take over my practice."

"Bah!" Morgan retorted at once. "You've another twenty good years in you, at least."

"If so, then there's no harm in humoring an old man, is there?"

Once more Morgan put the glass to his lips and drained it dry. His dark brow was creased in frown, his eyes squeezed tightly shut. He didn't want to have this discussion, didn't want to make promises that he might not be able to keep.

"Have I ever, in all these years, asked anything of you?" Dr Sinclair pressed.

"No, sir. I can't say that you have." At that moment, Morgan felt the full weight of the debt he owed his godfather dragging on him like a convict's heavy chains. But even as he hesitated, letting the silence grow until it filled up the space between them, he knew there was only one reply he could give.

"All right . . . all right, then. When the time comes, I'll do what you ask. I suppose it *is* my place to carry on for you."

"There's a good lad," Dr. Sinclair replied.

Sinclair was well-pleased with himself, even though he'd had to pressure the lad unmercifully. But his motives could not be faulted in the least, for he loved Morgan Glendower like a son, and he would not see him throw his life away, not while there was yet a breath left in his body.

It was nearly a month since she'd come to

Gran's, and there'd been no word from Brendan. Lexi ought not to have been surprised; Brendan had never been good at writing letters, and besides, she'd left him in an awkward spot — with an unanswered marriage proposal hanging between them. So she sat down and composed a letter to him: a chatty little note that told him little more than how Gran and Jacob were faring and how she'd been spending her days.

She would have liked, more than anything, to relate to him the tale of the singular Welshman she'd met, a man who could be at one minute full of warmth and charm and the next as cold as a winter's breeze on Lake Erie. She would have liked to ask her friend's help in sorting through the tangle of conflicting emotions that were aroused in her whenever she encountered Morgan Glendower. Brendan had always been a sharp hand and a good judge of character. He'd know just what to make of the man, but, with things as they were, Lexi could hardly ask him.

She did find the courage to ask one favor of him, however. Would he kindly stop by and ask Mrs. Fraser how her father was faring? There'd been no message from Papa at all, and Lexi feared that by now the household would be a shambles without her there to manage things. Papa had never had the time for anything but the business of making money. If he needed her, she'd go back. If only he'd write and tell her so. . . .

When Lexi finished the letter, she was so eager

for a prompt reply that she decided to carry it at once to Stevensville and post it at the general store. When she announced her intentions, Gran gave over a basket and a shopping list, for as she said, " 'Twould be foolish tae make a two-mile walk for but one wee letter!"

The day was gray and dreary. A chill mist had risen out of the valley with the dawn, but Lexi was not put off by the weather. In fact, she welcomed the change, for it added new dimension to her surroundings, softening the landscape and casting a deep hush over all. And so she borrowed Gran's wool shawl, put on her bonnet, and with the empty shopping basket on her arm, she set off for Stevensville.

Along the way, Lexi found that her thoughts were full of her father and the awful argument they'd had before she'd left home. She *had* behaved rather like a spoiled child, she realized as she looked back on it now, and he'd had every right to be angry with her. But now that some time had passed, maybe he might come to see, too, how hurt she'd been to discover that he'd made his plans without even discussing them with her. And maybe he'd write and ask her to come home. Lexi hung onto that thought as she continued on her way. Yes, maybe he'd ask her to come home. . . .

From her childhood visits to the town, Lexi remembered Stevensville as a thriving place with well over a thousand inhabitants, a busy sawmill on the banks of Black Creek, and a large cooperage that supplied barrels to the entire Niagara Peninsula. Spreading out from the crossroads that was the center of town had been an inn for travelers, half a dozen boardinghouses, two saloons, a livery, the merchants' bank, church, and general store, and, further on, the rows of neatly painted clapboard houses that belonged to the residents, some with fence rows and flowers planted in the yards.

Now, though, as she approached the crossroads, Lexi felt an icy chill run through her that made her clutch her shawl tighter. Gran had told her about the fire that had struck the town a little over a year ago, but she hadn't expected the utter destruction that met her eyes.

All of the tidy little houses were gone; the plots that had once been thoughtfully tended flower gardens were unkempt and overgrown with weeds. The mill had been laid waste and the cooperage as well. Stands of charred timber were the only testament to what had once been.

At the crossroads, Peterson's Inn was intact. This and two of the shabbier boardinghouses seemed to be the only survivors of the conflagration. Mr. Newcomb's general store was standing where it always had, with its familiar signboard hanging over the door, but the newly built veranda and fresh coat of white paint told Lexi that this was, in fact, a new structure rebuilt upon the ruins of its predecessor.

Lexi climbed the stairs. A bell jangled when she

pulled open the door and stepped inside. "Mr. Newcomb?"

The tall man who stood behind the counter penciling figures into a ledgerbook had lost a considerable amount of hair in the years since she'd seen him last, and the thick brown beard she remembered was now peppered with gray, but Lexi recognized him nonetheless.

"Mr. Newcomb!" she repeated. "It's good to see you again."

The storekeeper lifted his head to regard her and pushed his wire-rimmed spectacles back up his nose. "Is that you, Miss Merritt? Why, I wouldn't have believed it! Just wait till Hannah sees what a fine young lady you've grown into. Hannah? Hannah, come out here at once."

A buxom woman in brown calico pushed through the drape that served as a door to separate the back room from the rest of the store. "What is it that's so urgent, James? You know I'm seeing to that shipment of fabric that's just come in."

Hannah Newcomb straightened her apron and smoothed back the few stray wisps of silvery blonde hair that had escaped her chignon. "Oh, my goodness!" she exclaimed when she looked up at last to see their visitor.

She hurried across the room, folded her arms around Lexi, and hugged her tight enough to leave her breathless. "Now here's a sight for sore eyes. You're the picture of your mother, Lexi, the very picture. Jacob told us when he was in last that you'd come to visit, and we've been wondering ever since when you'd pay us a call."

"I'm sorry I didn't come sooner," Lexi replied, once she'd regained her breath. "But there's been so much to do. I honestly don't know how Gran manages all on her own."

"No need to worry about your old gran," Mr. Newcomb assured her. "She's a sharp hand. Makes me give her no less than top dollar for butter and eggs each time she crosses my threshold."

"And Jacob helps out. He's been a good son to her," Hannah put in, "even with his . . . difficulties."

Lexi set her basket on the counter and handed Gran's shopping list to Mr. Newcomb, who scanned it and began selecting the items from the shelves behind him.

"And of course, we all help out our neighbors around here," he said over his shoulder, "we've got to now — only the most stubborn of us are still left."

Lexi dropped her head, reminded of the desolation she'd seen on her walk through town. "Gran told me about the fire, but I never imagined there'd been such damage. . . ."

"So many lost everything that night," Hannah explained. "We were lucky. We'd put some money aside and were able to rebuild. But things here won't ever be the same again. They've not rebuilt the mill, and so most of the town folk have gone elsewhere. Old man Peterson's still hanging on . . . and the Millers, too. Some of the hardier folk have turned to farming, but as you well know the land in these parts is not good for much more than scraping out a living."

Lexi knew that it was true. Gran and Jacob had lived for all these years on the proceeds from the apple harvest, the sale of milk, butter, and eggs, and whatever small cash crop of wheat grain Jacob could manage.

"Oh, but enough of this sad and sorrowful talk!" Hannah said, scolding herself, and then came to slip her arm through Lexi's. "Let's you and I go upstairs. We'll have a cup of tea and a slice of my lemon cake, and you can tell me all about what's been happening in your life."

Lexi accepted Hannah's invitation—it would have been useless to do otherwise when Hannah had her mind set—and for the next half hour, she allowed the woman to wring every last drop of news out of her. How was her father faring? He was planning to marry, was he? Well then, what sort of woman was this fiancée of his? What was the latest news from Buffalo? What kind of fashions were the local shops showing this year?

On the subject of her father's engagement, Lexi carefully avoided sharing her true feelings, for, despite her more-than-generous nature, Hannah Newcomb was a notorious gossip, and Lexi did not want it known—unless she could find some way to prevent it—that her normally level-headed father was bound and determined to marry a fortune hunter.

Lexi had given Brendan's letter to Mr. Newcomb to post before she went up to have her tea, but when she returned later to say good-bye to him and retrieve Gran's shopping basket, he handed *her* a letter.

"What's this?" she asked, perusing the envelope.

"It arrived for you yesterday," he explained, "along with this."

Reaching behind the counter, he drew out a leather valise and set it on the counter beside the basket. Lexi recognized it at once and felt her face flush with color as she read the tag that was affixed to the handle and bore her name and Gran's address. It, like the envelope Mr. Newcomb had just given her, had been written in her father's hand.

"Oh? Yes . . . well, thank you, Mr. Newcomb," she stammered as she tucked the unopened envelope into her waistband, took up the shopping basket in one hand and the valise in the other, and headed promptly for the door.

"Are you sure you wouldn't want to leave that suitcase until Jacob can come fetch it with the wagon?" the storekeeper suggested.

"No," Lexi replied, swallowing hard as she struggled to maintain her composure. "No thank you, Mr. Newcomb. I can manage, really. Good afternoon."

With Gran's shawl thrown over her shoulders, Lexi carefully balanced her burden, hurried out of the store, past the crossroads and down the nearly empty street. The tears were gathering now, stinging behind her eyes, and with all her might, she willed them not to fall.

The morning fog had lifted, but the wind had picked up and carried on it a sharp chill. Thick, gray clouds were gathering overhead, and an ominous grumbling sounded in the distance. Ignoring the signs, Lexi trudged on.

All around her there was desolation: burnt-out shells of buildings that were already thick with the verdant green of vining weeds and undergrowth as the forest sought to reclaim the land. So many people's dreams had died here—all in the course of one cataclysmic night. But it wasn't these vivid reminders of the fire that had brought tears to her eyes.

She hadn't even read Papa's letter, but the fact that he'd sent along her heavily packed valise made his intentions all too clear. He did not want her to come back home; he did not need her at all.

Only after she'd left all traces of civilization behind and found herself safe in the shadows of the tall, black pines did Lexi stop to catch her breath. Setting down the valise, she rested herself upon it, put aside her basket, and reached into her waistband to remove her father's letter.

Her hand was unsteady as she tore open the envelope and drew out the single, folded sheet of paper to read it:

Dearest Alexandra,

I was disappointed when I woke to find you missing, with only a note to explain that you'd gone to your grandmother. But after some consideration, I have come to realize that perhaps yours was the wisest course. We both said some hurtful things on the night before you left, and perhaps this time apart will be good for us.

Your Gran has written to inform me that all is well and that you are thriving in the country. I am glad to hear it. As for us here, you needn't worry. Mrs. Fraser has stepped in and takes excellent care of the household, and my wife-to-be has been generous enough to offer help and advice as well.

It was she who suggested that we pack and send some of your things, as you left in such haste that you cannot have brought enough to see you comfortably through your stay.

Please write if there is anything you need or if you have decided when you plan on returning home. Do not feel that you must hurry on our account. If you are enjoying your stay, we will manage without you. I do hope, though, that you will come home in time for the wedding at Christmas.

Your loving Papa

Exhaling a low, shuddering sigh, Lexi got to her feet, slipped the page back into its envelope, and tucking the whole back into her waistband with a trembling hand, she picked up her basket and valise and continued on her way.

Chapter Seven

The rain began shortly after Morgan stepped off the train and went to retrieve his horse and buggy from the livery in Ridgeway. It was not part of any violent thunderstorm, with bold gusts of wind to shake the trees and lightning to pierce the sky, but only a rather commonplace sort of rain that dripped steadily from a steel gray sky, until it puddled across the low ground and filled the deep-cut wagon ruts of the road with rivulets of running water.

Snug and dry in his broad-brimmed hat and gutta-percha cape, beneath the buggy's wide leather canopy, Morgan turned the horse in a homeward direction and allowed his thoughts to wander. In the few days he'd spent in Hamilton, his godfather had tried every method at his disposal to make him decide to stay, but Morgan had stood firm in his intent to return to his cabin in the woods. It was only after the man resorted to emotional blackmail that Morgan had promised to eventually take over his practice for him—and then

106

only after Dr. Sinclair's death. It wasn't too much to ask, especially considering the man's generosity over the years. Besides, as Morgan himself had pointed out, Arthur Sinclair had a good twenty years left in him yet. Still, Morgan couldn't help feeling as though he'd somehow been bested.

He drove on in silent contemplation for several miles, until finally he turned off onto the western fork and caught sight of a lone figure just ahead, walking alongside the road. It was a woman. Her back was to him, but he could see as he drew nearer that she was wearing a plaid shawl, a sunbonnet whose brim was sodden and misshapen, and a faded calico dress, with skirts that were soaked with rain and mud-spattered. They clung to her legs as she trudged on, making each step more difficult than the last. And as if this were not handicap enough, she was struggling to carry a heavy valise in one hand and had a market basket balanced on the opposite arm.

It was only when he drew alongside that Morgan realized the woman was Lexi. Pulling up on the reins, he adjusted the horse's gait to match her pace. She turned to regard him, but the bonnet brim obscured her view, and so, frustrated, she reached to swipe it from her head, leaving it to dangle down her back by its strings as the rain washed over her face.

Morgan was able to study her more closely now. He saw the wisps of red-gold hair plastered against her brow, and pale skin that was beaded with crystal droplets of rain. The image of Lexi slipping on the rocks and landing bottom-first in the creek came to mind and made him smile. He spoke before he could stop himself. "What's this? Running away from home, are we?"

Lexi ignored this amusement he had at her expense and kept on walking. "If so," she retorted, without looking back, "then I'm headed in entirely the wrong direction, wouldn't you say?"

"Forgive me," Morgan entreated, sensing her disquiet. "It was no more than a jest and a poor one at that. Let me give you a ride home, Lexi. You'll be another half hour yet in the rain if you go on as you are. You'll catch your death."

"I can manage on my own, thank you," she replied, nearly stumbling before she recovered herself to continue on without slackening her pace.

Perhaps it was only the hollow tone in her voice that affected Morgan, but just then a strange uneasiness swept through him. Looking closer, he noticed that Lexi's skin was too pale to be healthy and that her lips, which were now pursed tightly together, had taken on a bluish tinge. Bringing the carriage to a halt, he tied off the reins and jumped down, carelessly spattering mud up over his high-polished boots in the process. Hurrying after Lexi, he caught her arm and spun her around to face him.

Her eyes were red and swollen, and it was apparent now that all the trailing droplets on her face were not on account of the rain.

"You've been crying."

"Leave me alone, Mr. Glendower," she begged,

sounding weary and miserable as she writhed against his grasp to free herself. "Just leave me . . . alone. I'm tired of playing games with you."

Morgan gripped her arm tighter. "I'm afraid I must insist that you come with me," he said as he pressed his free hand to her brow. "You're feverish. You need to get home and into a warm bed at once."

She shook her head vigorously. "I can't go home, not ever again. He doesn't want me there. He's made his choice. He's packed me off, so he might be alone with *her*."

The words did not make sense to Morgan, but there was the look of a lost child in those glazed green eyes of hers, and without even thinking, he gathered her close against him and whispered in her ear, "I don't know what's happened, Lexi, but whatever it is, it isn't worth making yourself sick over—and you *will* be sick if you stay out in this weather much longer. Please, let me take you home to your grandmother."

Lexi fully intended to resist—she was ashamed to have Morgan Glendower see her like this and determined to show him that she did not need help, not from anyone. She had taken a slight chill, no more than that, and as soon as she got home, she would take off these wet clothes and climb into bed. She just needed to lie down in her bed and then everything would be all right.

Despite her conviction, Lexi paused for a long while before trying to wrest free of Morgan again. His body radiated warmth, and she was so very cold. . . . Still, she was not prepared for the violent tremor that coursed through her next, nor for the wave upon wave of uncontrollable shivering that followed. She stood, helpless, as the strength ebbed from her body, and as the valise dropped from her hand, she collapsed against him, with her flaming cheek resting against the cool, slick surface of his gutta-percha cape.

Morgan drove the horse as fast as he could, given the weather and the poor condition of the road. Throughout the bone-jarring ride, though, Lexi did not stir. She lay, flushed and still, on the seat beside him, wrapped up in the carriage blanket and his waterproof cape.

When at last they reached the MacLennan farm, he bundled her into his arms, carried her up to the house, and freed one hand to beat upon the kitchen door. Mrs. MacLennan opened it promptly, and her face paled at the sight of them.

"I found her walking on the road from Stevensville," Morgan explained quickly. "She's soaked to the skin, and she's taken a chill, I'm afraid. She's running a high fever. We'll need to put her someplace warm."

Mrs. MacLennan ushered him inside. "Take her into my room," she instructed, pointing out the way.

Morgan did as she bade him, but as he rounded the corner into the hall, he came face-to-face with Jacob and drew up short. The young man's gray eyes went wide as he regarded Lexi's still form. When he spoke, his voice was a tremulous whisper. "Is she . . . d-dead?"

"Nay, lad," Mrs. MacLennan replied patiently over Morgan's shoulder, "but she's taken ill, and ye maun go for the doctor in Fort Erie at once. Can ye do that, Jacob? Can ye do that for me?"

Tears glazed Jacob's eyes. His lower lip began to tremble, but as he looked down at Lexi, he seemed to get hold of himself, for he squared his jaw and nodded vigorously. "Aye. Aye, I'll do it."

Morgan opened his mouth as if he might speak, but the words died in his throat as a cold sweat washed over him. He hadn't laid hands on a patient in two years, and he hadn't forgotten what he'd told his godfather only a few days ago. How could a man who could not heal himself expect to heal anyone else? Morgan dropped his head and swept past Jacob to enter the tiny bedroom, which stood at the end of the hall.

After he'd settled Lexi on the bed, he bent over her, and habit made him take up one of her wrists and put his other hand to her brow. The fever was still rising, her pulse was rapid, and her breathing had gone dangerously shallow. He stared at the curve of her cheek and the fan of red-gold lashes against translucent skin and felt sorely ashamed. This lovely young girl, who had offered him friendship and kindness, needed him now; how could he possibly stand by and not lift a hand to save her?

He turned to Mrs. MacLennan, who had followed him into the room and was standing directly behind him, watching his actions with a gimlet eye. "There's no need to send Jacob to Fort Erie, Mrs. MacLennan," he told her at last. "I'm a doctor."

Once the revelation had been made, Morgan took charge of the situation with cool efficiency. He left Mrs. MacLennan to remove Lexi's wet clothing and sent Jacob out to his cabin, giving the young man careful instruction as to precisely where he would find his medical bag and supplies. Then, shrugging off his frock coat, he returned to the sickroom, rolled up his sleeves, washed his hands in the basin on the bureau, and prepared himself for the long night ahead.

The fever persisted, and within only a few hours, Lexi was seized by intermittent spates of harsh coughing that wracked her slender body and left her weak and breathless. Once he had his stethoscope in hand, Morgan was able to assure himself of that which he feared—there was congestion in her right lung. He dosed her at once with veratrum and atropine to aid her blood circulation and gave orders to Mrs. MacLennan to put a kettle on the stove, charging her with the business of administering hot tea to the patient, whenever she was able to take it.

In the hours that followed, Morgan kept a close watch on Lexi and rested only when she did—either in the chair at her bedside or on the parlor sofa within the sound of her voice. He told himself that it was understandable he should be overly concerned with the fate of the first patient he'd had in two years, but there was more to it than that. The truth of it was that his feelings for Lexi Merritt ran deeper than he dared to admit, and he was discovering more about her as she lay ill than he had in the month that he'd known her.

On the first night when her fever was high, she had been seized by delirium, and she'd spoken again as she had when Morgan had encountered her on the road—of being unable to go home because she was unwelcome there. Mrs. MacLennan was beside him to hear it this time, though. When she noted the surprise in his expression, she explained to him that Lexi had been the mistress of her father's house since her mother died and took much pride in her place. But now that her father had decided to remarry, she felt as though she were being cast aside.

For his own part, Morgan would have thought she'd be happy that there would be another woman around the house to share in the work, but he supposed he could understand her fear of losing her place in her father's heart.

And then there was the letter he'd found on the floor beside Lexi's bed. It must have been tucked in her clothing and slipped free while Mrs. MacLennan was undressing her. But Morgan blithely ignored the fact that it was not meant for his eyes, and once he'd read the rain-smudged page, he understood so much more about her. He

113

understood why she had been trudging through the rain, carrying a heavy leather valise, and he understood why she'd been crying. That letter from her father must have seemed to confirm her worst fears, and then he himself had come along with his thoughtless jokes about running away from home. That was why she'd come out here in the first place, he saw now; she *had* been running away from home.

In the quiet moments that were left to him, Morgan chastised himself for the way he'd treated Lexi Merritt since they'd met. He had allowed his own troubles to blind him to all else around him, and regardless of what she'd done to convince him otherwise, he'd insisted on casting Lexi in the role of a carefree and amusing innocent. Now he could see that she had been reaching out to him, that she had been sorely in need of a friend—and all he had been able to offer her was resentment at her intrusion in his life.

The trilling of a songbird perched somewhere high in the leafy branches of the oak tree in the dooryard prodded Lexi awake. As she opened her eyes, sunlight washed over her in blinding waves, playing tricks with her still-blurred vision. For a moment, she thought she saw Morgan Glendower sitting in the chair beside her bed. Even after she'd blinked hard, though, the illusion did not disappear.

He looked particularly handsome sitting there, but not at all like himself. He wore a fine linen

114

shirt, neatly folded silk cravat, and dark blue waistcoat and trousers. Rather than the stoical Welsh woodsman she'd come to know, he had the look of a prosperous city gentleman today, and he was smiling at her in a way that warmed her from head to heels. From the first time she'd seen it, Lexi had been struck by that smile, and she was sorry he did not make use of it more often.

"Good morning!" the apparition said to her when he noticed that she'd awakened.

The voice was cheerful and pleasant, the eyes alight with enthusiasm. This was not the Morgan Glendower she remembered. It must be only another of her dreams, Lexi told herself; she seemed to be plagued by unusual dreams of late. But she addressed him regardless. "I've been ill, haven't I?"

"You might say that," he replied, "seeing as how you've been lying abed these past five days."

"Five days?" Lexi echoed.

"You caught a chill while walking in the rain. I'm sorry to say it developed into pneumonia."

"I—I'm afraid I don't remember much about that," she admitted uneasily, and raised a trembling hand to massage her temple as if it might help her to remember. ". . . except perhaps for the coughing fits . . . and how much it hurt to breathe. I do recall that Gran fed me soup and herb tea, and you—"

Lexi paused to catch her breath, and her brow creased as she sought to piece together the threads of her memory. "You took me home after you came upon me in the road, didn't you?"

Morgan nodded.

"And now you've come back to see how I'm faring. It seems I must thank you again, Mr. Glendower — both for coming to my rescue as well as for your thoughtful concern."

By now Lexi was nearly convinced that she was lucid, and as she realized that she was lying in bed, talking to this man while wearing nothing more than a thin muslin nightgown, a blush warmed her cheeks and she reached to pull the quilt up to her chin.

Morgan's mouth flexed into a wry smile, and he dropped his head to stare at his folded hands. "Actually," he began, "I've been here all the while — tending you."

"But where are Gran and Jacob?"

"They've gone off to help with the threshing at the Miller farm. Your grandmother baked half a dozen of her special apple pies for the occasion. She was apprehensive about leaving you at first, but I assured her that your condition was much improved, and she left you in my charge."

"In your charge?" Lexi repeated, incredulous.

"Yes," he replied. "It's not so unorthodox as it sounds, Lexi. I'm a doctor."

Lexi's eyes widened at the revelation. Maybe she was only dreaming, after all. She'd have had no trouble believing this broad-shouldered woodsman to be a soldier, she thought he'd even mentioned as much once, but a doctor?

She pulled a long, tremulous breath. "A doctor, you say? Well, now, this is by far the most interesting delusion I've had yet."

"You're not delirious, I assure you. The fever is gone, and I haven't given you a dose of morphine in more than eight hours."

"Well, you *do* look different," she admitted.

Morgan's expression darkened all at once, then he rose and strode to the window, putting his back to her. "Don't let the fancy clothes fool you," he retorted, as if it stung him to realize that she preferred what she saw before her now. "Underneath I'm still the same rough, thoughtless blackguard you've come to know. But that day in the rain when you crossed my path, I was on my way home from a visit with my godfather, and these were all I'd packed for the trip. You see, the old man likes to believe I'm prospering, and so I dress the part for him."

The confusion Lexi was feeling at the divergence in his behavior was mirrored on her face, and as Morgan turned back to regard her, he was at once sorry for the way he'd spoken. She seemed so fragile and otherworldly lying there, her pale face framed by a halo of bright gold curls that were strewn across the pillow. Before she'd awakened, Morgan had promised himself that for her sake he would tame the darker side of his nature and be the friend that she needed, and he *would* keep that promise.

"Forgive me, Lexi," he said contritely. "My bedside manner has gone rusty from disuse. I've a great respect for my godfather, I do, but I'm sure you understand how trying one's relatives can be."

117

The look she gave him told him that she did, indeed, understand, and after a long hesitation, she asked, "Did Gran send word to my father that I was ill?"

"You're going to tire yourself out with all this talk," he warned her.

"Did she?" Lexi persisted.

"There was scarcely time for that. You've kept us rather busy these past few days."

Morgan hated himself for lying to her. But how could he tell her that her father had gone on a shopping trip to New York City with his fiancée and could not be reached?

"It's probably for the best," Lexi said, sighing. "He's so busy with his work and plans for the wedding—I wouldn't want him to worry over me."

In spite of everything, Morgan managed a smile for her. "Why don't you take the advice of a friend?" he said. "Write to him yourself, explain what's happened, and tell him that you're feeling better now. If he hears from you directly, he's not so likely to be worried."

After considering his words, he added, "You *are* feeling better, aren't you?"

"A little tired, that's all."

Morgan's dark brow furrowed in spite of her assurance, and he strode to her bedside. Taking the watch from his waistcoat pocket, he regarded it soberly as he reached to press his fingertips against the pulse point on her neck.

Lexi's skin tingled with warmth at his touch, and she silently chastised herself for the reaction.

With things as they were, she couldn't very well go on thinking of Morgan Glendower as a man—even if he did seem more charming and attractive than ever. He was her doctor now, and to her surprise, he played the part convincingly. But then she ought to have guessed by the way that he'd cared for Jacob's wounded bird that there was more to him than he'd let on.

"Just the same, you're to spend the next few days in bed resting," he instructed as he snapped his watch case shut and put it back into his pocket. "Doctor's orders."

The pronouncement sounded so solemn and out of character that Lexi had to struggle to stifle a rebellious grin. "Ah, and now that you've become *Doctor* Glendower, you think you can order me about, do you?"

There was a devilish glint in Morgan's blue eyes when he turned them on her, and it took her quite by surprise. "Oh, I've my own selfish interests at heart," he told her. "I intend to have the prettiest girl in the county on my arm when I arrive in Stevensville for the Harvest Dance on Saturday."

Lexi feared that her jaw was lagging open in a most unflattering way as she sought to form a reply. "Is this . . . an invitation, then?"

Morgan smiled at her, with that smile of his that fairly lit up the room. "I hope you'll find it an incentive," he replied, "to speed your recovery."

Lexi hardly knew what to think. She'd only just heard Morgan Glendower call himself her friend, and now he was offering her an invitation to the

Harvest Dance. What could have brought about this change in him? And what precisely did he want of her? His words implied nothing more than friendship, but in his eyes, Lexi was sure she saw more.

Chapter Eight

There had been many formal occasions in Lexi's life. On her father's arm, she had attended countless balls and receptions and dinner parties; she'd mingled with aristocrats, statesmen, captains of industry, and society matrons. And yet, for some inexplicable reason, not one of these functions had caused as much apprehension in her as Morgan Glendower's invitation to the Harvest Dance.

When it came time to decide what to wear, Lexi found herself thankful after all that her father, or more probably his fiancée, had sent along her valise — and packed her blue silk among its contents. Although it would hardly have been considered acceptable evening wear in Buffalo, for this occasion it was just the right touch of elegance, with its pale azure hue and wide lace collar.

Gran helped with her hair, brushing it down her back until it gleamed with golden fire and tying it back with a simple grosgrain ribbon. And when she was ready at last, Lexi put on her white cashmere shawl and went out to wait for Morgan on the porch. Simply dressed though she was—without benefit of an elaborately dressed coiffure, or a fine French gown, or jewels at her throat—Lexi felt, for all the world, like Cinderella preparing to go to the ball.

For the first fifteen minutes, she leaned against the porch rail, hoping to make a pretty picture when his buggy came up the road. For the next half hour, she paced a long grassy stretch of the dooryard, rehearsing the words she would use to chastise him for his tardiness when he arrived. And finally, after more than an hour had passed, she sat very still on the porch steps and told herself that he wasn't coming.

His invitation had seemed so sincere, and yet she ought to have expected something like this. Morgan Glendower was the most quixotic, most contrary man she'd ever encountered, and she was no closer to understanding him now than she had been when first they met. This was not the first time he'd drawn her close only to push her away, but it would most certainly be the last.

When Gran came out, she was wearing a lace cap, her best black dress and the cairngorm brooch that had been a wedding gift from Grandpa MacLennan. She sat down beside Lexi, and without a word, she took up her granddaughter's hand.

"You look nice tonight, Gran," Lexi said, in the strongest voice she could muster. "All the gentlemen will be clamoring for a dance."

"Och! Get on wi' ye. I'm too auld for such non-sense."

A long silence ensued, and Lexi sensed that her grandmother was considering her words carefully. "He maun be ill, lass," she said at last, ". . . or in some difficulty, else he'd be here. I'll send Jacob o'er tae see what's amiss."

"No!" Lexi replied sharply. "You can't do that, Gran. You can't."

"Well, we canna sit out here the whole night long. What shall we do, then?"

Lexi considered only briefly before deciding. She squeezed Gran's hand tightly and forced a smile on her lips. "If Jacob's got the wagon hitched, I'll go along with the both of you. I'll have the best time ever at the dance—and without Morgan Glendower. You wait and see if I don't."

"Aye, lass, but what if he—"

Lexi got to her feet. "I won't hear it, I tell you. You don't understand him like I do, Gran. He's got too close and now he's sorry about it. Well, I don't need him, and I don't intend to sit around here waiting a moment longer. Let's go."

Perhaps it was for the best, Lexi told herself; perhaps Morgan Glendower had done her a favor, for the interest she had taken in him had distracted her from her purpose. Now she could focus her thoughts on the reason she had come to Canada in the first place. She was not here to hide away in the country; she was here to find the proof that her father's fiancée, Mrs. Palmer, was not the woman he thought her to be, and first thing tomorrow morning she would begin to make plans to travel to Hamilton to do precisely that. For tonight, though, she was going to the dance.

The Harvest Dance was held, as it was every year, at Peterson's Inn. Outside in the stable yard, a sugar kettle of whiskey toddy stood brewing over an open fire, and the nearby refreshment table was laden with cheeses and biscuits and a wide assortment of delicacies contributed by the ladies. Gran and Lexi added their own gingerbread and currant loaves to the offerings before joining the crowd.

Inside, the dining room was gaily decorated for the occasion with fragrant pine boughs and wreaths of wildflowers. With most of the tables removed to the barn and the benches set along the outside walls, there was plenty of room for the dancers.

As it turned out, Lexi did not lack companionship for the evening. A small company of British regulars on a surveying trip had come by to join the festivities, and this influx of eligible men kept all the young ladies in demand on the dance floor. Lexi found herself swept along from one boisterous gentleman to the next, joining in their conversations and laughter and dancing until her slippered feet were sore.

It was not so hard as she'd anticipated to prove to Gran, whose sharp eyes seemed ever fixed on her, that she was not missing the company of an enigmatic, ill-tempered Welshman. But convincing herself was something else again, and more than once, Lexi's absent gaze strayed to the open doors in search of a familiar face.

During the course of the evening, she discovered that the British soldiers in their midst were stationed at the military compound in Hamilton. Deciding it must be providence at work, no less, she thereafter devised a plan. She made a particular effort to catch the eye of the officers, and when asked to dance, she would discreetly query them about the late, lamented Colonel Palmer . . . and his beautiful French wife.

"So you're stationed at Hamilton, Captain Ames," Lexi said to the handsome blond officer with whom she'd just shared a reel.

He escorted her to a seat, then sat down beside her. "Yes, Miss Merritt. 'Tis as good an assignment as any I've had. The city offers plenty of amusements. Perhaps you'll come up one day soon and let me show them to you."

Lexi shyly dropped her eyes. "I'd like that, I think. I've never been there, though we did have a friend of the family stationed at Burlington Heights. Perhaps you knew him? His name was Palmer, Colonel John Palmer."

Lexi had no qualms about lying to the man. She'd been weaving tales for most of the night to varying degrees and was becoming rather good at it. Besides, she told herself, she was doing all of this for her father's sake, and if it took the sprinkling of a few white lies to uncover the truth, then so be it.

Captain Ames's smile died away at once, and he busied himself with smoothing the creases from his crimson tunic. "Colonel . . . Palmer, you say? Yes. Yes, indeed. He was an experienced officer with a . . . a strict sense of discipline."

Lexi knew, from what she had earlier been told by a garrulous old sergeant who'd served with him in the Crimea, that at best Colonel Palmer was a rigid and brutal commander who did nothing to earn the respect of the men who'd served under him. Clearly Captain Ames was being generous in his assessment.

Leaning nearer to him, Lexi whispered behind her hand. "Though I hate to speak ill of the dead, to be quite honest with you, Captain, *I* found him a humorless prig, and I don't blame that young wife of his one bit if she had to look elsewhere for affection."

Captain Ames's pale brows arched high, and he sputtered a short laugh. "Miss Merritt you are a delight! I must say I find your honesty refreshing."

"Why, thank you, Captain," Lexi replied, realizing full well what a hypocrite it made her.

Ames gave her a conspiratorial wink. "I think I can assure you that the lovely Mrs. Palmer did not lack for affection. Some of Her Majesty's finest young officers claim to have seen to that."

"You don't say."

Although she had suspected this all along, Lexi

met him with wide-eyed surprise. Her mind was racing all the while as she considered, though, how she could provide the proof that would convince her father. "I don't suppose you know any of them who might know how to contact her for me," she said finally. "I've posted several letters to her home in town, but have had no reply. I understand she's gone away somewhere."

"Well, she and Captain Bascombe were said to be well-acquainted. I could inquire of him, if you like."

"Oh, no," Lexi replied. "Don't trouble yourself about it, Captain. Perhaps if I come up to visit, we can pursue the matter further."

He seemed satisfied with that, and Lexi did not mention to him that her visit to Hamilton was already planned, nor that she would not be calling upon him at all. But now she had a name to take with her at least: Captain Bascombe.

Soon after that, Captain Ames withdrew from the field, and Lexi went to join Gran, who was exchanging pleasantries with the ladies of the town in a far corner of the room. She'd only just arrived there, though, when Jacob appeared at her side and began tugging at her sleeve. "Lexi? Will you . . . c-come with me?"

Experience had taught Lexi to be patient with Jacob. He enjoyed the excitement of these occasions, but they were ofttimes trying for him. Although, for the most part, their neighbors had come to know and accept him, strangers were not always understanding. "Is everything all right?" she asked him. "Has someone said something to upset you?"

Jacob shook his head so vigorously that it tossed about his mane of bright red hair.

"Is it time for our dance, then?"

"No. Just come with me . . . p-please," he urged her. "There's . . . s-something I have to show you."

Excusing herself, Lexi allowed Jacob to take up her hand. He led her across the crowded dance floor and out of the doors that opened out onto the broad veranda that circled the building. The sun had set, and dusk had settled in, wrapping the landscape in soft gray shadows.

"Are you sure you're all right, Jacob?" Lexi repeated.

Jacob did not reply, only led her around the corner, then dropped her hand, and with a broad smile he stepped aside.

Standing there on the veranda before her was Morgan Glendower. He was dressed like any one of the farmers here, who were wearing their Sunday best: a black frock coat and trousers, starched collar with string tie and a simple, blue-striped shirt. Lexi knew that he had finer items in his wardrobe, but clearly he did not wish to draw attention to himself tonight, and as she realized this, it tempered the anger she had built up against him.

"You'd best wrap that shawl tighter," he said

128

softly. "There's a chill in the air tonight, and your health is still fragile."

Jacob left them alone then, and Lexi found herself doing as Morgan bade her. She could not find her voice, though, and she dared not meet his eyes, so she turned to clutch at the porch rail for support and stared off into the darkening depths of the woods beyond the road. She was not certain—for all her bravado earlier on—that she was ready for this confrontation.

"I owe you an explanation," he said, and came up so close behind her that she could feel his warm breath as it ruffled her hair.

Lexi shivered in response, hoping he couldn't see the blush that stained her cheeks. "It isn't necessary," she told him, all the while trying to keep her words calm and even. "I understand. I do. I ought to have known you'd be uncomfortable here, with so many people."

"That's not it at all," he protested.

Lexi had not admitted, not even to herself, how sharp her disappointment had been when he'd not come for her tonight. But now those feelings washed over her, and she felt the hurt anew. It wrapped itself around her like a tightening iron band that squeezed the breath from her body. She ought to leave him without a word. She ought to go back inside. But she cared for Morgan Glendower much more than was wise, and so she stood her ground, awaiting his next move.

He reached out to gently touch her arm. "Look at me, Lexi. Please."

She did not want to obey him, and yet she did so. She turned, inclined her head, and as she looked up into those blue eyes of his, he smiled at her, and her heart fluttered anxiously in her breast. Lexi had known from the first that that smile would be her undoing.

"The explanation is simpler than you think, you know," he said. "I was on my way to fetch you this evening when an axle cap cracked on the buggy and a wheel came loose. It took longer than I expected to repair, and by the time I got to your grandmother's farm, you were already gone. Not that I blame you for leaving—Good God, you must have thought me the worst sort of scoundrel, and I am sorry for it, Lexi."

Lexi let out a long, low breath. Looking closer now, she noticed that there was indeed a dark smudge of grease on his jaw and dust on his trousers. "Gran wanted to send Jacob to check on you," she explained, and, ashamed, she averted her eyes. "But I . . . I thought that . . . Oh, it's I who should apologize to you, Morgan."

Morgan caught her chin between his thumb and forefinger, tipping it upward so that she could not hide her face from him. "I haven't given you much reason to trust me till now, have I?"

With that, he held out the hand he'd been keeping behind his back, offering up a colorful nosegay of wildflowers tied with a satin ribbon. The blooms had faded somewhat, but their sweet fragrance was more potent than ever. There were sprigs of golden buttercups, campion, and four-o'clocks, spikes of sweet white clover, and pale blue flax. "These are for you," he told her, "though I'm afraid they've all wilted now."

"They're lovely," she said softly. "Thank you."

Lexi's spirits rose as she admired the bouquet. She pulled a slender stem of flax from the bunch, fixed it in the buttonhole of Morgan's lapel, and slipped her arm through his. "Now that that's all settled, shall we go inside so that you might claim your dance?"

Morgan seemed to ponder the question for a long while before he shook his dark head. "I should think you'd be tired of dancing by now. I hear you've been at it all evening," he said, and frowned at her. "You must take care with those officers, Lexi. Don't let their fancy airs and fine manners fool you; they're after more from you than just a dance."

Lexi regarded him, and one pale brow crooked upward. It pleased her to think that he might be jealous. "And just how would you know with whom I've been dancing?"

"Jacob and I have been watching you through those windows over there."

"Spying on me, you mean?"

Tightening his hold on her arm, he leaned close and whispered in her ear. "I confess I haven't been able to take my eyes off of you. Surely you must know that you're the most beautiful woman here tonight."

Lexi could hardly chastise him for his admission, phrased as it was, and so she pretended to ignore it, though she could not deny that her heart was beating faster on account of his words.

"If you don't want to dance, then what shall we do?" she asked.

"How about a mug of Mr. Peterson's whiskey toddy? I hear it has wondrous medicinal qualities."

Lexi regarded him askance. "Oh, I don't know if I should. . . ."

"Nonsense. As your physician, I highly recommend it. It will warm your blood and do you a world of good."

Without giving her a chance to refuse, Morgan escorted her through the stableyard. Settling her onto one of the benches that were set out near the garden, he strode off in the direction of the refreshment table. He returned a short time later, two steaming tin mugs in hand, and as he sat down beside her and gave over one of the mugs, the pungent aroma of spices filled the air between them.

"There's a magnificent, round, yellow moon on the rise. Why don't you and I sit out here and enjoy it?"

"It's the harvest moon," Lexi told him. "It comes but once a year."

"All the more reason not to miss it, then."

Lexi raised the mug to her lips. The sweet liquid

slid easily down her throat and its warmth seeped through her. An hour ago she'd not have believed she'd be sitting here with Morgan Glendower, sipping toddy and staring up at the moon. Now, though, she felt closer to him than ever, as if brick by brick he was taking down the wall he'd built around himself.

"Tell me about your home, Morgan," she ventured, "about the place where you were born."

It seemed a safe enough topic. Morgan's gaze remained fixed on the rising moon, and there was a wistful note in his voice, but he did answer. "I come from Carmarthen. It's a very old town in the southwest of Wales, where the land is all rolling hills and green valleys. I was born in a comfortable, old house at the end of a narrow, winding street and lived there for most of my childhood, until my mother died and I was sent away to school."

"What made you choose to become a doctor?"

"There wasn't a choice to be made. All the men in my mother's family for hundreds of years have been healers and physicians. It's a gift that's passed from generation to generation."

"And you have this gift?"

Morgan's mouth twisted contemptuously as he stared into the bottom of his mug. "My mother believed that I had."

"Then why did you stop practicing medicine?"

Now he drew a long, measured breath before responding. "When war broke out in the Crimea, I went out to the army hospital at Scutari, thinking to put this 'gift' of mine to good use," he told her. "I was an idealistic, young fool, but I learned soon enough that even a son of Rhiwallon, in whose veins flowed the blood of the celebrated *Mddygon Mddfai* could not save the lives of those torn apart in battle, nor those whom filth and disease had claimed. In the end, I'd made no difference at all."

"I'm sure that isn't true," Lexi argued.

She could see Morgan's distress as he confronted his memories, but still she felt flush with her success. He had revealed more of himself tonight than he had in all the time she'd known him. Lexi drank down a generous amount of whiskey toddy to fortify herself, intending to press further while she had the chance. But Morgan took her by surprise when he posed a question of his own.

"Have you written to your father yet?"

"What? Why, no," she stammered, "no, I—"

"Your gran told me that you and he had had a disagreement," he explained. "You shouldn't let a misunderstanding come between you, Lexi. You'll come to regret it. Believe me, I know."

Lexi was distressed to find that the conversation had turned on her. She set her empty mug on the bench, but as she got to her feet, it rolled off and clattered to the ground. "But you *don't* know," she protested, pacing anxiously before him. "It's not so simple as that."

She did not want to have to explain about her

father. The subject was a painful one; why couldn't Morgan see that? Suddenly Lexi understood how he must have felt when she insisted on probing his past, and shamed by the realization, she stilled her pacing and fell silent.

Morgan came up close behind her and laid his hands gently on her shoulders. "What we need," he said softly, " — what we *both* need — is to forget about the past. Can you do that if I ask you to, Lexi?"

When she turned to him, with his question mirrored in her eyes, Morgan pulled her against him, and on their own, his hands slipped under her shawl and splayed possessively across her back. The feel of skin-warmed silk beneath his fingers and Lexi's soft, slight body in his arms muddled his thinking. He'd meant to be a friend to her, nothing more than that, but what he was feeling at this moment was something more than friendship, something far more dangerous.

As he listened to the gentle rhythm of her breathing and stared down upon her parted lips, Morgan was reminded of the kiss he'd stolen from her in the orchard; but he had changed since then. He was not playing games with an innocent young girl tonight, and he wanted — no, he *needed* — some sign from her.

"Lexi?" he said, hoping to prompt her.

But Lexi was finding it difficult to concentrate. A million and one thoughts were flitting through her brain, but she could scarcely string them together in any coherent order because of the distraction of his warm breath on her face, his deft fingers caressing the small of her back, his hard thighs pressed against hers. . . .

"Yes," she said, in a breathless rush. "Yes, if that's what you want."

At that moment, Lexi would have promised him almost anything, but she struggled to get hold of herself, for there was something he needed to hear.

"First, though, you must listen to me, and then—I swear—I'll not say another word about the past. That young doctor who went to Scutari had dreams of saving the world. What else could he do but disappoint himself? But I think you've forgotten just how much you have to give as a doctor; look at what you did for me when I was ill. The people here need your gift."

When he did not seem convinced, she continued, more forceful than ever: "There are three tiny graves on the hillside beyond Gran's farm, her three stillborn sons that might have had a chance at life if there'd been a doctor nearby. Why, you have only to think of Jacob, and how different his life might be if Gran had had a doctor to attend her. I'm not asking you to save the world, Morgan, just one life at a time."

Lexi waited for his reply, but when it came at last, it was in a form she scarcely expected: as a gentle touch of his lips on hers that very soon deepened with need, a kiss that left her tingling and giddy and shaken.

When he drew back for breath, Morgan caught her face up in his hands, and his blue eyes glittered fiercely, reflecting the radiant moonlight. "Take care, Lexi Merritt," he said. "I think I'm falling in love with you."

Lexi thought she would remember that moment forever. The music and laughter seemed far off in the distance. There were only the black shadows of the trees around them, their branches tinged with silver moonlight, and the scent of wild roses hanging thick on the air. . . .

"Listen," he said then. "Can you hear it? The fiddler is playing us a waltz."

"Do you want to go back inside?" Lexi asked in a small voice, and turned to go.

"No!" Morgan caught her hand, and drawing her to him once more, he began to lead her in the steps of the dance. "I want you all to myself tonight. I want to dance with you beneath a harvest moon, Lexi, and dream only of the future."

Chapter Nine

Lexi had promised Morgan that she would forget about the past, and she intended to do precisely that, just as soon as she returned from Hamilton with proof that the widow Mrs. Palmer was not all that she seemed.

When she apprised Gran of her plans, the older woman only frowned and shook her head, mumbling something or another under her breath about hardheaded children. Then Gran grudgingly informed her that Jacob would drive her to the depot in Ridgeway and would return to meet the train at precisely four o'clock in the afternoon. But if Lexi wasn't there on time, she warned, she might just as well count on walking home, for Jacob had more important things to do than wait around for her to indulge her foolish whims.

Gran's attitude was designed to make Lexi feel ashamed of herself — and it did — but not enough to cancel her plans. She'd come too far to let the matter drop now; she could not face her father again without proof of the allegations she'd made about his fiancée. So she put on the gray foulard traveling suit that she'd worn on the day she left home, along with her gloves and the stylish straw bonnet, with its black grosgrain ribbons and gauze veil, and she asked Jacob to drop her off at the depot so that she might catch the morning train.

After she'd arrived and had a look around, Lexi decided that Hamilton was a lively city, even if it was only a quarter of the size of her hometown of Buffalo. It had a busy waterfront to handle the trade of the Great Lakes sailing vessels, and its main streets were macadamized and bordered by gas streetlamps.

This was the closest Lexi had been to civilization in more than a month, and so she slowed her pace as she passed by the windows of the shops on King Street to admire the goods offered for sale. She was sorely tempted to spend the morning shopping, but she had not entirely forgotten the reason she'd come here.

Lexi knew that Mrs. Palmer kept a house in town. The woman had, more than once in conversation, mentioned her "quaint little cottage on Vine Street." Lexi had only to inquire with a nearby grocer to learn the exact address. Next, she went to the bakery, purchased a fragrant, rum-soaked sponge cake, and, after it had been put into a paperboard box and tied up with string, Lexi took the package in hand and headed off in the direction of Mrs. Palmer's "quaint little cottage."

"Quaint" would not have been the word Lexi would have used to describe the elegant, two-storied white frame house whose facade was shaded by a pair of gracefully arching willow trees. A neat hedgerow divided the property on all sides from the neighbors' and sheltered a well-tended rose garden still brightened by the colors of the last, overblown blooms of summer.

Although it was by no means so grand as her father's brownstone on Delaware Avenue, it was far from the rude, cramped townhouse Lexi had expected to find. And as she stood there on the crushed gravel walk that led up to the front door, Lexi felt her first tinglings of doubt. If the Frenchwoman's home had been some meager little dwelling, it would have gone a long way to prove Lexi's case that this woman was a fortune hunter, but as it was, she'd have to find her proof elsewhere.

When the housekeeper, a ruddy-faced woman named Mrs. Clifton, heard that Lexi was an old friend of her absent mistress who'd come for a surprise visit, she was kind enough to invite her in for tea. Lexi accepted, of course, but only upon the condition that Mrs. Clifton join her and share the cake she'd brought with her.

At Lexi's insistence, they sat in the kitchen, at the small table near a window that looked out into the garden. The atmosphere was cozy and intimate, and Lexi suspected that Mrs. Clifton would be more comfortable there—and therefore more likely to exchange confidences.

The woman had already explained that Mrs. Palmer had gone away just after her husband's death, and had been living in Buffalo for some time. And she'd voiced aloud her fear that her mistress might soon decide that she wasn't coming back, leaving Mrs. Clifton to seek out a new position.

"I'm sure that Mrs. Palmer will be sorry to have missed you," the older woman said as she poured them both a second cup of tea.

"I was planning on a visit to Buffalo in the next month or so," Lexi told her then. "Perhaps I shall call upon her at her hotel there. You did say that was where she was staying, didn't you?"

"Yes, miss. She'd like that, I'm sure. The loneliness is likely what drove her away from here. There weren't many visitors stopped by to see her after the colonel died."

Lexi had been sipping at her tea, but now she met Mrs. Clifton's faded blue eyes over the rim of her cup. This revelation was surely an important one. "Why not, do you suppose?" she asked, trying not to sound *too* interested. "I would think that all her friends would have come by out of courtesy, to pay their respects."

Mrs. Clifton frowned, seemingly intent on pushing the cake crumbs around her plate with her fork. "Well . . . to tell the truth, miss, there was some talk. Mrs. Palmer is a handsome woman, as you must know, and some of the folks around here thought she ought not to have been entertaining those gentlemen, what with the colonel lying upstairs on his deathbed."

Lexi's eyes widened, but before she could speak, the housekeeper continued. "Of course, it was all perfectly proper. I was here, and I would know, wouldn't I? The only gentlemen crossed that threshold were those officers who come to inquire after the colonel's health . . . and his doctor, of course."

"How awful it must have been for her," Lexi replied, and surprised herself to realize that she meant it. The eerie, tingling sensation she'd felt before was returning now. Could it be just as her father had told her, that the rumors she'd heard had all been based on lies?

Distracted by these niggling doubts, Lexi turned her attentions on the rose garden outside the window. There was something special about this garden, she thought, something that made one feel comfortable and welcome. It was not the arrangement. The beds were set out in ordinary square plots, divided by brick walkways that were strewn now with petals of faded, browning hues. But the bushes had obviously been tended with a loving hand, for they were still thick with blooms, the fragrant heads drooping from their own weight.

"Shall I slice you another piece of cake, miss?"

"What's that?" Lexi said as she was abruptly drawn from her thoughts. "No. No thank you, Mrs. Clifton, but do have another yourself, if you like."

"Don't mind if I do."

As the housekeeper cut another thick wedge of the rum cake for herself, Lexi endeavored to regroup her thoughts. She was not half so trusting as Mrs. Clifton. After all, who could say what went on behind the parlor doors when those young officers came to visit? No, Lexi was not going to give up that easily. "My, but that is a lovely rose garden," she remarked offhandedly, as she considered her next move. "Do you have a gardener come in to tend it?"

"My son Jamie does much of the weeding and trimming now that the missus is away," Mrs. Clifton replied, "but when she's here, she insists upon doing everything with her own two hands. I never saw a lady liked to plant and dig as much as Mrs. Palmer. Her heart and soul are out there in that garden."

Lexi was somehow irritated to learn this. "I imagine the colonel must have been proud of his wife's horticultural talents."

"Horti—horticul—How's that, miss?"

"Her ability to grow such beautiful flowers."

"Oh my, no. My, my, no. Colonel Palmer thought it weren't ladylike for the missus to be out there on her knees all the time, diggin' in the dirt."

Lexi absorbed the information carefully as she reached to spoon more sugar into her cup. "I had heard that the colonel was a formidable man."

"I hate to speak ill of the dead, but I must say it. He was a tartar! Ran this household with an iron hand, he did. There weren't anything too small to catch his notice. Still he must have been a good soldier, though. His young officers thought so highly of him."

"Yes, you did say that they called to inquire about his health when he was ailing," Lexi reminded her.

"They did at that, miss. If it weren't Captain Hoskins or Lieutenant Perkins paying a call, there'd be Lieutenant Wallis or Captain Bascombe. . . . His men had respect for him, all right. I guess what makes a good man don't always make a good soldier."

With this, Lexi's interest was piqued. None of the soldiers she'd met at the Harvest Dance had seemed overly respectful of Colonel Palmer; in fact, quite the contrary.

"Bascombe, did you say?" Lexi asked.

Captain Ames had made mention of an officer named Bascombe who he'd said was "well-acquainted" with Mrs. Palmer. Surely this must be the same man.

"Yes, Captain Ronald Bascombe," Mrs. Clifton replied. "A fine-looking young gentleman, with blond hair and long, curling mustaches. Do you know him, miss?"

No, Lexi thought, not yet she didn't, but she suspected that if she was looking for answers, it was to him that she must turn next.

It had been amusing to convince the officers she'd met on the night of the Harvest Dance that she had been acquainted with Colonel Palmer, and she'd considered it a challenge to see how much she could learn of Mrs. Palmer from her housekeeper. But when Lexi found herself seated in the post commander's office at the military compound on Burlington Heights, attempting to pass herself off as a distant cousin of Captain Bascombe, she very nearly lost her nerve. Only by reminding herself that she had to bring out the truth about Mrs. Palmer to keep her father from making a terrible mistake was she able to go through with this one last charade.

Thankfully, Colonel Hampton was a genial old man, easily charmed by a sweet smile and the exchange of a few pleasantries. Lexi was surprised to see how simple it was to discover from him that at this time of the afternoon, his officers generally had their tea in the dining room of the Royal Hotel, and then to cover her tracks by swearing the colonel to secrecy so that she might surprise her dear "cousin."

The Royal Hotel with its vaulted, frescoed ceilings, sweeping staircases, and pedestaled statuary was easily one of the most elegant buildings in Hamilton and therefore well-suited to the tastes of those aristocratic young English officers who were so unfortunate as to find themselves stationed in the "wilds" of Upper Canada.

Once she'd been directed to the dining room, Lexi scanned the crowd, picking out those men wearing the bright red of a British officer's tunic to study more closely. As it happened, Captain Bascombe was not so hard to find, mainly on account of the long, curling "mustaches" of which Mrs. Clifton had made mention.

Having sighted her quarry, Lexi wound her way purposefully through the crowded room, until at last she drew up before his table. The tablecloth was littered with crumbs and china plates and more than one empty cup, but his companions must have already departed, for Bascombe was sitting there alone, with one fair brow cocked quizzically as he regarded her.

There was no denying that he was a handsome man: lean and lithe, with classic features — a golden Apollo in an officer's tunic. But even so, as Lexi looked on him, she was struck by the thought that this man paled before her memories of a brawny, black-haired Welshman. What was she doing here? Hadn't Morgan asked her to forget about the past? Hadn't she promised?

"Captain Bascombe?" she began, when at last she found her voice.

"Yes?"

"My name is Alexandra Merritt, and I'd like to speak with you, if I may. I believe we have a mutual acquaintance — the widow Mrs. Palmer."

A secretive smile twisted on his lips as he reached out to toy with one waxed end of his mustache. "Ah, yes. A delightful little minx, she was. We all enjoyed her company immensely."

"So I understand," Lexi remarked under her breath.

Captain Bascombe did not bother to rise, only lazily waved a hand to indicate the chair opposite his. "By all means do sit down, Miss Merritt, and tell me what news you have brought of our charming widow."

Lexi took advantage of his offer, although she'd begun to suspect by his manner that this time she was playing out of her league. She perched herself on the edge of the seat, her spine stiff as an iron od, gloved hands folded neatly in her lap, and drew a long, calming breath.

"We've none of us heard anything of her since she left Hamilton," Bascombe explained. "But you must forgive my manners. May I offer you some tea? Or cake, perhaps?"

"No, thank you," Lexi replied. She did not wish to stray far from the subject she'd come to discuss. "To answer your question, Mrs. Palmer has settled quite comfortably in Buffalo."

"Buffalo, eh?" he said, taking up the teapot so that he might refill his own cup. "I always suspected Hamilton was too rustic for her tastes. And since none of us here suited her, I suppose she's gone off after bigger game."

That particular remark struck home, and it told Lexi quite a bit about what kind of relationship there'd been between Captain Bascombe and Mrs. Palmer. Until this moment, she had been afraid that he'd find a starry-eyed young gentleman who was still in love with the woman and unwilling to cooperate with her plans. But now she saw that there was a chance, after all.

"Yes, bigger game, indeed. I suppose that's what you'd call my father," she said, a bitter edge to the words. "He is ordinarily a perceptive man, Captain Bascombe, but unfortunately he is not immune to the charms of such a woman. . . ."

Bascombe's brows rose as he lifted his cup to his lips. It was the only hint that he was surprised to learn of Lexi's connection with his "charming widow." "You mustn't blame your father," he told

147

her with a friendly familiarity. "Few of us poor men can resist such a woman."

Lexi leaned across the table, gripping its edge tightly with both hands. She was sick to death of the widow Mrs. Palmer and of the necessity of playing these games, and so she proceeded to reveal herself in a voice that was cool and clear and calculating. "If I may be candid with you," she began. "I do not intend to allow a scheming French opera dancer to take over my home and squander what my father has worked his whole life for, and I will do whatever I must to prevent it."

Bascombe set down his cup and eased forward in his chair, his sharp gray eyes gleaming brightly beneath their heavy lids, as if he were seeing Lexi now for the first time. "Well, well, Miss Merritt, I do appreciate a woman who knows what she wants and I assure you that you have my sympathies in this."

"I'm grateful to you, Captain."

"May I ask what made you seek me out?"

"I'd heard from several people that you and Mrs. Palmer had been . . . close, and . . . well, to be quite honest, I led your colonel to believe that I was your cousin so that he might tell me where to find you."

Reaching across the table, Bascombe put a hand over hers and effected a concerned air. "And imagine that you have gone to all this trouble in the hope that I might aid your cause."

Captain Bascombe seemed only to be offering her kindness, but for some inexplicable reason, as Lexi

148

elt the warmth of his skin seep through the fabric
f her glove, a shiver of apprehension went through
er. "I was hoping for some kind of proof that
vould bring my father to his senses," she said.

"Ah," he replied sagely. "Love letters? Some ten-
ler token of her affection? That sort of thing?"

"Well . . . yes."

Once again Bascombe's lips stretched into a lazy
mile. He rose from his chair and held out a hand
o her. "Come along to my quarters, then, Miss
Merritt. I'm sure we can find something suitable, if
ve put our two heads together."

And so Lexi allowed him to escort her back to
he military compound. Perhaps she ought to have
questioned his motives at once, but as it was, she
vas so flush with the possibility of success at long
ast that she did not pause to consider precisely
vhat he stood to gain. She only assumed that as a
purned lover, Captain Bascombe must be out for
evenge, and although she might not have been so
quick to admit it, that suited her purpose exactly.

Although Lexi may have accepted the role of a
hy and naive farm girl for the past few months, it
vas far from who she was in truth. She knew well
nough that she had no business accompanying
Captain Bascombe back to his private quarters, no
natter how innocent the errand. But she could not
urn back now, not when she was so close to getting
vhat she'd come after. After all, Bascombe had as
nuch as told her that he had some tangible proof,
adn't he?

When they reached his quarters, Lexi stepped

warily over the threshold. She had been considering her position all the while as they'd walked here together from the Royal Hotel. The wisest option would be to conclude her business with Captain Bascombe as quickly as was possible, but now as she looked about the room, all her cautious thoughts fled and her jaw dropped in astonishment.

She had expected a crowded, little room with the simplest of accommodations—a bedstead and bureau, perhaps a washstand. What met her eyes was something else entirely. But for the bed with a tall, carved headboard that monopolized the far corner, this room could have passed for a formal parlor to rival those in her own neighborhood back home on Delaware Avenue. The walls were papered in a crimson scrollwork design, and there were Turkish carpets scattered over the floor. A dark oak mantelpiece framed the hearth and was topped by a pair of matching brass urns, and a portrait of a young Queen Victoria hung over the desk that stood near the windows. As she took it all in, Lexi told herself that this was the room of a privileged young man used to having what he wanted out of life.

Bascombe offered her a seat on the leather sofa that was set in the center of the room and went immediately to his desk. Lexi sat down to wait. Her hands were trembling as she threw back her veil and removed her gloves. Only a few minutes more and she'd have the proof she needed. Then she'd get on the train back to Gran's and be done with this.

But when Bascombe returned and sat down beside her, he was not carrying the papers she'd expected to see, but two stemmed, crystal glasses, each filled with amber liquid.

"The letters . . ." Lexi reminded him.

"All in good time, my dear," he said, as he handed her one of the glasses. "I thought a glass of Madeira to seal our bargain would be in order."

Lexi knew now that she was definitely playing out of her league, but what choice did she have except to humor him? She sipped at the wine and felt it burn her tongue and throat as she swallowed. A few more sips of this and she might forget why she'd come here altogether. There was a table nearby, and she reached over and set aside the glass.

Bascombe had already drained his glass and reached across her body to set it down beside hers. This move put him far too close for comfort. "Do you know that your eyes are the most remarkable shade of green?" he said in a low voice, running his fingers lightly along her shoulder and down her arm as he withdrew.

A shudder ran through her, but Lexi managed to keep her composure. "I should like to see those letters now," she said, edging nearer to the arm of the sofa.

Bascombe seemed genuinely surprised by the request. "But, my dear, I thought you knew. There are no letters."

Lexi's heart began to hammer in warning against her breastbone. "You said that—"

"What I said—precisely—was that if we put our heads together, we could find something to suit your purposes, and I still believe that. I'm sure

151

somewhere in the drawer of my desk I can find an invitation written in her hand. . . ."

Revulsion swelled into anger as Lexi understood finally what sort of man she was dealing with. She got to her feet and paced the full length of the carpet, all the while struggling for words. "And just what do you intend? That we use them to forge a packet of love letters?"

"You needn't sound so self-righteous," he retorted. "After all, 'twas you who said you'd do whatever you must. Have you lost your nerve so quickly?"

"I never meant to imply such a thing. I thought you understood what I wanted. What I cannot understand is what you hoped to gain by all of this."

But even as she posed the question, Lexi feared that she already knew the answer.

Bascombe's eyes narrowed as he stood up and began to advance on her. "Besides a suitable display of gratitude from you, I should have had repayment finally for the fruitless months I spent chasing after the little French whore," he replied, his voice dropping dangerously low. "Did you know that's what we called her? Old Palmer's 'French whore'?"

Lexi realized now the gravity of her situation and knew that her best chance of coming out of this unscathed would be to keep him talking . . . and at a distance. "And so you mean to say that you didn't—"

"I'm afraid I was never so fortunate, though I never did anything to discourage the rumors. There were plenty of others who enjoyed her favors, I assure you. She even managed to beguile one of them into poisoning her husband when he became too much trouble. You may tell that to your father, if you like."

Lexi had been inching backward toward the door as he spoke, but as soon as she reached behind her to twist the doorknob, Bascombe closed the distance between them, trapping her between his body and the door, his fingers closing ruthlessly over the soft flesh of her arm. She looked at him, hoping for mercy, but there seemed to be no warmth, no heart in him at all—only the cold, hard perfection of a marble statue.

"I couldn't possibly believe anything you've told me," she said, writhing under his grip, "not even if I wanted to. Now let go of me!"

"I've heard that American women are like fine thoroughbreds," he said in an intimately low tone, "that even when making love they're full of fire and spirit. Perhaps I'll find out for myself if it's true. I'm an excellent horseman, you know."

"How dare you suggest such a thing! All I need do is scream and I'll have the whole regiment here smashing down your door."

"Oh, I don't think you'd want that. It's your word against mine, isn't it? And what will Colonel Hampton think of you when he discovers that you aren't really my dear cousin, after all?"

Lexi knew that he was right and vented her anger by twisting against his grip. The more she struggled, though, the more it seemed to fuel his ardor. When he forced himself more intimately against

153

her, her strength evaporated. She deserved this, she told herself, for being such a fool, and for trying to ruin the reputation of a woman who'd likely done nothing more than fall in love with her father.

"I only came here for the letters," she insisted, and pulled an unsteady breath. "That's all. I thought that you—"

At this, he drew his head back and regarded her sharply. "Don't play the innocent with me, you little hypocrite! Lying your way in here, inviting me with those eyes of yours. You and that Frenchwoman are more alike than you care to admit. You don't want her infringing on your territory, that's all. You want to keep your precious papa all to yourself—to manage his life and keep a firm hold of his purse-strings."

"That's not true!" Lexi cried. "It's not!"

Bascombe shrugged. "Believe what you like," he said. "It makes no difference to me."

His eyes perused her boldly, his mind clearly turning to other matters now. Releasing his grip on her arms, he captured her face roughly in his two hands. "As I've said, I don't mind helping you out . . . for a price."

For some time now, she'd been aware of his intent, but still it caught Lexi off guard when he shoved her back against the door, and his mouth closed over hers. All at once, she was suffocating. As his touch seared her skin, tears stung her eyes and choked her throat. She tried to turn away from him, but he caught her lip between his teeth, and a stab of pain and the salty taste of blood made her give up the attempt.

It took a few moments for Lexi to realize that her arms were no longer pinned, but when she did, she gathered all the strength remaining in her, and when he drew back for breath, she balled her fists and struck him a blow to the midsection. The effect was not overwhelming, but it was enough to knock the wind out of him and send him back a step, enough for her to slip free and put the door between them.

For an instant, Lexi stood like a frightened doe, afraid to make a move as she awaited his reaction. To her surprise, when he saw that she had escaped him, he began to laugh. The sound was far from pleasant, though; it was hard and hurtful, and pierced through her like shards of broken glass.

"Run on home to Papa now," he sneered. "Back where you belong."

His laughter rang in Lexi's ears long after she'd slammed the door shut and hurried off down the boardwalk, long after she'd straightened her bodice, retied her bonnet, and replaced the veil over her paling face. She did not look back.

The train ride home left Lexi with more than an hour to contemplate all that she'd been through. Acres of golden farm fields rolled past her window, and thick forests rich with autumn colors of crimson and flame. She looked out over it all, but did not see. Her mind was occupied with other thoughts.

Her father had been right all along, and Gran

and Morgan, and—as she was forced to confront it—very likely so was the despicable Captain Bascombe. She had not been thinking of her father's happiness when she'd condemned Mrs. Palmer without any proof, she'd been thinking only of herself.

Lexi felt miserable. Her arms were stiff and likely bruised, her lip swollen and sore, but these small pains she well deserved. What affected her more was her shame at having behaved for so long like a spoilt child. How could she ever face her father—or his fiancée—again?

Chapter Ten

The sound of a steam whistle in the distance brought Morgan to his feet, and while he waited for the train to come into sight, he paced a small section of the platform, his bootheels striking sharply against the wooden planks with each anxious step. He'd been waiting all day to give Lexi his news, imagining what her reaction would be, hoping she'd be pleased. God, what was happening to him? He sounded like a besotted schoolboy waiting to give his sweetheart a handmade valentine.

As he watched the passengers get off the train, Morgan almost failed to recognize her, dressed as she was in an elegant gray traveling suit, her heavy, golden hair knotted up under a smart, chip bonnet, which was draped with a gauzy veil that concealed her features. It struck him then that she could be a stranger, there was so much about her that he did not know. He wanted to know everything, every detail of her life. And this from the man who had preached to her to forget about the past. He already knew that she had a good heart, he reminded himself, and that ought to be enough.

"Lexi!" he called out then, waving an arm over his head to attract her attention.

She came to him cautiously, and it seemed as if she were hiding something beneath the self-assured carriage and graceful step. How could he ever have imagined her to be a simple farm girl?

"Morgan?"

He reached out and took both her gloved hands in his. "I stopped by your gran's farm to see you. She said you'd gone to the city to do some shopping. Jacob was busy with his chores, and so I offered to come and fetch you."

She dropped her head to avoid his eyes, even though he could scarcely read anything at all of her expression beneath the shadowy veil. "Thank you," she said softly.

"Where are your parcels?"

There was a long pause before she replied. "I didn't find what I went looking for."

"Well, come along, then," he said, and escorted her to the buggy.

He handed her up, joined her on the seat, and once they were on their way, they drove for several miles without a word between them. A gentle west wind carried the bright songs of the woodland birds and rattled the leaves still clinging to the trees, but Lexi scarcely seemed to notice any of it.

Morgan forgot about the surprise he had planned as he concerned himself instead with what might have caused this change in her. He'd never known a shopping trip to have such an effect on a woman, even an unsuccessful one. Was she having second thoughts about the two of them, regretting what they'd shared that night at the dance? No, there had to be another answer. Mrs. MacLennan hadn't told him where Lexi had gone precisely. But if she'd taken the ferry across the river to Buffalo . . .

"Did you go to see your father today?"

"I didn't go to Buffalo at all," she replied. "I went to Hamilton."

The very mention of the city where he'd known such misfortune made Morgan uneasy, but he put his own emotions aside. "Your first trip there?" he asked, trying to draw her out.

She only nodded.

"What did you think of it?"

"I—" The word caught in her throat and she swallowed hard before continuing, ". . . never want to go back."

A shiver of dread ran through Morgan as a thought came to mind. Lexi had been so interested in the life he'd led before he'd come here. Might she have inquired about him in Hamilton? Might someone have told her the whole sordid tale?

He stopped the carriage in the middle of the road and tied off the reins. He had to see her face, and turning to her, he reached to lift the veil of her bonnet. "What is it? What's wrong?"

Even before the words were out, he noticed the glaze of unshed tears sparkling in her eyes and her bottom lip, reddened and swollen and marked by a line of dried blood, and he forgot his foolish imaginings. He caught her shoulders, too roughly, perhaps, for she winced as he did so. "What happened to you in Hamilton, Lexi. Tell me!"

"I went meddling into my father's affairs, digging up the past," she told him, sliding her arms up around his neck as she buried her face against his shoulder. "Oh, you were right, Morgan. You were right when you said we have to forget about the past."

He tilted her chin upward and tenderly ran the pad of his thumb over her lip. "But who did this?" he asked. "Who hurt you?"

"It doesn't matter. It's nothing. It was my fault, and it's over now."

With a tremulous sigh, she lifted her eyes to his. Lacing her gloved fingers behind his neck, she drew him down to her, until he felt her breath caress his face in a warm, sweet wave. "Please . . . don't make me remember, Morgan," she said softly, borrowing the same smooth words he'd used on her that first night in the orchard. "Help me forget."

Her eyes were bright with longing, her parted lips an appealing invitation. Morgan could not have refused such a plea, even if he'd wanted to. Obliging, he took her in his arms and brushed his lips over hers, mindful of her bruised mouth, yet ready to offer the comfort she needed.

When he kissed her again, her mouth softened, opening under his to signal a surrender he suspected she did not fully intend. She was only trying to erase the memory of whatever had upset her today. Reluctantly, he drew back. "I want to help, Lexi," he said, "but not this way. Talk to me. Tell me what's wrong."

She did not seem to hear him. She pressed nearer still, and her hands slipped beneath his frock coat,

160

her fingertips skimming with an achingly light touch over the fabric of his shirt, along the curve of his rib-cage, and upward across the taut muscles of his back. She seemed obsessed with the reaction she was causing in him, and he could not deny her power. A shudder of pleasure coursed through him, and he groaned, sensing defeat.

"Please," she urged, her voice a seductive whisper.

On their own, Morgan's fingers moved to loosen the pearl button at her collar. A pulse was beating in the hollow of her throat, and he bent to press his lips against it. Her perfume permeated the air between them, and when he inhaled, it went to his head like a drug. And then his hands moved over her, and he was touching her face, her shoulders, her breasts. The need of her was rising in his blood. God, how many nights had he lain awake and dreamed of this? Of her?

"I don't want to go back to Gran's right now," she said, breathing the words against his ear. "Take me home with you, Morgan."

She didn't know what she was doing. She couldn't know that once she'd sparked this dangerous fire, it was bound to burn fast and hot, consuming them both. And she'd hate him for it in the end.

Gathering all his strength, Morgan grasped her shoulders and set her firmly aside on the carriage seat. "You don't want this," he told her. "You're just hurt and confused."

"I do," she insisted, and her soft, wounded lip began to tremble. "I want . . ."

Her voice drifted off and he could see that she'd realized that he was right. Watching her, Morgan nearly

161

changed his mind, but he knew that one of them had
to keep a clear head, else the fragile bond between
them might be snapped forever. And so he set his jaw
and made her look into his eyes.

"God knows I care for you, Lexi. I'll give you
friendship, comfort, consolation, whatever you need.
But don't ask me to make love to you while you're
dazed and hurting," he said fiercely. "Don't ask that
of me."

"I—I'm sorry," she murmured, sounding so lost
and lonely that it touched his heart.

Weakening, he offered a shoulder to her, and in an
instant, Lexi closed the distance he'd put between
them, and melting against him, she wept like a child.

When the storm was over and the tears had subsided at last, he reached into his pocket and handed
her a handkerchief. "No more meddling?" he asked
gently. "No more digging up the past?"

Lexi nodded, and easing upright, she dabbed at her
eyes.

With a trembling hand, Morgan reached for the
reins, snapped them up, and the buggy rocked into
motion once more. The silence was a comfort to him
now. He stared at the road ahead and cleared his
mind in an effort to restore his calm. But a thousand
questions rushed in to fill the void. Why was his heart
pounding like he'd just run a mile? Why did it pain
him so to see her hurting? What did she want of him?
And what about the future he'd planned?

The thought jogged his memory. "I nearly forgot,"
he said. "I've something to tell you."

Lexi looked up expectantly.

"Ever since the Harvest Dance, I've lain awake at

night, unable to sleep for thinking about what you'd said to me, about the good I could be doing here . . ."

"And?"

"And I realized that you were right. For too long now, I've been thinking only of myself. It's time I started doing something worthwhile with my life."

She touched his shoulder, and he was relieved to see her smiling. "Oh, Morgan, do you mean it? You're going to take up practice here? Gran will be so pleased to hear it, and the Newcombs, of course, and the Petersons . . ."

"And what about you, Lexi Merritt? What do you think of my plans?"

The deepened voice, the slow, careful way in which he phrased his question, ought to have told her how much he needed to know her feelings. But Lexi was still too out-of-sorts to comprehend. She only blushed and dropped her gaze.

" 'Tis you who ought to be the doctor, you know," he went on. "I never thought it possible, but somehow you've managed to heal this wounded soul of mine and make me hopeful of the future. The world could use such skills as yours."

There was more he wanted to tell her, more he needed to ask, but this was not the time.

"I only did what my heart told me to," Lexi replied softly.

It was enough to give him hope, and he cast her a meaningful glance. "Promise me then that you'll never stop listening to your heart."

* * *

Morgan's decision necessitated the building of an infirmary, and he planned to set to work on it at once. He explained to Lexi that he would start simply at first, with a small addition to his cabin that would house his store of medicines and equipment and enable him to see those patients who might call upon him.

When Lexi gave the news to Gran, the old woman reacted with a knowing smile, as if she'd been expecting it all along. But she didn't have much else to say, and Lexi considered that unusual, indeed, for Gran was seldom speechless on any subject.

A few days later, however, she packed up a hamper with cold chicken and cider and blackberry pie and insisted that Lexi take it out to the cabin for Dr. Glendower's lunch, for as she said, it "wouldna do at all for a man tae work so hard as he wi'out his proper nourishment." She also instructed her to inform him that Jacob was at his disposal, should he need the help, and that she would arrange for the neighbors to come on Saturday to help him finish up the job.

From the first, Gran had shown a special fondness for Morgan Glendower. Now, as Lexi hiked to his cabin through the waving fields of golden grass with the hamper on her arm and the tingling warmth of the sun on her back, she found herself glad of it. If the truth be known, she'd developed quite a fondness for him herself.

At first he'd been a challenge, a mystery that needed solving. But as they'd grown closer, Lexi realized that what mattered most of all was that he *needed* her. It was important to Lexi to be needed; she'd always shied away from men who'd wanted nothing more than a showpiece on their arm. Morgan had told her that she'd changed his life, and while that may well have been, she was beginning to see that she'd been changed as well. Whenever she was with him, her heart was lighter. For the first time in more years than she could remember, she felt as free as a child, and it thrilled her to realize that she was in love.

As she reached the crest of the hill, Lexi stopped, set down the hamper, and listened. There was an odd sound coming out of the valley below, the repeated, hollow *thunk* of metal on wood. Following it, she found Morgan felling timber in the wooded glen that stood beyond the cabin. For a while, she stood at a distance and watched as each powerful swing of his ax hit its mark, splintering a widening wedge in the tree trunk and causing it to shudder along its whole length. His broad shoulders flexed against the fabric of his shirt, and each cord and tendon in his hard-thewn forearms stood out as though they'd been carved in stone.

With a loud crack, the remainder of the wood splintered, the tree swayed, and Morgan stood well aside to watch it fall. When the flurry of dust and crumbling brown leaves stirred up from the forest floor had subsided, he turned and caught sight of her at last. With one sure stroke, he buried his ax blade in the log that now lay before him and hastened up the hill.

Hooking her waist with one strong arm, he swung her easily into his embrace, and heedless of the dust and perspiration streaking his face, he kissed her heartily. "I've been hoping you'd come. It's damned lonely out here, with only the sparrows and jays to keep me company."

Lexi savored the warm, salty kiss, and breathing in his musky scent, she hugged him tightly and laughed for the pure pleasure of it as he swung her around once more. Until now, she'd never heard Morgan admit to being lonely out here.

"Gran packed you a lunch," she informed him, as he set her on her feet once more. "There's enough for an army. It seems now that you're going to be *our* Doctor Glendower, she doesn't want you wasting away."

"Bless her soul. I have to admit I'm losing my taste for my own cooking: burnt beans and biscuits that would be better used as paving stones."

"Shall I go inside and set out lunch for you, then?"

"Why don't we walk down to the creek and make it a picnic instead?" he suggested. "The almanac says we're in for an early winter this year; we ought to enjoy these last warm days while we have the chance. Maybe I could even bring my fishing rod . . . if you think your gran wouldn't mind my poaching on her land, of course."

Lexi grinned. "Right now I think Gran would forgive you anything short of murder," she said, "and even that—if she thought the victim deserving."

Morgan's brow furrowed. For a moment he seemed distracted, but the mood soon passed.

"Good, then, it's settled," he said. "Just let me wash up and fetch my rod, and we'll be on our way."

While she waited for him, Lexi went down to the glen to retrieve the wool coat that he had carelessly left behind, draped over a tree stump. As she tossed it over her arm, something fell out of the pocket. It was a small book, bound in worn, brown leather, whose curious title was written in gold letters along its spine: *Mabinogeon*.

Walking back to the cabin, Lexi opened its cover and thumbed through the pages, perusing. The text sounded old-fashioned, and although the words were in English, many of the proper names seemed to have too many *l*'s and *y*'s and *w*'s. The stories within appeared to be a collection of tales of King Arthur and his knights; there were chapters chronicling the adventures of Kynon and Owain and Gawain. . . . Lexi's interest was piqued, and so, settling herself down on the porch steps, she began to read. She was soon so engrossed that she did not think of Morgan until she heard his voice as he came up behind her.

"Do you see those stakes I've set out over there?" he said. "That's where the infirmary's to be."

Lexi blinked in confusion as she looked up from the page to see Morgan hovering nearby. He'd taken the time to clean up, for now he wore a fresh cotton shirt, and his thick hair was damp with moisture and smoothed back from his face.

"What's that?" she asked.

"The infirmary," Morgan repeated patiently, "the room I'm planning to build."

"Oh, yes. I'm sorry. I guess I wasn't listening. I went to fetch your coat and this curious little book fell out of the pocket, the *Mabi— Mabinoge—?*"

Morgan smiled as she stumbled over the word. *"Mabinogeon,"* he corrected. "It's a collection of old Welsh tales that have been translated into English."

"It's wonderful. Do you think you might let me

borrow it sometime? Gran doesn't keep much reading material other than the family Bible. I suppose she thinks it a frivolous pastime." With that, she sighed heavily. "That's one of the few things I miss about home."

"Take it with you now," he offered. "In fact, I've a trunk full of books inside. Feel free to borrow any of them, any time you like."

Lexi met his eyes and smiled. Thanking him, she slipped the volume into her apron pocket as they set out on their way.

Chapter Eleven

They picnicked in a pleasant spot by the creek, far away from the incessant rush of water tumbling over the rocks farther upstream. Here the banks were wide and the waters formed a deep, still pool. After they'd eaten their fill, Lexi took off her shoes and stockings, and tucking up her skirts, she waded out to perch herself on a large flat boulder that rested in mid-stream to warm herself in the sunlight.

Morgan followed suit, shedding boots and stockings and rolling up his trouser legs before he went to prepare his fishing rod. Once he'd baited his hook and cast the line in the water, he stepped out into the shallows and found his attention captured by his companion.

She was reclining on the rock, stretching herself like a tawny cat, propped on her elbows, with eyes closed and gentle face turned skyward. The sunlight glinted off the burnished tendrils of hair that had escaped her heavy topknot and kissed the warm ivory of her skin.

He was pleased with himself for having suggested this outing. Lexi seemed so calm here, so unlike the pale and distressed young woman he'd picked up at the depot in Ridgeway only a few days ago.

169

The rose-colored calico stretched taut over her breasts as she arched her back and drew up her knees, and a pair of shapely calves emerged from beneath the dampened drape of her petticoats. With a contented sigh, she eased herself upright and slipped her bare feet back into the waters. Morgan swallowed hard, unable to look away. She was the loveliest creature he'd ever encountered, and he wanted her all for his own.

For days now he had been making his plans, with but one end in mind—their future together. But he'd been hurt once before, and he needed to be sure before he spoke.

"What are you thinking about?" she called to him, when finally she noticed him studying her.

"Did you know that you were sitting, dangling your feet in the water just as you are now, on the first day I saw you?" he replied. "It reminds me of the story of *The Lady of Llyn y Fan Fach*."

"Is that one of the stories of the *Mabinogeon?*" she asked.

"No, 'tis an old folk tale my mother used to tell me when I was a boy. She claimed it was the story of her own family, in fact, and how a certain young lad among them came to take a fairy to be his wife."

Lexi's eyes went wide, but then she frowned and reached down to splash some water at him. "Now you're teasing me."

"I'm not," Morgan protested. "She swore that it was true."

He tried to regard her with a serious air, but one corner of his mouth insisted on twitching rebelliously as he pretended to concentrate on reeling in his line, then cast it out further.

"Will you tell it to me?" she entreated, stirring up the waters around her as she fluttered her feet.

"Well . . ." he began slowly, summoning up his memories of the tale. He hoped to make it as vivid for her as it had been for him when he'd first heard it as a young boy all those years ago.

"It seems that this young man was tending his cattle beside a lake one day when there appeared the most beautiful lady he had ever seen, sitting there on the surface of the water, combing her hair.

"He fell in love at once and asked her to marry him. She answered him by saying that if he came to this same spot twelve months hence, she would return with her twin sister, and if he could tell them apart, she would marry him. Once he'd agreed, she dived into the waters and disappeared."

Morgan paused, looking over to see Lexi's reaction to the tale so far. A pensive smile curved on her lips. "A rash young man, this ancestor of yours."

"Ah, but he had twelve months' time to reflect on his ladylove," Morgan reminded her, "to savor and recall her every feature."

"And when she returned with this sister of hers, did he choose correctly?"

"He did. Being an observant fellow, he'd not failed to notice that his lovely fairy laced her slippers in a most unusual fashion, and in that way he was able to tell them apart."

"A triumph for true love," Lexi replied, clapping her hands together, "and I suppose they lived happily ever after."

"They might have, but for the *tri ergyd diachos*."

"I beg your pardon?"

171

"Three causeless blows," Morgan explained. "On the day that they wed, the fairy warned him that if he should ever strike her three causeless blows, she would leave him forever."

"Where's the harm in that? If he truly loved her, surely he would not strike her at all."

" 'Twas meant figuratively, I think," he said, "and as he was soon to discover, it was she who decided if there was cause. The first blow was struck when he chastised her for crying at a wedding. 'But this pair's troubles have just begun,' she said. The second came when he became angry to hear her laughing at a funeral, although she explained that 'Once people die, their troubles are over.'

"The final blow came when he teased her because she did not move fast enough to fetch his horse as he'd asked her to. And with that, she announced that the third blow had been struck. She bid him farewell, went back to the lake, and disappeared beneath its waters forever."

A long silence ensued. Lexi sat motionless, staring intently at her distorted reflection in the rippling waters of the creek. Morgan wondered what she was thinking, and as he began reeling in his line, he sought to prompt a reaction from her. "The fish aren't biting today. I think someone's stirred up the waters hereabouts and chased them all away."

Setting his fishing pole back on the bank, he heard a splash behind him as Lexi got to her feet. He turned back, crossed his arms over his chest, and met her expectantly. But Lexi did not reply to his jibe. Gathering up her skirts, she crossed the shallows to stand before him, a scowl marring her gentle features.

172

"That's an awful ending for a fairy tale, Morgan. Are you sure you haven't forgotten something?"

"We never know when something we do or say might strike someone the wrong way and bring an end to our happiness," he mused. "It's very much the truth, isn't it?"

As Lexi considered his observation, she thrust her bottom lip out; it made her look like a petulant child. "Yes, I suppose so," she agreed reluctantly. "But do you mean to say that there isn't anything more to the tale? No happy ending at all?"

Morgan laughed. He could not help but be amused at her enthusiasm for a mere fairy tale. No wonder he'd fallen in love with her. He wanted to take her in his arms, right then and there, but he stopped himself. He had to know what was in her heart.

"There is something more," he said. "The fairy and her husband had a son named Rhiwallon, who often visited the lake, hoping that his mother would appear to him. And finally one day she did.

"She told him that it was his duty to aid mankind through healing and relieving pain. She taught him about the healing plants and gave him a bag that contained all manner of medical prescriptions, and thereafter he became the most celebrated physician in the land."

He felt a pleasing warmth rush through his veins when she smiled. "That's right," she said. "I remember now. You did say that all the men in your mother's family for generations had been physicians. And it's all on account of a fairy tale. I think I like your story after all."

When she spoke again, her voice was soft and tenuous. "I'm nearly certain there are no fairies in my family tree, Morgan, but even so. . . . Do you think that maybe I might help you with your work sometime . . . if you should need me?"

His chest tightened as he drew a wavering breath. Was this the admission he'd been waiting to hear?

"What about your father?" he asked. "And your life in Buffalo?"

With this, Lexi dropped her gaze, seemingly intent on the cold, clear stream that eddied around their ankles. "Buffalo is a part of the past. There's nothing for me back there anymore."

She stepped nearer. Letting her skirts slip free to drag in the water, she wound her arms about his neck. And when she lifted her eyes to his, he knew. "I hope my future's here," she said, "with you."

Without warning, Morgan swept her into his arms, and Lexi gasped in surprise. Carrying her up the bank, he stumbled and, whether by intent or design, pitched forward, sending them both tumbling onto the old tartan blanket that they'd earlier spread over a bed of fallen leaves.

As he settled over her, he cupped her face in his hands, seeking assurance in her eyes. "Are you certain this is what you want? A rude little cabin in the woods with a soul-weary country doctor for your companion?"

"More than anything," she said.

Morgan tried to swallow the lump that had formed in his throat. "God knows that I'm a selfish blackguard to let you say it, but I need you, Lexi."

He did not give her the chance to change her mind. His mouth settled on hers; it was soft and warm and

174

wonderful. He kissed her again and again, and with each kiss, he seemed to grow stronger, his lips demanding more of her, while she grew more passive, her brain muddled and foggy as she gave over to the delicious, languid feeling.

Lexi was alarmed by what was happening to her. During the most important years of her young life, she had been without a woman to confide in, and so when she'd heard the girls at school talking behind their hands about what went on between a man and a woman, she'd turned to Mrs. Fraser with her questions. The older woman had been patient and kind, but she'd never told her that she would feel like this.

Morgan was propped on one elbow, and so the weight of his body on hers was not uncomfortable, but rather made her curious. Her breasts were crushed against the sheath of his well-muscled chest, both legs entwined with his in the jumble of her sodden skirts. Through the thin layers of fabric, she could feel his hard thighs against her own and his need pressing intimately against her.

With his free hand, he was exploring now, as if he sought to commit every curve and hollow of her body to memory. Lexi trembled at his touch. Her mind had gone dangerously dull, and so she threw back her head to draw a cleansing breath and looked up, but the fringe of vivid autumn leaves overhead seemed to be spinning furiously around a patch of blue sky.

Twining her arms over his shoulders, she clung to him to stop the whirling in her brain and inhaled the clean scent of his soap, the sharp tang of pine, damp earth, and decaying leaves. Morgan was murmuring soothing words in her ear as he turned his attentions on the buttons of her bodice, loosing them one by one until the valley of her breasts and the lacy edge of her chemise lay exposed.

He drew back, and there was a gleam of triumph in his eyes. He bent to trace his lips slowly across her cheek, the line of her jaw and along the arch of her throat. Before she knew what he was about, he had untied the ribbon of her chemise and his lips were moving over the soft swell of her breasts, his tongue grazing one pink crest and then the next.

Lexi gasped as the excitement of contact burned across her skin like quickfire. A desire she had never known before began to build within her, a tingling of awakening awareness. "You make me feel . . . alive," she told him, her voice filled with awe.

"But there's more," he said, as he kissed her face, her eyes, her hair, "so much more."

Brushing back the tangle of her skirts, he followed the line of her thigh. His fingertips were hard and insistent, the rough calluses on his palm catching threads on her thin lawn drawers. Through the fabric, Lexi could feel the heat of his hand as it edged surely upward.

She was beyond rational thinking now. She only knew that she did not want him to stop touching her. She did not want this moment to end. Her hands fluttered to his collar, fingertips anxiously working loose the buttons of his shirt, sliding beneath the fabric to range over the smooth, hot surface of his skin. Curious, she pressed her palms against his chest to feel the crisp mat of hair, the skin pulled taut over well-defined muscles, and beneath it, his heart beating, steady and strong.

176

O   G E T   Y O U R

4 FREE BOOKS

AIL THE COUPON BELOW.

GET 4 FREE BOOKS

"Show me," she said, her voice hushed and deep against his ear. "Please."

Morgan labored to pull a full breath. His vision was blurring; his entire body had gone rigid with tension, and the warning bells were clanging furiously in his head. If they did not stop at once, he'd not be able to answer for the consequences.

He held himself painfully still, squeezing his eyes shut in a struggle for control. "You don't know what you're asking."

Oblivious to the danger, Lexi pressed her lips against his and, in one smooth motion, ran her hands up, then outward, swiping the fabric of his shirt and his suspenders off his shoulders and pinning his arms at the elbow. As he sought to free himself, Lexi toyed with his trouser buttons.

"I do," she said. "I may be . . . inexperienced, but I'm not a child. Love me, Morgan. Right here, right now. I've never wanted anything more."

Morgan's head was reeling. He'd been waiting for this moment, waiting for her to come to him. And now she had. Where was the harm?

Before reason could raise a voice within him, he kissed her again, intoxicating himself with the honeyed taste of her, and her scent, all sweet grass and violets. Meanwhile, he worked with swift precision, unfastening the tapes at her waist that bound the fragile scrap of lace-edged lawn that stood between them and casting it aside. Her thighs were smooth as warm silk beneath his fingers, and his brain darted ahead to imagine them wrapped securely about his hips.

Don't rush, he warned himself, as he fought to ignore the throbbing cadence of blood pounding at his temples, don't frighten her. Banishing the image from his thoughts, he reached instead to pull the pins from Lexi's hair, feeling the weight of it as he combed it free with his fingers, and watching in fascination as a ray of sunlight that had slipped in between the leaves overhead caught the curling strands and made them glint with red-gold fire.

With calm restored, Morgan focused on her needs, scattering feather-light kisses across her brow, taking her mouth with a leisurely thoroughness before sweeping lower, where his tongue sought the rosy tips of her breasts, encircling each in turn. And all the while, one hand was trailing upward along the soft flesh of her inner thigh to that most sensitive spot. A cry of surprise caught soundlessly in her throat as he touched her, teasing her with sure, even strokes.

Morgan knew that Lexi was an innocent, in this regard at least, and he wanted this first time, their first time, to be a pleasant memory for her. But the tickle of her quick, light breaths against the bared slope of his shoulder was maddening, and when, bold with passion, she reached out to free him from his trousers, her fingers intimately enfolding him, a groan vibrated deep in his chest. He could bear it no longer.

For a moment, he stilled. There was only the rasp of their uneven breathing filling the air, and then, lifting one knee, he parted her thighs and settled between her hips. Lexi felt the heat of him hard against her, a pressure that was answered by the wild, desperate aching his touch had sparked in her. There was no denying what was to come. But still her eyes widened as if only now did she realize his intent, and she made a small, whimpering sound.

"Don't be afraid," he whispered, his tone breathless but soothing. "Trust me, love. I would never hurt you."

She almost believed him, but with his first thrust, the pressure turned to pain. She shut her eyes and buried her head against his neck, ashamed to let him see her disappointment. After all that had come before, she'd been so certain that this final culmination would be wonderful. He felt her stiffen, and cradling her in his arms, he murmured softly. "Trust me, Lexi, please."

He made a move as if he might withdraw, but it was only to plunge deeper. Lexi gasped, expecting to hurt anew, but to her surprise, the pain receded, replaced by hot, sweet warmth, and an inexplicable urgency. The pressure was within her now, building as he filled her, her body pulsing madly with each rhythmic thrust.

Shamelessly, she arched against him, wrapping her legs around his waist to draw him nearer still. Never had she imagined that it would be like this. The blood was singing in her ears, her whole being centered on fulfillment. And when at last it seemed she could stand no more, the tremors began — small, tight circles that started deep within, widening like ripples on the water, and with each new wave a surge of exquisite pleasure. "Oh, Morgan, yes!"

She managed a ragged breath before his mouth captured hers once more in a bruising kiss, and his body stiffened and shuddered with the violence of his own release.

They lay together in one another's arms for a long while, spent and shaken, their limbs entwined in the tangle of skirts and cast-off clothing and blanket, afraid to move or speak lest they should break the spell. A chill breeze swept through the glade, rattling the crimson oak leaves overhead, and sending a shower of them down on the lovers.

Morgan stretched out a long arm, and picking them up one by one, he weaved them into the shimmering strands of Lexi's gold hair, scattering them wreathlike over her brow. " 'Tis a fairy crown for you to wear," he said at last.

When Lexi tried to speak, she found her voice nearly choked with emotion. She had never felt so safe, so complete. She wanted to lie here in his arms forever. "Will it always be like this?"

"Always," he promised, gathering her closer.

"We shall go and speak to your father tomorrow. Once we have his blessing, we can be married as soon as you like."

Lexi grew very still as she considered facing her father and telling him that she was going to marry this man, who she hadn't even known existed when she'd fled from home just a few months ago. He'd think her rash, surely; he'd say she was only reacting to the upheaval in her life and his own plans to marry. But that wasn't so. She was in love with Morgan Glendower. She wanted nothing more than to spend the rest of her life with him. There was no doubt of that, none at all.

Morgan frowned as he noticed her hesitance. "Will he be disappointed with me as a son-in-law, do you think?"

"You? Oh, no. That's not it," she quickly assured him, and then sat up and began to rearrange her clothes, her hands trembling so badly she could scarcely manage the buttons.

"Put on that suit you wear to impress your godfather, and he'll like you well enough. I'm the problem. Before

180

I left home, he accused me of behaving like a spoiled child, and well, I suppose I was, just a little. But now he'll think I'm being impetuous, that I can't be trusted to make a clear decision. He'll think that I'm only using you because I'm weak, and it's not true, Morgan. I swear it."

Her eyes were glazed with tears when she turned to him, two pools of liquid green, and she was hugging her knees and rocking back and forth.

He reached for her and drew her tightly against him. "I know. I know, Lexi. You weren't weak when you found me out here, hiding from the world. You had strength enough for us both, strength enough to bring me back to life. I'm not afraid to admit it, and you mustn't be afraid either, not now. We'll face him together, and we'll make him see."

Held fast in his arms, with his steel blue eyes fixed on hers, radiating confidence, she could not help but take comfort. But somewhere deep inside of her — whence it sprung she could not say — an uncomfortable sense of foreboding had began to take shape.

Chapter Twelve

Jacob was sitting on the porch steps, waiting for them, when they returned to the cabin at last. Hawkeye lay at his feet, sharp eyes following them closely even as his head rested atop his front paws.

Lexi felt her cheeks flame as she remembered where she'd been and what she'd done there, and her tongue went strangely numb. But Morgan seemed, by contrast, very much at ease.

"Well, Jacob!" he called out heartily when he saw him sitting there. "What brings you here? We went for a picnic. I hope you haven't been waiting long."

Jacob shook his head vigorously. "Nay," he replied. "I've only . . . j-just come."

Morgan put aside his fishing rod and the picnic hamper, and as he climbed the porch steps, the young man handed him an envelope.

"I went tae Stevensville, an' . . . M-Mister Newcomb said . . . I maun gie this tae ye," he explained haltingly.

Morgan took it from him, examining the handwriting on its face before he tore it open and unfolded the sheet that was tucked inside.

"My godfather has been taken ill," he explained

as he read, a note of restraint in his voice. " 'Tis a seizure of some kind, the housekeeper says. He's asking for me."

Lexi came up beside him and lay a hand on his arm. "Of course, you'll have to go at once."

"I'm sure he'll be fine," he said, but even as he spoke, she sensed a hesitance in him. "He's a crafty old goat, probably worked this whole thing out just to get another week's visit out of me."

"You're probably right," she agreed, for his sake.

He turned to her and clutched her arm. "You'll wait for me at your gran's until I return? As soon as I've assured myself that he's well, I'll come back for you and we'll go to Buffalo and speak with your father."

"Don't worry about me," she told him. "Just go and do what you have to."

And so the next morning, wearing a confident smile, Lexi waved good-bye and sent him on his way, blithely unaware that all too soon afterward, she'd come to wish that she'd never let him go.

"Thank heavens you've come. He's been asking for you for three days now."

The housekeeper threw the door open wide, and Morgan swept in, set down his valise, and handed her his hat. "Where is he, Mrs. Edmunds?" he inquired briskly.

The old woman regarded him askance. "Why, he's in his bed, of course. Where in heaven's name did you think he'd be, sick as he is?"

"With my godfather, one can never be sure. He's likely to have pronounced himself recovered and gone off fishing."

With his black leather doctor's bag in hand, Morgan started up the stairs.

"Not this time he hasn't," Mrs. Edmunds called after him as she reached to put his hat on the hall table. "At first they hardly kept him off his feet at all, but this latest attack scared him, I think."

Morgan halted mid-stride on the landing. "Latest attack? Do you mean to say that this has happened before?"

"At least twice lately that I can recall."

"And you witnessed these attacks?"

Mrs. Edmunds nodded. "Once at dinner, and another time while he was at the desk in his study. He went pale as a ghost, stiffened all up, and clutched at his chest."

"And afterward, he seemed very tired and complained of the cold?"

"Why, yes," she replied. "But however could you know that?"

Morgan did not reply, but his dark brow furrowed as he continued up the steps and then crossed the upstairs hall. He stood before the closed door of the bedroom for a long moment, considering. Perhaps he'd been wrong to have made light of his godfather's talk of a weak heart all these years. He'd been so certain that it had been no more than a ploy for eliciting sympathy, but there was no mistaking the portent of these symptoms.

He rapped sharply on the door and strode in, noticing at once that the bed was empty, the bedclothes cast carelessly aside. The afternoon sun was streaming in between the open draperies, and his godfather's broad leather wing chair was set before the windows. A long curl of smoke rising upward over the curved chair-back gave a clue to his whereabouts.

Morgan waved a hand to clear the air and sputtered a choking cough. "It's no wonder you're ill," he chided, "what with your penchant for rich foods, expensive brandy, and those bloody awful cigars."

Arthur Sinclair peered around the chair. He was sitting there in his nightshirt, a lap robe thrown over his knees. His face was more ashen than Morgan would liked to have seen, but the old man's expression brightened as soon as he saw him, and he reached to stub out the offensive cigar in the china dish on the table beside the chair.

"Well, my boy, it's about time you showed up. We were beginning to give up hope of ever dragging you out of those woods of yours."

Morgan came around to stand before him. Regarding his godfather with a distinct air of disapproval, he set his bag down on the table, opened it, and drew out his stethoscope.

"How long have you been suffering with angina?" he asked as—without bothering to ask permission—he went to listen to the old man's heart.

"A few years, more or less."

"And have you consulted one of your colleagues

about this? You know what they say about the doctor who takes himself as a patient. . . ?"

Sinclair bobbed his head. "I do, and I have."

"And the prognosis?"

"Heart muscle's weakened," he replied, as if they were speaking of some anonymous patient. "I've six months, a year at best."

The news took Morgan by surprise. Arthur Sinclair had been like a father to him, more father than his own had ever been. His throat constricted tightly, and he felt as if a heavy weight were pressing on his chest. A rage born of helplessness welled in him, and he tossed the stethoscope back into his bag, swiping a hand across his brow. "I ought to have seen this; I ought to have noticed the signs."

"I took care that you should not. I'd intended to carry on myself as long as possible. No need to worry you with my problems. There's nothing can be done about it anyway, my boy."

Morgan paced restlessly before the windows, kneading the back of his neck with one hand. "We'll do what can be done, by God," he shot back. "We'll see to it that you rest—no more late nights at the hospital, no more patients at all. And I'll have Mrs. Edmunds change your diet immediately."

"No," Sinclair replied firmly. "I don't intend to spend my last days on porridge and weak tea. But there's still plenty of time for us, plenty of time to get you settled in here, acquaint you with my patients. . . ."

A cold chill swept over Morgan as he remembered now the promise he had made to his godfather to take over his practice when he was gone. He'd never imagined the day would come so soon. And then slowly the realization dawned on him. "You knew about this when you dragged that promise out of me, didn't you?"

"You didn't expect me to stand by and watch while you wasted your youth—your talents—out there in the wilderness, did you?" Sinclair said, his voice rising dangerously. "This is where you belong, Morgan, and it's your responsibility to carry on in my stead after I'm gone."

Morgan thought of Lexi now. He could offer her a life of ease here, in this house—a comfortable, respectable role as the wife of a hospital surgeon. But he knew, even as he formed the thoughts, that she would reject this kind of life. In his mind's eye, he pictured the pleasure on her lovely face as she'd stretched out in the sun, or dangled her bare feet in the cool creek waters, or lay with him on a pile of autumn leaves. She'd run away from her life in Buffalo, and after only one day in Hamilton, she'd returned to him pale and trembling. No, Lexi would never be happy here.

Morgan did not miss the tightly clenched fists or the bright flush of color that spread upward across his godfather's face. These were not good signs, and in spite of the temptation to continue this argument, he did not respond.

* * *

Three weeks he'd been gone. Three long, lonely weeks without a word. Gran kept Lexi busy enough in the daytime, what with chores and mending, and then there was the peeling and drying of the apples to do and the putting up of preserves for the winter. But the nights, oh, the nights were endless, and they left her prey to dreams that made her miss him all the more.

She'd read Morgan's *Mabinogeon* from cover to cover several times, and she slept with it beneath her pillow each night after the reading of the words became too sharp a reminder of him. And then finally she'd remembered what he'd told her about a trunk he kept—a trunk filled with books, he'd said, and she was welcome to borrow them anytime.

So the very next day, Lexi set out, bundled up in her wool shawl against the morning's chill, the frost-covered grass crunching beneath her shoes with each eager stride. Her heart leapt when at last she saw the welcoming sight of his cabin. But there was no beckoning curl of smoke rising from the broad stone chimney today, and the shutters were all firmly closed. Nevertheless, Lexi ran all the way down the hill, and by the time she'd climbed the porch steps and pushed open the heavy wooden door, she was breathless.

Inside, the cold seemed more intense. She left the door open as she entered to let in the light and went at once to perch herself upon the straw-covered mattress. Reaching for the quilt that was folded at the bottom of Morgan's bed, she clutched it to her breast. Squeezing her eyes tightly shut, she inhaled deeply. The fabric was full of his scent and for a moment, she imagined he was there, holding her in his arms. But when she opened her eyes once more, the loneliness pricked sharper than ever.

She had never been inside Morgan's cabin before; they'd always lingered on the porch, and curious now, she allowed her eyes to roam, studying the tall stone hearth capped by a rough wood mantel, upon which stood an assortment of canisters and glass bottles, a pair of tin mugs, and a small clock that seemed entirely out of place, with its ornate face and a fancy wooden cabinet that was decorated with gilt engraving. He must have brought this from home, Lexi mused when it caught her eye.

There was little furniture besides the bed, only a simple square table with two straight-backed chairs and a pair of leather trunks set side by side in the far corner. Lexi put the quilt back in its place, rose from the bed, and went to kneel on the planked wood floor before the trunks. She lifted the latch on the largest of the pair. Folded neatly inside were items of Morgan's city wardrobe: neckcloths, silk embroidered suspenders, stockings, handkerchiefs, brocade waistcoats, jackets, trousers, finely woven linen shirts, and underclothing.

Beneath all these, a flash of crimson caught her eye, and setting aside the stack, she drew out a British officer's tunic, faced with a long row of shiny buttons. Staring down upon it, she cringed with the memory of her trip to Hamilton and her encounter with the despicable Captain Bascombe. But this was not Bascombe's tunic, she reminded herself, this had belonged to an army surgeon. This was Morgan's uniform.

He'd told her once that he'd been to war, told her how it had sickened him. Reverently she touched the white-banded epaulet at the shoulder and ran her hand along the sleeve, wishing she could feel the hard, smooth muscle of his arm beneath her fingers. With a tremulous breath, she refolded the tunic and the other things and put them all away.

She turned to lift the lid of the second trunk. Inside this was set a tray that contained a pencilbox and notepaper, a sewing kit in a folded leather pouch, and a small parcel, wound up in a large white handkerchief. Lexi knew that she ought not to be snooping through Morgan's things. He'd invited her to borrow his books, not to examine his private belongings; but where was the harm if it made her feel closer to him?

She unwrapped the handkerchief to reveal an old meerschaum pipe and an ornate pocket compass, whose case was engraved with the words *Presented to Colonel Thomas Glendower, well deserving of the respect and admiration of his men. June 16, 1847.*

Morgan had never mentioned his father; Lexi had come to believe there was bad blood between them, and yet still she knew with an unexplained certainty that these thoughtfully preserved mementos had belonged to him. Carefully, she rewrapped the pipe and compass and put the parcel back in its place, pleased that she'd pried, for these particular items had told her a great deal about the man she'd come to love.

Removing the tray, she saw the books at last, stack upon stack of them, just as Morgan had said there'd be. Many were medical journals, not the sort of reading material she was after. But there was Shakespeare, too, and Dickens, Thackeray, and Scott. A small volume of poetry bound in red morocco caught her eye, and she reached for it. *English Poets,* it was entitled, and as she drew it from the trunk, she noticed that something had been pressed between the pages.

Lexi's legs had begun to go numb from kneeling on the rough plank floor, and so she got to her feet and carried the book to the table near the door. The light was better here and she sat down to examine it.

No sooner had she cracked the spine than a folded lace handkerchief slipped from the pages, settling onto the table, and at once Lexi was aware of the scent of a spicy perfume. It pricked at her memory, familiar somehow.

All that remained to mark the page in the book of poems was a folded sheaf of paper. Lexi drew it out, opened to the marked page, and saw there a poem by Shelley, in which the first and last stanzas had been underlined in bold pen strokes:

Rarely, rarely comest thou,
  Spirit of delight!
Wherefore hast thou left me now
  Many a day and night?
Many a weary night and day
'Tis since thou art fled away.

I love Love—though he has wings,
  And like light can flee,
But above all other things,
  Spirit, I love thee—
Thou art love and life! O Come!
Make once more my heart thy home!

Lexi felt an icy chill run through her that was not caused by the frosty autumn air. She had never read this particular poem before, but the meaning of the underlined passages was plain enough: an abandoned soul, crying out for a lost lover's return. And as she looked again upon the penstrokes that called attention to the lines, she knew she dared not consider who had made them. But she'd come too far now. Curiosity made her reach for the folded page and read the words that had been set down in a neat, feminine hand.

Morgan,

You were my friend when I had none. You alone saw the truth in the misery that was my life and brought light and warmth to me when I so sorely needed it. For that I shall always be grateful to you.

I hope you will understand why I must go away

and why we must never see each other again. It is not because of what they say about you and I. People will always talk, and I have borne gossip before. But I will not see you destroyed by this. When I am gone, the talk will fade and you will have your life back. I am returning your book to you, with the hope that if it should remind you of me, you will remember me fondly, as one who will always be your friend.
Celeste

Lexi let the page slip from her hand as a myriad of disjointed pieces fell one by one painfully into place. She was hearing voices now, memories echoing through the stillness of the cabin. ". . . what he finds there is love with another man's wife." "Was she very beautiful?" "Yes. God, yes. The most beautiful woman he'd ever seen."

Lexi put her head in her hands. How could she have forgotten? And then she heard the fiddler's music and the crickets chirping, and again Morgan's voice, deep and even, urging her to forget about the past.

But no, not this. This she would never forget. As tears blurred her eyes, she pulled a ragged breath and felt the bitter sting in her nostrils of the perfume that she remembered all-too-well now, and the name of the woman who, without knowing, had taken from Lexi everything she loved . . . Celeste Palmer.

Chapter Thirteen

Morgan noticed the sliver of lamplight under his godfather's bedroom door as he passed it by, but it took a few minutes more for him to gather his thoughts . . . and his courage. As it was, he'd nearly reached his own room at the end of the hall before he hesitated mid-step, turned on his heel, and strode back to rap sharply on the heavy paneled door.

It had been three weeks now, and he was more convinced than ever that he could not make a home for himself and for Lexi in Hamilton. But he hadn't found the words to explain that to his ailing godfather. In fact, he hadn't found the words to tell him about Lexi at all.

Sinclair bade him enter, but once inside, Morgan stood there with head bent, brow furrowed, and hands shoved deeply in the pockets of his frock coat, feeling somewhat like an errant schoolboy, even as he chastised the older man. "You oughtn't to be keeping such hours, you know. You need to conserve your strength."

"I'll have the whole of eternity for resting," Sinclair replied, without looking up from the papers he had spread across the bed. "For now I want to finish these case notes. It will make things easier for you, when the time comes. Old Mrs. Archer here has a list of complaints that stretches back fifteen years or more."

There was no putting it off any longer. Morgan had to speak now. He came to stand beside the bed, crossing his arms firmly over his chest. "Yes, well, we need to talk about that, sir."

"Did you meet with Doctor Mason today?" his godfather asked, as if he hadn't heard.

"I did, and while he was showing me around the wards, he mentioned a specialist in Toronto, who might — "

"No specialists! I've been poked and prodded enough for one lifetime. We'll do what can be done here, and leave the rest in God's hands."

Morgan saw where this was headed, but this time he refused to be led into a pointless argument. If his godfather was going to be upset, then it might as well be with good reason.

"I'm getting married," he blurted out, realizing only afterward how abrupt the announcement must have sounded.

This time, Sinclair did not bother to pretend he hadn't heard. He put aside his papers, pushed his spectacles back up on his nose, and regarded his godson closely. "But you've only been back a few weeks, my boy. You've hardly had time to develop any ties."

"She's not from Hamilton, sir," Morgan explained. "She's American. Her name is Alexandra Merritt, and her grandmother's farm lies next to my property near Stevensville."

At this, Sinclair's brow arched. "You intend to marry a farm girl?"

"A farm girl who quotes Latin poets and chides me for neglecting my duty as a physician."

As the old man's lips twitched, Morgan felt relief wash through him. "Oh? She does, does she? Well, she sounds like a sensible girl, at least," Sinclair decided. "And Mrs. Edmunds will be pleased. She's always said this household needed the feminine touch."

Morgan had cleared the first hurdle, but the most difficult was yet to come. His met his godfather eye-to-eye. "We won't be living here in Hamilton."

"What's that?"

"I should have told you at once, I know, but I was reluctant to upset you. This life is yours, not mine. There are plenty of other doctors in Hamilton to take your place and see to your patients. It's true that two years ago I may have run from here for all the wrong reasons, but what's come of it is right.

"I'm not wasting my talent in the wilderness, sir. There are people living out there, a community of souls who could better benefit from my skills than old Mrs. Archer and her imaginary ailments. Yes, I may have calluses on my hands, but it's because

196

'm building something, a life of my own."

Sinclair nodded sagely, but his expression did not change. He seemed bent on keeping his thoughts to himself. "And this young lady of yours. Did she help you come to this conclusion?"

"She did. She seems to see things very clearly."

And then Sinclair smiled. "I hope you realize what a lucky young man you are to have found someone who cares so much. She's done more for you than I ever could, try as I might."

"I'm asking you to release me from my promise, sir," Morgan pressed boldly.

"I've only wanted what's best for you all along," Sinclair replied, "and any fool can see that you won't find that here. Go on back to that young lady of yours then. Just don't forget to send me an invitation to the wedding."

Morgan felt as if a heavy weight had been lifted from his shoulders and thanked his godfather as he turned to go. He'd thought the interview was concluded and so was surprised when, as he reached the door, Sinclair called out to him.

"Morgan?"

"Yes, sir?"

He turned back, and in that first instant, Morgan would have sworn he'd seen the glint of a tear in the old man's eye. "Your father would have been proud."

There was a letter from Brendan waiting back at

the farm, and before Gran could question he
about her pale face and red-rimmed eyes, Lex
snatched it from the table and hurried up to he
room to read it.

Dear Brendan was cheerful as ever, his exuber
ance set down on the page with each hurried
scratch of the pen, each half-finished sentence
And as always, he was offering a dear friend's ad
vice: *"Come home for the wedding, Lexi, and
make peace with your father, for both of you.
sakes."*

It was time to go home. The summer was wel
over, and fall was fading fast. The brightly colored
leaves had all turned to dust and blown away, and
there was the sharp bite of winter in the air.

Gran would understand. Gran had told her more
than once to mend this rift with her father before
it was too late. It would be hard to face him, to
admit that she'd behaved like a selfish, spoiled
child. But she would do it.

Once she'd thought she loved him too much to
let him throw his life away on a woman who was
unworthy of him. Once she'd have done anything
to prove to him that she was right. But now, with
proof within her reach, Lexi's mind had changed
And she was not certain whether the change had
come about because of the kindness she'd sensed
in Celeste Palmer's letter or because she could no
willingly subject her father to the same pain that
she'd suffered in reading it.

* * *

Morgan jumped down from the buggy, fiddled for a moment with the latch on the dooryard gate with his numbed fingers, then, thinking better of it, grabbed hold of the top rail and leapt over. He crossed the yard in a few long strides, climbed up on the porch, and rapped his knuckles in an anxious rhythm against Mrs. MacLennan's kitchen door.

Almost at once, the old woman threw open the door and then finished wiping her hands on her apron. Morgan found himself unable to stifle his eager grin. "Good afternoon, Mrs. MacLennan."

"Good afternoon tae ye, Doctor Glendower. Do come in out of the cold," she bade him, standing back. "Seems winter is nigh upon us."

Morgan stepped inside and shut the door behind him. He filled his nostrils with the wonderful smell of newly baked bread as the heat of the kitchen stove rushed against his face like a warm, welcome breeze. "I'd like to speak with Lexi," he said.

At this, the old woman paled. "But . . . she's gone. She didna tell ye?"

"No, but I've been away, surely she mentioned that."

Mrs. MacLennan crossed the room abruptly to stir the kettle whose contents were boiling noisily atop the stove. "Aye, a sick relative, wasn't it?"

"My godfather," Morgan explained, his disquiet increasing by the moment. "Where did she go, Mrs. MacLennan?"

"Home tae her father. Jacob took her tae the depot the morning afore last."

Now it was Morgan's turn to be confused. "But I asked her to wait for me. We were going to go together."

Mrs. MacLennan seemed determined to avoid his gaze. "Perhaps she couldna wait any longer. Her father's tae be married soon, ye know."

"Yes, perhaps," Morgan agreed, though still not convinced. "She left no message for me?"

The old woman shook her head. "Somethin's not quite right in all this," she admitted to him at last. "She scarcely spoke a word tae any of us afore she left. Could be was only nervous about goin' home, could be only that."

But Morgan had an awful feeling. It stayed with him as he drove back to the cabin, as he unhitched the mare and settled her into the shed that served as a stable. And when at last he walked into the cabin and tossed his bags on the floor, the feeling grew stronger, even before he noticed that something was amiss.

The trunk in which he stored his books was opened, and on the table, three small items lay in a neat pile. He drew close enough to identify the handkerchief, a book of poems, and a letter. As soon as he saw them, he knew what they were, and God help him, he feared he knew what had happened. Lexi had come to borrow his books.

Beside the little pile was a sheaf of notepaper upon which had been penciled several words. Morgan's heart wrenched as he read them: *THREE CAUSELESS BLOWS.*

No sooner had Lexi stepped out of the dressmaker's shop than a pair of strong hands gripped her shoulders, and she found herself staring into the accusing amber eyes of Brendan O'Neill. He was wearing a gray woolen cap, heavy coat, and muffler, but his face was ruddy from the cold, and his expression was uncharacteristically sober.

"Just what *am* I to be thinkin', Lexi Merritt? It's more than a week you've been back home now and not yet thought to send word to your oldest and dearest friend. I'd never have known it at all if it weren't for Mrs. Fraser comin' into the shop this mornin'."

As he spoke, Lexi began to wring her gloved hands within the capacious folds of her fur muff. "I'm sorry, Brendan," she answered softly. "I've meant to call on you or to send a note, truly I have . . ."

Brendan hesitated, his head cocked to one side as if he were gauging her reaction. His grip on her eased a bit, and when at last he spoke again, his voice was gentler and full of concern. "What is it, darlin'? What's wrong?"

She ought to have known that he'd sense the change in her; maybe she did know and that was why she'd been avoiding him. In any case, Lexi found herself strangely afraid to speak again, afraid he'd sense her heartache in even the simplest reply and force her to tell him everything.

"Send your driver home and walk with me," he urged. "We'll talk for a while, just like we used to."

She could hardly refuse, but even as she headed for the carriage waiting at the curbside and addressed the coachman sitting up on the box, she told herself that things could never again be as they used to be. "Thank you, George. You can go on ahead. Mr. O'Neill will see me home."

She returned to the place where Brendan was waiting on the boardwalk, watching her. "How's a man to be lookin' into those lovely eyes of yours if you insist on hidin' yourself behind all these damned fancy fripperies?"

Reaching to lift the layers of lace veiling, he tossed them impatiently back over the brim of her green felt bonnet. Lexi took a moment to arrange the folds in a less hapless fashion, then slipped her arm through the one he proffered.

"Now, tell me," he said as they started along the boardwalk arm-in-arm. "What's wrong? Is it trouble at home? Have you settled things with your father?"

Lexi nodded, keeping her eyes carefully trained on the planking beneath her feet. "I've told him how sorry I am for all that I said, and I've made my apologies to Mrs. Palmer. I'm even helping with the wedding arrangements."

"But somethin' else is troublin' you. Don't think

I don't know you well enough to see it."

"You mustn't worry over me so, Brendan," she replied, conjuring a weak smile as she met his eyes finally in an effort to convince him. "I'm tired, that's all. The wedding's to be at our house, and there are so many details that must be attended to."

Brendan said nothing, but his grip on her arm tightened as he escorted her across the street just ahead of a rumbling delivery wagon. He seemed to relax, though, as soon as they reached the park.

There was nothing attractive in the natural landscape this time of year; the stretch of lawn was brown and the leafless oak and elm trees that bordered the lot stood like cheerless, black sentinels. But the well-worn path cut through a thick copse of evergreens that afforded some amount of privacy from the bustling city around them, and it was here that Brendan paused and turned to her. Before Lexi could anticipate what he was about, he'd caught her up in his arms.

"It pains me to be seein' you like this, Lexi. I want to bring back that smilin' young girl that I remember so well."

His eyes were alight with warmth, his expression full of confidence in his purpose. She ought to have felt comfortable in his arms, after all the years of friendship, but Lexi felt only a strange sense of panic rising in her.

"I could make you smile," he whispered, touch-

203

ing her face gently with a gloved hand then reaching to tuck a stray wisp of hair back under the brim of her bonnet, "if only you'd let me."

There was only the soft brush of his mustache and then his lips were on hers. His kiss was different this time, though, soft and coaxing. Her eyelids drifted shut, and for an instant, Lexi relaxed as her mind rushed back to a sun-dappled grove, a tartan blanket and falling leaves. . . .

"Ah, Lexi, me darlin'," he whispered, "I've waited so long."

The voice brought Lexi sharply back to reality. This was not Morgan's voice. These were not Morgan's arms around her. Horrified by what she'd just allowed to happen, she twisted free and stumbled backward awkwardly.

"No, Brendan, I can't, I —"

She pressed a trembling gloved hand over her mouth before she could say anything more. Brendan's crestfallen expression made it plain that he was hurt and confused. She knew that she owed him some kind of explanation. But how could she begin to tell him?

She pulled a dangerously quavering breath as she sought to form the words. Hot tears were stinging her eyes, spilling down her cheeks. "You were right," she muttered. "I'm miserable, so wretchedly miserable."

"Has someone hurt you?"

"No. It's all my fault. While I was away, I . . . made a fool of myself . . . over a man."

Some unreadable emotion flashed in Brendan's eyes. When he stepped toward her, it was apparent he intended to comfort her; but like a frightened animal, she edged backward in response. "Please!" she implored him, "please, don't touch me again—not that way."

Keeping his distance, he extended an arm out to her. "Take my hand, then," he told her, disappointment threading through his words. "I won't hurt you, Lexi. Sure and I never meant to hurt you."

Regarding his pale expression, Lexi was overwhelmed with guilt and shamed to realize that her emotions still lay so close to the surface that a single wrong word or act could open the floodgates. And she'd thought that after a week at home she was healing.

"I know that, Brendan," she replied, firmly grasping the hand he offered. "And I'm sorry. I never meant to burden you with this. Would you please take me home now?"

As they started down the path once more, Brendan reached inside his coat and handed her his handkerchief. "It might help if you were to tell me about it," he suggested.

Lexi took the handkerchief he offered, wiped the tears from her face, then began to twist it between her fingers. "No," she replied at last, careful this time to keep a tight rein on her emotions. "Some things are best forgotten. Give me a few more weeks, and I'll be myself again."

"A few weeks?" he echoed, his confidence reasserting itself. "I can manage that, to be sure, for I'm a patient man."

Chapter Fourteen

Morgan had spent Christmas Day alone in a Buffalo hotel room, and he'd tried for all of the following week to see Lexi, but each time he'd called upon her, he'd been told that she was not at home.

He knew that if he could speak with her, even for a few minutes, he'd be able to make her see that Celeste meant nothing to him, that he'd been an impressionable young fool when he'd sent her that book, and that there was only one woman he had ever loved enough to pursue with this much determination. But it seemed that Lexi was just as determined not to give him the opportunity to change her mind. And so Morgan decided finally that the situation called for desperate measures.

On his most recent visit, he'd been cooling his heels in the Merritt parlor before he was sent away, and he'd noticed the commotion about the house. Inquiring of the maid, he discovered that Lexi's father was to be married the very next day and that the household was making preparations for the reception, which was to be held at home.

So on the following evening, armed with this knowledge, Morgan put on his formal broadcloth suit, with white tie and waistcoat, and as the guests began to arrive, he presented himself at the Merritts' front door and was duly escorted inside. He left his coat and hat with the maid in the foyer, then followed the other guests through a long central hall that was hung with painted landscapes and decorated for the occasion with sprays of hothouse flowers.

Even though he'd been inside the house before when he'd attempted to see Lexi, he was no less impressed by his surroundings on this occasion. She had never told him about her home. He'd once asked her if her father was a farmer, then later amended his views to decide that he must be a prosperous merchant. But Morgan would never have guessed Daniel Merritt to be president of one of the largest banks in Buffalo, nor that the home that Lexi had run away from was a spreading three-story sandstone mansion in the city's most fashionable neighborhood.

And yet she'd accepted his offer to share a life in a rude log cabin in the woods. All at once, a notion occurred to him, sharp as a knife twisting inside. Perhaps when she'd come face-to-face with her choice, she'd reconsidered his offer and was only using this business with Celeste as an excuse.

By the time he stepped through the doors into the ballroom, with its walls of dark wood paneling and mirrors, and crystal chandeliers blazing over-head, Morgan was feeling uneasy. But he steeled himself against his doubts and took his place in the long receiving line.

Even at a distance, he recognized Daniel Merritt at once, for there was something of him in his daughter: the wide-set eyes and a particular curve of the mouth. Regarding him, Morgan noted that the man was positively beaming, and no wonder —his new wife was obviously a prize that he cher-ished greatly. They stood, arm in arm, conversing politely with each guest who passed through the line.

The bride wore a gown of a pale rose color, and her thick chestnut hair was caught up in a caul set with pearls. There was something almost familiar about the color of her hair and the way she held her head, but Morgan did not long consider these thoughts before his attention was captured by the young woman standing beside her.

His jaw tightened, and he swallowed the lump that had formed in his throat. He scarcely recog-ized her in her expensive gown of emerald green watered silk, with her burnished hair drawn up in coiffure of cascading curls, a collar of green ones at her throat, and a proud tilt to her chin, but it was indeed Lexi. She looked older, more ac-complished than he could have expected, but no less beautiful.

And he was not the only one who'd realized at, he saw now as he surveyed the room. More

209

than one young buck had cast his roving eye on her. Possessiveness welled in him before he realized that he had no right — not yet, at least. But soon enough he'd have his chance to mend the rift between them . . .

As the receiving line moved forward, Morgan glanced again at the bride and groom — but this time the bride had turned his way, and he saw what he hadn't seen before. It was Celeste!

He felt the color draining slowly from his face. Dear God, now he understood. What must Lex have felt when she'd found that book and Celeste's letter in his cabin?

The world had turned upside down, and the urge to find a quiet place to sit and consider these consequences was strong within him, but he could not make a move now without alerting them all to his presence, and so he drew himself inward and prepared to meet his fate.

"Congratulations, sir," he said, putting out his hand to the bridegroom when it came his turn in line.

Daniel Merritt regarded him politely, but a brow rose up over the top of his wire-rimmed spectacles as he tried to put a name to the face before him.

"Doctor Morgan Glendower," Morgan said, to help him out, and at that moment, Celeste turned to them. Her eyes widened as they fixed on Morgan, and she paled, momentarily flustered.

"Daniel, this is Doctor Glendower from Hampton," she explained to her husband, as soon as she was able. "He's the army surgeon who took such good care of John. You may have heard me mention him."

There was a note of caution in Celeste's words, and Morgan realized she must be uncertain of his intent, so he sought to reassure her. "I'm living out near Stevensville now, sir," he said, addressing himself to Mr. Merritt. "Your daughter and I became friends while she was staying with her grandmother. When I found myself in Buffalo for the holidays, I felt I must come and offer my congratulations."

"How kind of you to think of us," Celeste said, sounding more than a little relieved.

"And you're a friend of Alexandra's, you say?" Merritt, too, seemed relieved as he turned to his daughter, who was absorbed in conversation with an elderly gentleman. "I'm sure she'll be pleased you were able to come. Alexandra?"

Lexi was thankful to hear her father's voice; she'd been listening to Mr. Brewster for nearly ten minutes now. He was a well-meaning old gentleman, but his memory was failing, and so he always managed to repeat everything he said at least twice. She needed this kind of excuse to send him on his way.

But when she turned to her father, Lexi caught her breath—and the smile she was wearing froze on her face. Morgan was standing there beside her father and Celeste, and all of them were looking expectantly at her. She felt numb as she forced herself to put a hand out to him. "Doctor Glen-dower, how nice of you to come."

Her tone was coolly polite, but surely the breathlessness in her voice gave her away. Even now, her fingers were warming beneath his and her heart was twisting painfully in her breast. Oh, how could he have come here? And why? She had to escape him, but she knew by the glittering purpose in his eyes that he did not intend to release her.

"There's no need for you to stand here entertaining all the old folk, my dear," her father said to her then. "Why don't you show Dr. Glendower around?"

"That would be exceedingly kind of you, Miss Merritt," Morgan piped in, sounding every bit the well-mannered British gentleman.

She wanted to slap his face, she wanted to scream at him to get out, but under the circumstances, all she could do was oblige her father and accept the arm that Morgan offered.

Lexi kept silent until they'd put enough distance between them so that they'd not be overheard and then addressed him in a harsh whisper. "How could you come here tonight? I warn you, Morgan, if you've any intention of upsetting my father—"

"I came here because I had to speak with *you* and no other reason," he replied. "I swear to you until I walked into this room I had no idea that Celeste was the woman your father was marrying.

Lexi winced inwardly as the hurt flooded

through her anew. Somewhere in the back of her mind, she'd held out the foolish hope that she'd been wrong about all of this, that she'd misconstrued the damning evidence she'd seen in his cabin. But with his words, he'd wiped out the last of those hopes.

"Is there somewhere we can speak privately?" Morgan asked her then.

"I can't leave now. What will everyone say?"

"There are so many people here, they'll hardly notice if we go missing. Besides, your father asked you to show me around, and I don't think you want to stand out here in the middle of the crowd and have this discussion."

"Lexi darlin', there you are, and as always, the prettiest girl in the room."

Brendan O'Neill drew himself up squarely before them, but his attentions were focused only on Lexi. As for Morgan, he kept a firm hold on Lexi's arm, regarding the intrusion and Brendan dispassionately; the only change in him was a single raised brow.

"Brendan, this is Doctor Morgan Glendower, who's come down for the wedding from Canada," Lexi explained.

"Ah, a friend of the bride, then?" Brendan remarked, sounding more at ease.

He could not have known how deep a nerve he'd struck, but Lexi felt the stab at her heart, just the same, and beneath her hand, the muscles in Morgan's arm went taut. "I'm a friend of

213

Lexi's, actually," Morgan told him. "Her grandmother and I are neighbors."

"Are ye now?"

"Yes," Lexi quickly interrupted, sensing the rising tension between them. "And, Morgan, this is Brendan O'Neill. He's a . . . very dear friend."

Lexi's gaze shifted nervously from one man to the other. Even dressed in his evening clothes tonight, Brendan looked no less brawny and rough-and-tumble than he always did. But Morgan, by contrast, seemed relaxed and reserved, and she found it amazing that he was able to move with ease from one social sphere to the next as if he belonged equally to both.

"A pleasure to meet you, Mr. O'Neill," Morgan returned, but Lexi was not at all sure that he meant it. "Now, if you'll excuse us . . ."

Morgan advanced a step, and reluctantly, Brendan moved out of the way. But he cast a last warning glance at his adversary before meeting Lexi with a serious air. "I'm here if you'd be needin' me, darlin'," he told her.

In that moment, Lexi knew that Brendan had identified Morgan as the man who'd caused the change in her, and the realization left her cold with apprehension. Brendan had always been as tenaciously protective of her as he had of any of the members of his family, and if he thought there was a chance of her being hurt, she knew he'd not hesitate to cause a scene. It would be wise to keep these two as far apart as possible.

"Shall we go?" Morgan prompted.

"Go on and enjoy the evening," she said to Brendan. "I'll be fine."

Lexi allowed Morgan to lead her from the room and directed him down the hall to her father's study. Once inside, though, she made certain to leave the door ajar and strode to the hearth at the far end of the room, where a blazing fire provided heat and, at present, the only light in the room. She intended to put as much distance between them as she could while Morgan pleaded his case, for she feared she could not trust herself to remain calm and rational if he were to touch her.

To steel herself, she formed a mental picture of him holding Celeste in his arms, whispering the same sweet words that he'd used on her. She reminded herself of the anguished sentiment of Shelley's poem, which Morgan had used to liken her new stepmother to a "spirit of delight" and to beg for her return. The exercise proved immediately successful. A numbing coldness seeped through her veins, in spite of the fire at her back, and she was fully composed as she turned to face him. "I don't know why you've come. There's nothing to discuss."

"No," he said, seeming to agree with her as he restlessly paced the length of the Turkish carpet that covered the floor between them. "You saw that damned book and Celeste's letter and you've judged me guilty—without the benefit of a trial."

Lexi knew he was right; still, there was no mis-

215

taking what she'd seen, no mistaking the hurt it had caused her. She never wanted to feel a hurt like that again; it would be better not to feel at all.

"I suppose you believe that I murdered her husband as well. And why not? Even without proof, everyone else did."

Lexi hadn't even thought of that; it was too ridiculous to credit. But as Morgan continued to advance on her, she took an anxious step backward in reply.

With this, he halted. She saw in his eyes a wild, wounded look, and when he spoke again, his tone was dispirited. "When I emigrated to Canada, I was just out of the Crimea. I was hurting. I needed . . . something sweet and fresh in my life, something that would erase the stench of death. Can you understand that?"

"I don't blame you for loving her, Morgan," Lexi told him, trying to make amends. "She's a wonderful woman; I found that out for myself when I went to Hamilton. But she's made her choice now, and I hope you can let her find happiness with my father."

"For pity's sake, listen to me, Lexi!"

In two long strides, Morgan closed the distance between them and swept her into his arms. "There was never anything between Celeste and me, beyond that which I wished for in my own imagination," he insisted, his arm tightening across her back as he willed her to look in his eyes. "I was an impetuous young fool. But all of that happened two years ago; I'm a different man now. I love *you*."

Lexi couldn't think clearly with him so near; her senses were too full of the spicy, clean scent of him and the feel of his hard body pressed against her. She had to protect herself, had to ignore what her heart and her body were telling her, lest she be hurt again. She had to have time to think.

"No, please, Morgan—"

In an instant, the door swung open and crashed back against the paneled wall, revealing Brendan in bold silhouette.

"Get your hands off her, ye filthy British bastard!"

Lexi knew that under ordinary circumstances, Morgan was the most reserved of men, but considering what had just passed between them, his emotions were perilously close to the surface. She sensed the danger too late.

Morgan whirled around, placing himself protectively in front of her. "This is no concern of yours, O'Neill," he growled. "Now get out!"

"The devil I will. You've taken advantage of an innocent child, used her for your own selfish purposes, and now you think you can come back for more, d'ye? Sure an' I'll see ye in hell first."

Balling his fists, Brendan strode forward. His eyes narrowed, gleaming with reflected firelight. Lexi could not see Morgan's face at all, but when his spine stiffened suddenly, she anticipated what

217

was coming and rushed to put herself between them.

"Stop it! One more word, and you'll have the guests rushing in here to see what's amiss. I'll not have you spoiling this day for my father."

Brendan adjusted his stance. "Leave me to deal with him, and I guarantee he'll not be botherin' ye again."

"What gives *him* the right to act as your protector?" Morgan asked her. "I need to know, Lexi. Just what precisely is his claim on you?"

Lexi's head was spinning at such a pace that she feared she'd lose her balance. She covered her ears with her hands, unable to listen to any more. "You're not thinking of me at all," she said to them both. "Here you stand, the two of you, snapping and snarling like hungry wolves. Well, I'm not a scrap of meat to be fought over! Can't either of you understand that?"

A long silence ensued. Morgan's features settled into an unreadable mask. "Perhaps I should leave, then," he proposed.

"Yes, perhaps you should."

With that, he squared his jaw, and his eyes went cold. "I ought to have known when I set foot in this fine, fancy house that you'd not leave it all behind for me."

Lexi stood there paralyzed, distracted by the rapid cadence of her own breathing as Morgan strode past her and out of the room. He did not look back.

Only after he was gone, though, did she begin to consider the finality of what she'd just done. If he *was* telling the truth, if there *had* been nothing between him and Celeste, then he'd come all this way to make things right between them, and she hadn't even given him the courtesy of listening before she'd turned him away. And she knew him well enough to know he'd not give her a second chance to hurt him.

"Well, now, that's done. He'll not be botherin' ye again," Brendan said, expelling a hearty sigh as he came to stand at her elbow. "Shall we go and join the others?"

Lexi turned from him and swallowed the tears that were gathering in her throat. Lifting her skirts, she swept across the room and dropped into the leather wing chair that was set before the hearth.

Brendan followed, but had scarcely drawn up beside her when, with her gaze still fixed on the flickering flames, she spoke to him. "Get out, Brendan."

"But, Lexi . . ."

He reached out to touch her arm, but she would not even look at him.

"I said get out."

The very next morning, Lexi checked at all the hotels where she thought Morgan might be staying, but when at last she found a desk clerk who

219

remembered the name, he informed her that Morgan had already checked out.

Within the week, a letter arrived. When she opened the envelope, she found but a single, folded page inside, torn from a book of poetry that was painfully familiar to her. Upon the page was a poem by John Keats, and several stanzas had been underlined in bold hand:

I met a lady in the meads,
 Full beautiful, a faery's child;
Her hair was long, her foot was light,
 And her eyes were wild.

I made a garland for her head,
 And bracelets, too, and fragrant zone;
She looked at me as she did love,
 And made sweet moan.

And there we slumbered on the moss,
 And there I dreamed, ah! woe betide,
The latest dream I ever dreamed
 On the cold hillside.

I saw pale kings, and prices, too,
 Pale warriors, death-pale were they all,
Who cried—"La belle Dame sans merci
 Hath thee in thrall!

Chapter Fifteen

Buffalo, New York, April 1866

Lexi made a small, neat stitch, extended her arm to pull the length of wool floss through the canvas in the tapestry frame, then fashioned another stitch and repeated the process.

She did not look up as her stepmother entered the sitting room, only continued making stitches, one by one by one. The dull rhythm helped to pass the time and kept her mind from wandering down dangerous paths.

"Alexandra, so there you are," Celeste began. "Your father has sent word that he will be late this evening, and so it is just you and I for supper, *chère*. I've asked Mrs. Fraser to make the veal fillet tonight. She tells me it's your favorite."

"Thank you," Lexi replied. "That was very kind."

Celeste was hovering near the sofa where Lexi was seated, and when Lexi looked up at last, she noticed the hesitance in her stepmother's expression.

"May I?" the older woman asked, motioning to the empty spot beside Lexi on the sofa. "That is, I should like to speak with you for a moment, if you wouldn't mind."

Lexi met her with a warming smile. In these past few months she'd learned firsthand just how wrong she'd been about Celeste. "Yes, please, do sit down."

With a crisp rustling of taffeta skirts, Celeste settled beside her. "How lovely," she said as she admired the floral pattern upon which Lexi was working. "You do such fine work, *chère*. Perhaps one day you might teach me?"

"If you'd like."

Celeste was still for a moment, as if considering her next words carefully. "What I should like more than anything," she said at last, "is for us to be friends, to be able to speak honestly to one another. Do you think that we could?"

Lexi hesitated for a moment over her stitch, and an odd uneasiness crept over her. Much as she'd come to admire her stepmother, there were some subjects she feared she could not bear to discuss. "I should hope so," she said, but the note of caution was plain in her reply.

"Since I came to live here, you've been so . . . quiet. I have asked your father if he's noticed the change, but he tells me it's nothing to be concerned about. Still, I cannot help but think that somehow I am the cause of your unhappiness."

Lexi felt a flood of relief rush through her to realize that Celeste hadn't come to discuss Morgan after all, and then it occurred to her how selfish she'd been to think only of her own feelings. Setting down her needle, she turned to her stepmother.

"Oh, no, that's not it at all," she told her, taking up her hands and squeezing them tightly. "And I apologize if I've made you feel unwelcome. Your coming here has been a blessing for us, you must believe me. I haven't seen Papa looking so vital in years."

"But you, *ma chère,* grow paler by the day. You do your charity work or sit here alone in this room and stitch away the hours, and it tears at my heart to watch you. I know that something is wrong, terribly wrong. If it is not that I have taken your place, then what?"

"There's nothing wrong, truly," Lexi assured her.

"But you are young and beautiful, Alexandra. You ought to be enjoying your life," Celeste insisted. "Why do you send away those young men who come to call? And why will you not even speak to your old friend, Mr. O'Neill?"

How could Lexi possibly explain? How could she tell Celeste that she did not deserve her pity, that she herself had thrown away her one true chance at happiness?

She was tired of keeping her feelings bottled up inside, woefully tired of sitting and stitching day after day to pass the time. Before she knew what was happening, Lexi had thrown herself into her stepmother's arms.

"I understand what it is to be in love," Celeste said, gently smoothing Lexi's hair with her hand, "to put your heart in someone else's keeping only to find that your trust has been betrayed."

"It's not that. I'm the one that's to blame. I didn't trust him. I lost my temper and sent him away," she said, before she could stop herself.

"You speak of Doctor Glendower, yes?"

Lexi drew back in surprise. "How could you know?"

"Your eyes gave you away, *chère,* and the blush in your cheek, on that night of the wedding when he took your arm. He did not come all this way on my account, you know."

Filled with shame, Lexi dropped her head. "Yes, I think I know that . . . now."

"You were angry with him, though, when he told you that he'd once had a . . . *penchant* for me. It cannot have been easy for you."

Lexi sensed that Celeste was only guessing about the particulars, but her guess had hit painfully close to the mark.

"He didn't tell me," she explained. "I found your letter."

"*Pauvre petite,*" Celeste replied, shaking her head. "But you mustn't be too hard on him, *chère.* He was such a kind and decent young man then, such a good doctor, but the war had hurt him

224

badly, and he was looking for something to make him forget. I tried to be his friend, but he needed more than I could give."

Lexi had been holding her breath. Now it left her in a quivering sigh. "He is . . . a hard man to understand."

Her thoughts drifted back to the man as he was when first she'd met him — cold and angry and wanting nothing more than to hide from the world. "I don't know what to do," she said.

"Go to him," Celeste urged her. "He needs you, even if he will not admit it."

Lexi had been proud of the changes she'd brought about in Morgan, proud of the man that he'd become — but now everything had changed. In turning him away, she'd wounded him deeply and likely destroyed the last bit of trust left in him.

"It's no use," she told her stepmother.

No doubt Morgan had gone back to his refuge in the wilderness, and this time for good. There would be no drawing him out again, for in his mind, Lexi would be forever remembered as *"la belle dame sans merci,"* the beautiful lady without mercy.

"It's outrageous, that's what it is!" Daniel Merritt sputtered from behind the pages of the *Buffalo Courier.*

"What's that, Daniel?" Celeste inquired, between sips of her morning coffee.

"Those damned Fenians have been—"

"Daniel!"

"Oh, beg pardon, ladies. Those . . . confounded Fenians have been trying to stir up trouble for months now, and it looks as if they've done it at last. Tried to attack the British on Campobello Island. Only managed to set fire to a few warehouses, though, and steal a British flag from the customs inspector before they were driven off."

Lexi and Celeste exchanged confused glances. "I'm afraid that we don't always understand when you're speaking politics, Papa," Lexi said to him. "Who exactly are these Fenians?"

Mr. Merritt folded his paper neatly and set it on the nearest corner of the breakfast table. "The Fenian Brotherhood is a group of Irish-Americans whose goal it is to fight the British in order to secure freedom for Ireland," he explained patiently.

"But then why attack a Canadian island?" Celeste wanted to know. "Why not confront the British on Irish soil?"

"The first rule of battle is to attack an enemy at his weakest point," he replied, sounding for all the world as if he'd had some practical experience, when they all knew that his knowledge of the late war had consisted of determining which investments would prove the most profitable for the bank. "Experience has proven that the British presence is far too strong in Ireland, but the Canadian provinces with their thousands of miles of unprotected border are another matter entirely."

Lexi had been concentrating on the eggs and

sliced ham upon her plate, but now she set down her fork and addressed herself to the conversation. "And so they propose to march northward and conquer the whole of Canada in the name of Ireland?" she asked, incredulous.

"I'll admit that it sounds rather preposterous until you consider that the Brotherhood has a pool of over one hundred fifty thousand veteran soldiers of Irish descent from which to draw — war-hardened fellows like your young friend, Brendan O'Neill."

"Brendan would never be so foolish as to ally himself with such a brainless mob," Lexi replied, but then her thoughts were suddenly filled with the memory of Brendan as he faced off against Morgan, his temper flaring and logic the furthest thing from his mind.

"Well, at any rate, the newspapers seem to think that the danger has passed," her father continued. "After the bumbling invasion attempt at Campobello, I believe we've heard the last of the Fenian Brotherhood. All their fiasco seems to have spawned is a new desire for confederation among the Canadian provinces."

A smile curved Lexi's mouth as she considered how this news would please Morgan. She remembered how ardently he'd spoke on the subject of confederation over supper at Gran's on the first night they'd met. But once she'd opened the floodgates, she could not prevent all the other memories of that night from pouring in as well. As they did, a knot began to twist in her stomach, and she wondered if she would ever be free of the memories. How much better it would have been if she'd never run away to Gran's, never met Morgan Glendower at all, and then she'd not have been able to hurt him with her lack of trust.

When Mary the parlormaid swept into the room to hand Mr. Merritt the morning mail, Lexi's bitter thoughts scattered like dry leaves in the wind. She shivered against the cold emptiness she felt within and reached for her steaming tea, wrapping her fingers around the china cup as if to ward off the chill.

"Here's something for you, Alexandra," her father said as he riffled through the stack. He drew out the envelope and handed it to Celeste, who then passed it on.

Lexi set down her cup. Her chest tightened painfully, as she recalled the last missive she'd received by mail. Only when she noticed the feminine handwriting was she able to draw an easy breath once more. Tearing open the envelope, she pulled out the page and unfolded it.

"What is it?" Celeste asked, when she noticed Lexi's furrowing brow.

"It's from Hannah Newcomb," she explained. "She's a friend of Gran's from Stevensville. She says that Gran was doing her spring cleaning and had a tumble while washing the windows."

"That sounds like your gran, all right," Mr. Merritt replied. "Was she hurt?"

228

"Well, she's broken her ankle, and her arm is badly bruised, but Mrs. Newcomb says that her disposition hasn't been damaged a bit. She is already hobbling about, against the doctor's orders, and trying to handle everything on her own."

Celeste's expression mirrored her concern. "Perhaps you ought to go to her, *chère*," she suggested.

"That's what Mrs. Newcomb says," Lexi said, and referred again to the handwriting on the page. "Well, more precisely that I ought to 'get myself on out there at once before Gran breaks her fool neck.' "

"You know that your grandmother and Jacob are welcome to come and stay with us for as long as they'd like," her father reminded her.

But Lexi knew that Gran would never leave the farm. This was *her* responsibility; Gran and Jacob were *her* family, and of course, she'd go to them at once.

"You know that Gran would never agree to that. I'll pack my things and leave in the morning," she said.

It was less than two hours later when Mary came to inform her that Mr. O'Neill was waiting to see her in the red parlor. Expecting that, as usual, she would be instructed to send him away, the girl's eyes widened in surprise as Lexi informed her that she would be down to speak with him in a few minutes. And as for Brendan, he was no less surprised when she actually appeared between the double doors.

"Lexi!" he exclaimed. "Saints be praised, I feared you'd made up your mind never to forgive me."

He advanced toward her, arms outstretched, but something in her look made him halt midway and let his hands drop to his sides.

Lexi passed him by and settled herself on one of a pair of chairs set before the windows. "Shall I ring for tea?" she asked coolly when he came to join her.

"I'd not be wantin' to play tea party with you," he said, all his frustrations caught up in the words. "We need to talk, you and I."

It was all that Lexi could do to maintain her icy demeanor. From the first, she'd decided to blame Brendan for all her misfortune. After all, if he hadn't bullied his way into the study on the night of her father's wedding, she might have had the opportunity to listen to Morgan. But then she came to admit that she couldn't fault Brendan for being protective of her; he always had been. The truth of it was that she'd been so hurt that she was only looking for an excuse, any excuse, to strike out at Morgan.

Brendan was fidgeting in his chair like a child who was being allowed in the parlor with the grownups for the very first time. His hands gripped the wooden armrests so hard that his knuckles blanched. And all the while, his eyes were on her, as if he were trying to gauge her mood. When at last she smiled at him, he seemed to take heart.

"You've changed since you've come back home," she said gently.

"Aye," he agreed. "You'll get no argument from me on that. The war has made me a hardened man and all the more determined to go after what I want in life. I want you, Lexi. Can't you see that?"

"I don't think you know what you do want, Brendan. I think that you need more time to settle back in, to renew old acquaintances and meet new people. There are plenty of young ladies in Buffalo who'd welcome the attentions of a fine man like you."

But he wasn't listening to her. "I know you're angry with me for what I said to your doctor friend, but there's no use denyin' he deserved it after what he done to you."

Lexi felt the color rise in her cheeks; she wished she'd never confided in him at all. "Doctor Glendower cannot be held to blame for what I've already explained to you was my own foolishness."

"Any gentleman worthy of the name would never take advantage of an innocent young lady," he retorted. "What he's done can't be undone."

With this, Lexi sprang from her chair and crossed her arms tightly over her breasts as she began to pace, hoping the action would dissipate her anger. It did not. "Do you mean to say that now I'm damaged goods, am I?"

Brendan was staring hard at his hands, which he began to wring together in his lap in a nervous fashion. "No man would be happy to hear that the woman he's chosen as his own—" His face paled as he realized what he was saying, and he promptly sought to repair the damage. "But you know that I would never let that—"

"Well, you needn't worry, Brendan O'Neill. I have no intentions of getting married, not to *anyone*," she said, glaring back over her shoulder at him as she emphasized the word.

"Please, Lexi," he said, starting after her. "I've only come to say I'm sorry, and now I've gone and made things worse. I know I'm a jealous fool, whose tongue needs tearin' out by the roots, but I'd not have you thinkin' that I don't have respect for you. Sure an' I've more respect for you than any woman I've ever met."

"Then please, Brendan," she said as she turned back to face him. "Stop trying to play the jealous lover and just be my friend."

He dropped his head contritely. "If that's truly what you want of me."

"It's all I've ever wanted."

Lexi hoped she'd gotten through to him finally, but she couldn't be sure, for when he looked up again, he met her with a mischievous grin. "Then, will you have supper with me tomorrow night . . . purely as my way of making amends, you understand?"

She shook her head as she walked back to her

chair and sat down. "I can't. Gran's had an accident, she'll be laid up for several months, and so I'm going back to help with the farm. I'll be leaving tomorrow morning."

"And how long will you be stayin'?" he inquired, taking his own place in the chair beside her.

"I'm not at all certain that I'm coming back at all. Papa has Celeste to take care of him now; he doesn't need me, but Gran and Jacob could use the help. Besides, I like living in the country."

"And—mind, I'm only askin' this as your friend—you're sure that part of the reason you're goin' back there is not on account of *him?*"

Lexi had no qualms about meeting his amber eyes; she had nothing to hide. "Whatever there might have been between us once is over now, I assure you."

Perhaps the tone of her voice was sharper than she'd intended it to be, for Brendan winced as she spoke. "You haven't forgiven me, have ye?" he said.

"Of course I have."

He shook his head. "Nay, I don't believe that you have. But I'll think of some way to make amends, you just wait and see."

Chapter Sixteen

Lexi stood at the rail and watched as the frothy trail of the ferry's churning wake stretched out across the water and the familiar sights of Buffalo receded, blurring into the early morning haze.

The last trip across to Canada that she'd made on this ferry hadn't been planned at all; she'd carried only a hastily stuffed carpetbag and two stale biscuits tucked in her pocket for a meal. But this time she'd had some time to arrange matters. As soon as she'd decided to go, she'd sent word for Jacob to pick her up at the station in Ridgeway, and then, after she'd said her goodbyes to Brendan yesterday, she'd had the maids help her pack her things and gone off to do some shopping.

Outside of her own needs, she'd concentrated on those items not so easily gotten from the Newcombs' in Stevensville: a tin of imported chocolate, canned figs, a large bottle of lemon extract. . . . She bought a new taffeta petticoat for Gran and a walking stick for when she was up and around again, and a sketchbook and pencils for Jacob, so he'd not have to make his drawings on Gran's linen tablecloth.

And then, of course, there were the books: a set of popular classics, Macaulay's entire *History of England,* the works of Alexandre Dumas, Emerson's *Essays,* and an assortment of modern novels. It would not be hard at all to leave Buffalo and make a home with Gran in the country, Lexi told herself, so long as she had her books to help pass the quiet hours.

By the time she'd finished packing last night, she'd filled up three large trunks and several valises. She grinned rather shamelessly now as she recalled that when she'd arrived at the ferry dock this morning, her coachman and the porter had had a time of it getting them all on board, and in order to salve her guilt, she had to offer them both an excessively generous tip.

As the ferry drew nearer the Fort Erie side of the river, there was less of the smell of factory smoke and coal dust in the air and more of the sweet scent of spring. The spreading limbs of the trees that girded the shoreline were thick with buds, and the pastureland beyond the split rail fences near the wharf had already turned a verdant green and was dotted with heads of pink and white clover.

With every moment that passed, Lexi was feeling more and more certain that she'd made the right decision. Gran needed her now, and she needed something purposeful in her life.

The ferry was not particularly crowded this morning, and so she was a little uneasy when, out of the corner of her eye, she caught a glimpse of a brawny man sidling up beside her. "Good morning to ye, Lexi."

There was no mistaking that voice. "Brendan?" she said, her face paling in surprise as she turned to regard him. He was wearing his army kepi on his head, a dark blue work shirt, corduroy trousers, and he had a faded knapsack slung over his back. "What are you doing here?"

"Didn't I tell you I'd find a way to make amends?"

"Whatever do you mean?"

"Me ma's gotten so used to runnin' the store that there's hardly a use for me there, and, well, I figured that with your gran ailin', you could use a hand with the plowin' and plantin' an' such. Mind you now, I'm not sayin' I'm experienced at that sort o'thing, but I've got a good strong back and a sturdy pair o'hands, and I'm ready to do what I can to help."

Lexi was more than a little confused. She almost told him that as Gran was not a plow horse, her accident would hardly keep Jacob from plowing and planting the same as he did every spring. But before the words came out, she realized what Brendan was trying to do with his offer. Just as he'd vowed that he would, yesterday, he was finding a way to make amends for the way that he'd treated her. And even though, somewhere in the

236

back of her mind, a voice was telling Lexi that he might still harbor some hope of changing her mind about a match between the two of them, she had to believe that his intentions were genuine.

"And don't go worryin' yourself about what the neighbors will be thinkin'. I'll be comfy enough in the barn, same as any hired hand."

What could she say? Although she feared the arrangement might make her uncomfortable, after what he'd put her through lately, there was really no harm in it. This time of year another hand would certainly be welcome; it would mean that Jacob would not have to bear the burden of putting in the wheat crop all on his own. And once Brendan had discharged this debt he thought he owed her, he'd go home to his family, and that would be the end of it.

After they'd boarded the train for Ridgeway, Lexi shared the lunch Mrs. Fraser had packed with him, and he asked her questions about Gran and Jacob and the farm. She'd told him a little over the years, but now he was interested in details. How far was the farm from the railway depot? And how many acres were there that needed planting? And how many people lived in Ridgeway? And Stevensville? And were all of Gran's neighbors friendly folk?

Soon enough, Brendan was able to see for himself that the village of Ridgeway was a quiet spot, not much more than the depot, several storefronts, two taverns, and twenty or so houses scattered along the main crossroads. On the banks of a nearby creek stood a flour mill that served the neighboring farms.

Jacob was waiting at the depot as instructed, and after Lexi had introduced them to each other, the pair proceeded to load her heavy trunks into the wagon, with no small measure of grunting and sweating.

"And just what the devil have you got in these trunks of yours, Lexi?" Brendan asked as he and Jacob slid the last of the luggage into the wagon bed. "They feel as if they're loaded down with bricks. Aw, but you can't be thinkin' of bringin' your papa's house over here a brick at a time, can ye?"

Lexi rolled her eyes. "Don't be silly, Brendan. It's only books . . . and other odds and ends I'm going to need."

Jacob, however, found Brendan's antics highly amusing, and he favored him with a broad grin, which unfortunately only encouraged him to continue.

"Well, now, did you hear that? Odds and ends, she says. I tell you, Jacob, never trust a woman to do her own packin' or she'll try and stuff in every last blessed thing she possesses, includin' the family cat and the kitchen stove."

Lexi sat between them on the wagon seat for the whole of the drive home. Each time she turned to Brendan, he was wearing a mischievous grin, and then she'd look at Jacob, only to catch him snuffling a little laugh. It seemed that the two had developed an instant camaraderie and that she was destined to be the butt of their humor. It shouldn't have surprised her, really. Brendan was accustomed to dealing with his younger siblings, and Jacob, regardless of his age and size, did still have the mind of a child.

It had been a long day, and by the time the wagon pulled up in the yard, Lexi was sorely tired. The last thing that she needed to see, as she looked up to the porch, was Morgan Glendower standing there with an oddly expectant look on his face.

For an instant, her heart leapt in her breast, and she forgot all the heartache that had passed between them. But before too long, she was sharply reminded, for his expression went cold as soon as he noticed Brendan beside her on the carriage seat.

In the time it took for Brendan to hand her down, Morgan had disappeared from his place on the porch. She did not see him as she led Brendan into the house, nor as she entered her grandmother's room.

Gran was lying in her bed, her eyes half-closed. She was propped up by a pair of pillows, and wearing her best muslin nightdress, with a long silver braid trailing over one thin shoulder. One bandaged foot was sticking out of the blankets and set upon a small cushion.

"Gran?" Lexi called softly. "How are you feeling?"

At the sound of her voice, Gran came to life. "You needn't hae come, lass. I'll be up and around in a few days."

"No doubt you will," Lexi agreed, as she swept in and perched herself on the edge of the bed, taking up her grandmother's hands. "But I want to make certain that you don't overdo it. Besides, I've decided I'm better suited to the country. Do you think you'll mind having me around?"

Gran pulled her near. "Ah, Lexi, I couldna ask for a better tonic."

"Do you think you're up to meeting someone?" Lexi asked her then.

"Aye. But what's this about?"

"A friend of mine has come with me from the city: Brendan O'Neill. You remember me mentioning him?"

Again Gran nodded.

"Well, he's come out to help Jacob with the planting," Lexi explained, and then leaned nearer to whisper. "Be nice to him, Gran. He's an old friend, and he wants to do this as a special favor to me."

Lexi did not miss the cocked brow or the glint in Gran's eye as she went to the kitchen to fetch Brendan, and it made her uneasy. Gran's body may well have been slowed down a bit by her accident, but her mind was sharp as ever, and there was no telling what she'd say to Brendan. But there was nothing to be done about it; she'd just have to introduce them and see what happened.

On the positive side, Lexi had a good deal of faith in Brendan's abilities as a charmer. One had only to look how quickly Jacob had taken to him.

" 'Tis a pleasure to meet you at last, Mrs. Mac-Lennan," he said as he came into the room. "I see now where Lexi comes by her beauty."

"Dunna bother tae waste your silver tongue on me, Mr. O'Neill," Gran told him plainly. "I'm a bristly old goat wi' no taste for flummery. But I understand you've been a good friend tae me granddaughter, and that says enough for ye. You're welcome here. Now tell me why ye've come."

Lexi winced at her grandmother's blunt words, then watched in fascination as Brendan followed Gran's lead, adapting himself to suit her demeanor. He bowed his head and a wave of thick auburn hair swept across his brow, then he clasped his hands behind his back, and his expression turned sober and sincere. "I've a close family o' me own, mum, and Ma's always raised us to help one another. Lexi, well, she's no less than family to me, and I'll help her wherever I can. I'd be askin' for naught but meals and a warm place in the hayloft. Besides all that, for years your granddaughter's been tellin' me how pleasant the country life can be, and I been thinkin' that it's high time I come and see it for meself."

"I canna say how pleasant a place you'll find it after you've trudged knee-deep in clods behind a stubborn plowhorse," Gran said then, the burr in

241

her words sounding sharp after Brendan's melodious brogue, "but we'll welcome your help, so long as you'd like to stay."

Lexi hooked Brendan's arm, drawing him away before Gran could interrogate him further, and took him back out to the kitchen, where she gave instructions to Jacob to show him around the farm. She had hoped that Gran might drift off to sleep before she returned, but, of course, it was only wishful thinking. Gran was waiting for her, her sharp eyes fixed on the doorway, arms folded across her chest.

"He's smitten wi' ye, lass. Or are ye too blind tae see it?"

"He's a friend, Gran," Lexi replied briskly as she busied herself with smoothing the blankets on the bed, "an old and dear friend. There's nothing more to it than that."

"Aye, an' that may be what you think, but that Irishman's of another mind altogether. But enough of that now, where's Doctor Glendower gone off to?"

Lexi hesitated, hastily glancing back over her shoulder as if she expected to see him standing there. "I—I don't know. He was on the porch when we arrived, but then he disappeared. Perhaps he's gone home."

"Nay, he wouldna leave without sayin' good-bye. He comes by every day to check on me. Did you know that, lass? Aye, he's doctorin' for everyone hereabouts now. The neighbors helped him finish off that infirmary of his, and he's thrown himself into the work."

Gran's shawl had slipped off the bed and was pooled on the floor. Lexi's gaze fastened on it and she bent down to pick it up, so that her grandmother would not be able to see the change in her expression, for the truth was that she was surprised. Somehow she'd expected that after their last encounter, Morgan would have gone back to his cabin to brood again and shut out the world.

She had not forgotten how hard it had been to draw him out in the first place, and she'd imagined that — after the way that she'd hurt him — he'd have gone back to being what he was before. But then maybe she'd been giving herself too much credit, maybe she'd only been naive to think that she'd effected the change or that she'd even meant that much to him.

"He comes by every day to check on me," Gran persisted. "Did I tell you that? He's a good man. You couldna ask for better."

Lexi couldn't listen to any more. She had to get out of this room before Gran wore her down and she ended up making admissions that she didn't want to make. "I'll go out and look for him, if you like," she offered.

"Aye, you do that, lass, and tell him that maybe I will take that laudanum, if he'll leave the bottle with you."

She couldn't say where he'd been hiding for all of this time, but when Lexi left Gran and went back into the kitchen, she saw Morgan through the open door, sitting on the porch steps. He looked comfortable enough. The sleeves of his striped cotton shirt were rolled to his elbows, which were resting on his bent knees as he sat there staring out toward the barn. There, Jacob and Brendan were alternately engaged in taking the grand tour and making merry. As Lexi well knew, Brendan had a way of finding levity in even the most commonplace of chores.

But Lexi's thoughts were not on Brendan now, they were on Morgan. She came up behind him, so close that her skirts nearly brushed his shoulder, and when she breathed the familiar scent of him, of pine soap and perspiration, she was suddenly caught up in a web of painfully sweet memories, and she had to twine the fingers of both her hands tightly together in order to quell the powerful urge to run them through his thick black hair.

"Gran said you wouldn't leave without saying good-bye," she said softly.

"I wouldn't." The voice was cool and restrained. He did not turn to face her.

"She says that she'd like you to leave the bottle of laudanum. Is she in much pain, do you think?"

Morgan reflected for a long moment before replying. "That's hard to say. It was a bad break, but it ought to heal good as new, if she's careful. She oughtn't to be walking at all. See to that, will you?"

"Of course."

"And do keep a close eye on her," he warned. "When Mrs. Newcomb came by to prepare supper last week, she found your grandmother hobbling about the house, trying to do the housework."

"I know. Hannah wrote to me about it, else I'd never have known about the accident at all."

Morgan was sure that he detected a slight touch of asperity in her voice. Could it be that she'd expected *him* to write? Maybe her irritation was not unfounded, he told himself as he thought on it; maybe he should have been the one. But no matter the reason, he simply could not bring himself to open the door that she had so firmly closed.

And now he was glad that he hadn't, for it appeared that Lexi had cast her lot elsewhere. She had come back here flaunting that damned Irish protector of hers, and he was already making himself at home.

Four months had gone by, yet the very thought of her still had the power to wound him, and it angered Morgan to realize it. Just now, when he'd heard the whisper of silk skirts behind him and caught a hint of the sweet scent of violets floating on the air, his body had responded with a startling violence, a rush of heat flooding through his veins. It angered him all the more.

The conflicting emotions roiled within him, forcing him to his feet. He strode into the dooryard to put some distance between them.

"*I* suggested that Mrs. Newcomb contact you," he explained, with no apology in his tone. He wanted to strike out at her; he needed to sever the hold she had on him. Drawing upon all the strength within him, he turned back to her, forcing his face into an expressionless mask. "Oh, and you may tell your new lover that he needn't watch for me over his shoulder while you two are tumbling in the hayloft. I'm bright enough to know when I've been dismissed. I'll not be troubling you again."

It was an awful thing to say, and no sooner had the words escaped his lips than he regretted them, even if they were true. Lexi blanched, and in one quixotic instant it struck him how beautiful she was, in her cherry-colored silk dress, with her hair all plaited and coiled and lustrous pearl earrings dangling from her dainty lobes. But her soft bottom lip was trembling and her eyes were liquid emeralds, swimming with tears. And he had done this to her.

Chapter Seventeen

Anna MacLennan was a slave driver, no doubt of that at all. Lexi was sure that in a former life, her grandmother had been one of the gang bosses who oversaw the hauling of blocks of stone by slaves to build the pyramids, or a lieutenant to the lord of the manor who assured that the hapless serfs spent their every waking hour toiling in the field.

In two weeks, she'd seen to it that Lexi finished washing all the windows, beat the dust from the parlor carpets, wiped down the kitchen walls, top to bottom, and then scrubbed all the floors, white-washed the chicken coop, and replaced all the straw. And after she'd nearly burnt the skin off her hands with Gran's lye soap, wrenched every muscle in her back and shoulders, and worn her fingernails down to the nub, Lexi began to think that there was something to be said for the useless life, after all.

On this particular morning, while Gran supervised from her rocking chair on the porch with her bandaged foot resting on a cushioned stool, Lexi was planting the kitchen garden. She'd already turned the soil with the spading fork, raked it smooth, and strung the rows. Now, with her skirts tucked up to keep the hem from dragging in the dirt, she knelt down on a reed mat and set to work planting a row of the bean seedlings that she'd just taken out of the cold frame.

Overhead, only a few wispy clouds chased across the bright blue sky. The soft breeze that fluttered the brim of Lexi's sunbonnet carried the clear trill of a sparrow from somewhere in the wood. The sun was warm on her back, and the smell of rich, moist earth tickled her nose. With a rhythmic precision, she scooped out a hole, dropped in the seedling by its roots, mounded the soft earth around it, patted it down with her fingers, and went on to the next.

She continued the process with the cucumber seedlings, and then the melons, and before long she'd created a veritable army of little garden soldiers, all standing in neat rows, their leafy green heads bobbing in the breeze. As Lexi surveyed her work, a smile came to her slowly. There was a certain satisfaction in seeing the product of her labor set out before her. That's what she'd always liked about living with Gran. Although it was hard, the work that she did had a direct effect on their lives. It wasn't the same as making stitches on a tapestry or planning a formal dinner party. Maybe she'd forgotten about that lately, but staring at the neat garden rows was a strong reminder and only strengthened her resolve to stay.

"Mind ye now, lass. Dunna put the beans afore the carrots in the row," Gran called out. "They'll block the sunlight."

"Yes, Gran," Lexi replied, waving a hand over her head to show she'd understood.

After repositioning the reed mat she'd been kneeling upon, she settled down once more and removed the envelope of carrot seeds from her apron pocket. She made a furrow along the string line and carefully shook the tiny seeds out of the envelope, spreading them all along the row. So intent was she upon her work that she did not even notice the long shadow that fell across the spot where she was working.

"Mistress Mary, quite contrary, how does your garden grow?"

At the sound of the smooth, deep voice, Lexi stiffened, but did not stop her work or turn around. "Good afternoon to you, Doctor Glendower."

"I see your grandmother is resting at last. Do you have her tied to that chair?"

At this, she could not help but smile, but still she did not turn her eyes upward, only continued planting the row. "She'll stay put so long as I dance to her tune. Let me slack off, though, and you'll see her hobbling over here fast enough to see what's what."

"Then, by all means, do continue," he said.

A brief glance in his direction told her that he was dressed for business, in his dark blue frock coat, waistcoat, and trousers. But he did not hurry on his way. Even after several minutes had passed, he was still standing there, with his forearms resting on the top rail of the garden fence, as if he intended to stand there all day watching her. He did not speak again, though. Perhaps he could think of nothing hurtful to say to her today.

Gran called out, finally breaking the silence. "Lexi? Lexi? Dinna just sit there digging in the dirt, lass. Bring Doctor Glendower o'er here and then fetch us some tea."

Before Lexi could get to her feet, Morgan had come in by the gate and was offering her a hand. She accepted it. What else could she do? But the moment she felt the firm pressure of his fingers closing over hers, the rough calluses, the heat of his skin, she was sorry that she had. The memories were still too close to the surface. She hated herself for responding with a warming blush and swore that even if it took every ounce of her strength, she'd blot them out.

As soon as she'd regained her footing, she released his hand, and after brushing the dirt from her skirts, she hurried up the path to the house. She swept past Gran and went into the kitchen without so much as a glance in her direction. She'd had quite enough of her grandmother's bullying for one day.

With a frown marring her brow, Lexi snatched

250

up the sink brush and scrubbed at the dirt under her fingernails, muttering all the while about iron-handed, ungrateful relatives. She knew well enough that she was only using her irritation with Gran to distract her from the deeper turmoil within herself, but it was safer somehow.

She filled the kettle, carried it to the stove, and slammed it down, feeling a strange satisfaction as more than a few droplets of water splashed out of the spout and skittered across the hot stovetop in a hiss of steam.

Yet even as she bustled about the kitchen giving vent to her spleen, Lexi did not miss the sound of Morgan's heavy tread on the porch steps, nor the familiar timbre of his voice as he sat down beside Gran and inquired after her health.

"Much better today, thank ye, Doctor. An' it wouldna be so but for your kind attentions," Gran replied, sounding for all the world like a smitten schoolgirl.

"You give me far too much credit," Morgan told her. "A simple broken bone couldn't keep a woman like you down for long, Mrs. MacLennan."

Lexi could have sworn she'd heard a giggle. She'd never have believed her grandmother capable of making such a sound. Oh, this was really too much!

"Lexi? Hurry wi' that tea, lass, and bring Doctor Glendower a slice of that seed cake you baked yestere'en."

Only by biting down on the tip of her tongue

was Lexi able to prevent herself from dealing a sharp reply. She drew a measured breath to calm herself and went on arranging Gran's good china cups on the tray, then silently crossed to the pantry to fetch the cake. Slicing several thin wedges, she arranged them on the china plate.

"She's a good lass," Lexi heard Gran remark to Morgan then, even though she'd lowered her voice, "to leave all the comforts of her father's house and come here tae care for us. Just look at all she's done: cooked and scrubbed and washed and mended — an' have ye e'er seen a garden with rows as straight as that? Aye, she'll make some man a fine wife . . ."

Lexi had already taken the heavy tray in hand and was heading for the door, but when she heard her grandmother's final remark, she felt her heart thud in her breast. With her cheeks flaming, she halted midstep. How could Gran say such a thing? Well-intentioned though she might have been, she was as transparent as glass, and she didn't understand how things were — not at all. Lexi had not yet been able to bring herself to tell her grandmother what had occurred between her and Morgan; likely she never would. As the minutes passed, there was no denying the uncomfortable silence from without.

"I'm sure Mr. O'Neill thinks so," Morgan said at last.

That remark seemed to effectively silence Gran. Lexi tilted her chin upward at a proud angle as she pushed through the screen door and settled the tray on the table next to her grandmother's chair. She was doing her best to pretend she hadn't heard any of their conversation as she poured out their tea, but deep within, yet another layer was added to the shell that had been forming around her heart.

"Where is Jacob today?" Morgan asked, changing the subject at last. "Busy planting?"

"He and Mr. O'Neill have finished wi' the planting," Gran explained. "They've gone off to Stevensville for supplies."

"It seems that the admirable Mr. O'Neill has been a great help . . . to all of you."

Before Lexi could decide what precisely Morgan meant by the remark, Gran had wisely turned the subject of the conversation in another direction entirely.

"Why don't you join us for supper this evenin', Doctor?" she suggested. "Lexi's promised us baked ham wi' sliced potatoes and corn bread."

Lexi willed her hand not to tremble as she lifted a cup from the tray and handed it to Morgan. Gran had no idea what she was proposing. Thus far, Morgan and Brendan had managed to keep a discreet distance between them, but an evening with the two of them sitting across the supper table from each other was bound to end in bloodshed. Morgan simply had to refuse.

"It does sound tempting, but I have to go into Stevensville to see Mrs. Peterson," he said. Lexi breathed a scarcely audible sigh of relief. "Her rheumatism has had her laid up in bed for more than a week now."

"You maun stop on your way back home, then," Gran continued, undaunted. "We shall expect you at seven, and I willna have 'nay' for an answer."

Morgan shook his head and a smile curved on his lips, as if he found Gran's persistence amusing. "As you wish, Mrs. MacLennan. I promise I shall be on my best behavior."

Only when her eyes met his did Lexi realize that the last comment had been directed at her.

"Oh, I've nae doubt of that," Gran replied, accepting the cup that Lexi held out to her, and then she turned to her granddaughter. "Where's *your* tea, lass? Pour yourself a cup, sit down here by us, and we'll talk a bit."

But Lexi had no intention of doing that. She couldn't listen to any more of Gran's machinations; she had more than enough to worry about already. "I've no time," she replied, as she stepped down from the porch and headed back toward the garden. "There's far too much work to be done."

It was late afternoon when Morgan finally finished with his patient and left her bedside. A lifetime of hard work and exposure to the harsh Canadian winters had taken its toll on Mrs. Peterson, but Morgan prescribed what he could to relieve her pain. He suggested to her daughters that she ought to be made to rest and recommended the application of warm flannel compresses to her swollen joints to make her comfortable until the inflammation subsided.

After he'd done all that he could for her, her husband, the innkeeper, invited him to stay and have supper. But Morgan had not forgotten his promise to Mrs. MacLennan, and so he politely refused. He did accept Peterson's offer of a pint of ale in the dining room of the inn, however, where a number of the local men had gathered to exchange the news of the day.

"You were with the Queen's Army, weren't you, Doctor?" the storekeeper, Mr. Newcomb, inquired of him as soon as he'd sat down with them. "Tell us what you think of this Fenian business. Have we anything to be concerned about?"

Morgan had enough problems of his own with Irish troublemakers, or at least one in particular, and he was far too weary to address such a question. It had been a long day, and considering what awaited him at the MacLennan farm, he expected the evening would prove trying at best. He was sorely in need of a restorative, so he lifted his glass to his lips and downed a generous swallow of the dark ale before giving Newcomb's question any serious thought.

In the meanwhile, Mr. Peterson offered an opinion of his own. "The militia has been sent hither and yon chasing Fenians for months now. Folks see them creeping through the bushes and behind every tree. Why, I'd not be surprised to hear but that they check beneath their beds before going to sleep at night. And what's come of it, I ask you? Nothing, that's what."

"If these Fenians should decide to come," Morgan said, speaking up at last, "they'll find few friends on this side of the border, I can tell you that. Our own Canadian politician Mr. Thomas D'Arcy McGee was Irish-born himself, and he speaks for many when he says that 'our first duty is to the land where we live.' That's something we must all remember, gentlemen."

"What about the raid on Campobello?" Newcomb returned. "If they tried such a thing once, they might again."

Morgan drained his glass, enjoying the sharp bite of the rich, dark brew on his tongue. He felt much stronger now. The blood in his veins was not half so sluggish as it had been, and his thoughts seemed clear and focused. It might have been the direction of the conversation or it might have been the effects of the ale, but whatever the cause, his spirits were rising. "As I see it," he said, his words radiating a calm assurance now, "their incompetence in that affair only proves how little we have to fear from Irish rabble-rousers."

"Here, here," Peterson agreed, and signaled to his daughter to refill Dr. Glendower's glass.

"But," one of the local farmers piped in, "I hear tell that there was a letter printed in the Buffalo newspaper calling the American Irish to arms.

And there was a mass meeting of them Fenian folk in New York City a couple of months back. What do you think that was about?"

"Making plans and carrying them out are two different matters," Morgan replied. "And if anything should come of this, it will be the Americans who are to blame for not keeping the troublemakers on their own side of the border."

On that note, he lifted his glass and swiftly emptied it again. Yes, he was feeling a good deal better now, even with the prospect of facing Lexi and her thickheaded Irish protector across the dinner table. Before he'd realized it, he'd allowed Peterson to pour him yet another ale and lifted his glass as the innkeeper toasted: "God save the Queen!"

"So, then, you don't believe there's any danger at all, Doctor?" Newcomb inquired yet again.

"Oh, there's a danger, all right," Morgan told him, "but not from the Fenian Brotherhood. The American government is just waiting for the excuse to cross our borders and annex our provinces, one by one. It's called 'Manifest Destiny,' gentlemen, and so long as we continue to squabble amongst ourselves and hide from Fenian bogeymen, there's every chance we'll wake up one day and find ourselves a part of the United States and all her problems."

Morgan considered for a long moment and then boldly raised his glass to offer a toast of his own. "To a united Canada!"

Until now, Morgan had not stopped to wonder why, if Jacob MacLennan and Brendan O'Neill were supposed to have been in Stevensville purchasing supplies, he had not encountered them on the road, nor seen them at all in the time he was there. After he'd bid good-bye to the gentlemen at the inn and climbed into his buggy, though, he started south on the main road and caught sight of their wagon as it crossed his path some distance ahead, and it made him wonder. The two were heading back to the farm—that was clear enough—but they'd not been in Stevensville at all. They were coming from the east.

Morgan found himself considering as he drove. If they'd not found what they'd needed in Stevensville, they might have gone to Ridgeway—but Ridgeway was south, not east. The road they'd been traveling wound up eventually in Fort Erie, but that would have been a long way to go for supplies that could surely have been gotten closer to home. And as far as Morgan knew, there was nothing else on the road in between but woods and a few small farmsteads. And he had to admit, it made him curious.

By the time he reached the MacLennan farm, he'd forgotten all about it, though. He was far more concerned with preparing himself to meet the cold, unforgiving chill in Lexi's eyes. It made him shudder just to think on it. And if that weren't enough to unnerve him, there was always Mrs. MacLennan's determined curiosity or Brendan O'Neill's outright animosity. Morgan told himself that he ought to have refused this invitation. What perversity was there in his nature that made him keep going back to her, even after she'd chosen another? Perhaps the truth of it was that he didn't want to believe that Lexi and Brendan O'Neill were lovers.

How had everything gone so wrong? Morgan knew that Lexi had been hurt when she'd found out about Celeste, and he could hardly blame her for that. But he could not erase the past, and she could not seem to forget it . . . or forgive him.

Hurt and anger had caused him to strike his own share of blows since then—there was no denying it—and as a result, a chasm had opened up between the two of them. Lexi scarcely acknowledged him at all lately, and when she did speak, she was chillingly polite. Could she have come to hate him so much?

Morgan pulled a painfully deep breath, wanting to fill his lungs with clean, fresh air and his mind with hopeful thoughts. To his surprise, he felt a new confidence welling in him. Maybe he'd been wrong about her relationship with O'Neill. Maybe when he'd looked at Lexi, he'd seen something more mirrored in the depths of those emerald green eyes of hers, something that gave him hope.

He realized full well that this newfound strength of his was likely borne of wishful thinking and one glass too many of Mr. Peterson's strong ale. But if there was a chance for them yet — if there was . . . Somehow tonight, he intended to find out.

Chapter Eighteen

Lexi kept her gaze carefully trained on her dinner plate as she sliced her food into neat morsels. It was the safest way to avoid any sort of confrontation, for everyone's eyes but Jacob's seemed to be fixed upon her. The kitchen table was far too crowded for comfort tonight. Morgan was seated so close that his sleeve brushed hers several times during the meal, and Brendan was scarcely more than an arm's length across the table.

Thus far, the conversation had been polite, but Lexi was still uneasy. She knew her grandmother well enough to know that the woman was up to something.

"What've ye planned for tomorrow, Jacob?" Gran asked innocently enough.

Lexi was certain that Jacob sensed the tension in the room, even if he did not understand it. For a long while now, he had only sat there, with his ruddy head bent, concentrating upon the buttering of his biscuit. But he responded to his mother's question at once, lifting his head to reveal a prideful grin.

261

Even now that Brendan had come to help, these small decisions were left in Jacob's hands, and it pleased him to believe that he was in charge. "We shall start on a new . . . p-pasture fence, I think. Brendan and I are good b-builders."

With that, Gran turned to Lexi. "Ye havna yet seen the fine infirmary Doctor Glendower has built, have ye, lass?"

"It's naught but a small room," Morgan was quick to amend, "and I couldn't have done it without the help of all the neighbors."

"Aye, but the folks here appreciate what you're doin' for us, Doctor," Gran continued. "Tae our minds, there canna be a higher callin' than that which you have chosen."

Morgan thanked her, and a silence settled briefly over the table until, all too soon, Gran began anew. "And what business did you say that you were engaged in, back home in Buffalo, Mr. O'Neill?"

Lexi realized what her grandmother was up to and moved to diffuse the situation. "You know very well, Gran, that Brendan's family owns a dry-goods store," she answered for him. "It's a very successful business."

"We've plenty of fine merchandise, all a body could ever need," Brendan added. He seemed pleased that Gran was finally taking an interest in his life. Clearly her attempt at sarcasm had eluded him.

Lexi found herself coming to his defense, before Gran could strike again. "Brendan's been off fighting a war, you know. He's given four years of his life to his country."

"Four years," Gran echoed. But her air of astonishment belied something else entirely. "Ye maun be a hardened lad by now, Mr. O'Neill."

"Aye, Mrs. MacLennan, that I am. But 'twas all for a noble cause, and I'd be ready to do it again if called upon."

"Would ye now?"

Lexi felt a tingling of apprehension rush through her at the tone of Gran's remark. She caught a glimpse of the spark in the old woman's faded blue eyes, but before she could guess what her intentions were, she had already made her next move.

"Dr. Glendower is a veteran of the Crimea. Isn't that so, Doctor?"

"It is," Morgan replied, without elaborating.

"Well, then, I wonder if you'd be likely to say the same as Mr. O'Neill here?"

Lexi knew well enough what Morgan's opinions of war were. Hadn't he told her that he'd come all this way to escape the awful memories? But thankfully, Morgan was a man of calmer mettle. Perhaps he, too, had sensed what Gran was up to, for he considered for a long while before forming his reply.

"I'm afraid I cannot consider any cause as noble which requires so many human lives to be lost."

At this, a flush of color spread upward across Brendan's broad face. " 'Tis hardly possible for those who've never felt the yoke of tyranny about their neck to understand that there are those of us who would be proud to give our lives that others might be free," he retorted.

Lexi was surprised at his eloquence, but that feeling was soon replaced by a growing dread when she realized that he had struck a nerve in Morgan, who now glared across the table, one dark brow raised in suspicion. "And I trust, Mr. O'Neill, that it is the newly freed American slaves of whom you speak with such noble intention?"

The animosity was building fast on both sides. Surely this was what Gran intended: to put both men who she believed had a claim on Lexi's heart in the same room and set them at one another, so that Lexi might compare their natures.

But Gran did not understand. It was not a question of whom Lexi loved best. Brendan had always been her friend and confidant. She could have loved him no more if he'd been her own brother, but she was not *in* love with him and never could be. And as for Morgan, she'd lost her chance with him on the day she'd sent him from her father's house. He'd made it more than clear since then that he'd closed his heart to her. There was no going back.

To prevent the situation from escalating further, Lexi got to her feet and hastily began gathering up the plates. Surely they'd not continue to play at this farce if she removed herself from the stage. "I'll just take care of these dishes," she said.

"Here, let me help you."

Before she knew it, Morgan was on his feet beside her and had taken the dishes from her hands and carried them to the sink. Lexi retrieved the large enamel kettle from the stove as he cleared the rest of the table and busied herself with filling the dishpan with steaming water.

Jacob left the table soon thereafter and went out to the barn to tend the animals. There was a long, quiet moment before Lexi heard Brendan's chair scrape the floor behind her, and then as he got to his feet, Gran spoke to him. "Oh, Mr. O'Neill, I wonder if ye'd be so kind as tae go out and check the south pasture gate? I canna be sure, but I thought when I looked out earlier that I saw it standing open."

"Aye, ma'am. I'd be happy to do it."

Lexi cast a glance at him over her shoulder, and the look that Brendan met her with as he headed for the door was full of hope. It made her admit to herself at last that he had come here with more in mind than making amends. She ought to have known it all along. He was still determined to win her favor. But how could she make him understand that what he wanted could never be?

As for Gran, she did not even try to hide her satisfied smile as she rose up from her chair and leaned upon her cane to address Lexi and Morgan. "I'm feelin' a wee bit tired this evening, so I'll be off tae bed and leave you two young people tae finish up here."

And with that, she quit the room, without so

much as a backward glance. She'd achieved her intent: Morgan and Lexi were left alone in the room.

Lexi pushed up the sleeves of the pale-green sprigged muslin dress that had once been her mother's and tried to focus on the task at hand. But each breath she drew was light and shallow, and her heart was fluttering within her like a windblown leaf. She would not let Morgan know how deep her feelings for him still ran; she would not! Steeling herself against her own reckless emotions, she thrust her hands into the still-steaming dishwater, only dully feeling the scalding heat seep through her skin, and blinked away the tears that pricked her eyes.

"Let me help you with the dishes," Morgan suggested, making the first move. "It's the least I can do to thank you for the fine supper."

"No," she protested. "No, I couldn't ask that of a guest."

The truth was that Lexi was not certain that she could bear to have him stand so close beside her for all that time. But there was a flicker of emotion mirrored in his eyes when she spoke of him as a guest—was it a wounded look?—and so she conjured up a smile for him, albeit a tenuous smile, and added, "Please, sit and have another cup of coffee, and you can keep me company."

He accepted the offer of coffee, but carried the cup with him as he paced the room restlessly, and an awkward silence settled in between them.

"Lexi, we need to—"

The tone of his voice was deep, serious . . . intimate. Inexplicably afraid of what he might say, Lexi interrupted him before he'd gotten the words out. "Would you bring me that pan from the table?" she asked coolly.

He did as she bade him, then went back to pacing silently. Lexi channeled her energy into scrubbing the worst of the grease from the bottom of the pan, feigning calm all the while, but when the measured tread of his footsteps ceased, she held her breath, fearing he meant to speak again.

"Who made these sketches?" he asked.

Lexi turned to him and saw that he'd picked up Jacob's sketchbook from the place where it lay on a chair in the corner. She let go a sigh of relief.

"It was Jacob. Do you remember that night that we caught him drawing on Gran's tablecloth?"

"Yes," he replied, and the single word was filled with such relish that Lexi half-imagined he was calling to mind other things about that night.

He was standing there with the sketchbook in hand, but for a moment he shut his eyes, and a smile played about the corners of his mouth. Then, as if suddenly reminded of reality, his jaw tightened, and the smile faded away.

"I thought he might have a talent," she continued, turning back to her dishes and trying to erase that last glimpse of Morgan's harsh profile from her mind. "He certainly had an interest, and so when I came out this time from Buffalo, I brought him a sketchbook and more pencils."

She heard him flipping through the pages. She herself had already seen most of the pictures that Jacob had drawn. Although there was no denying that they were simply composed, he had put a lot of care into their creation. There was one of his black dog, Hawkeye, and another of the flour mill in Ridgeway. He'd tried to capture the broad wing-span of a hawk as it circled high over the trees on the ridge, and he'd even attempted a portrait of Brendan. Lexi smiled as the picture came to mind.

"Brendan's been very good for him," she said then, without thinking. "He's encouraged him to try new things. They've roamed all over hereabouts, laughing and exploring and playing at hide-and-seek like two carefree children."

"Why is he here, Lexi?"

Morgan's question, phrased so solemnly, made Lexi stop what she was doing and turn to him, wiping her hands on her apron. "Why should that matter to you?" she heard herself ask.

"It does matter . . . very much."

Those simple words unnerved her more than she would have believed. She fixed her eyes on her own whitening fingers, which were clenched tightly in the fabric of her apron. "He thinks he's in love with me," she admitted.

"And you?"

"I think that he's confused, that he came back from the war looking for something to erase all the awful memories, and I was close at hand. But that isn't love."

They exchanged a long look, and Lexi swallowed hard as she realized what she'd just said and how closely this situation mirrored Morgan's relationship with Celeste. But he didn't speak of that; his mind was on other matters.

"That isn't what I meant, Lexi. I meant — what do you feel for him?"

She drew a labored breath. Why was he asking her all these questions? What was it he was after? For weeks, he'd been cold and distant, and now he was acting as if he cared. "I thought you'd already made up your mind that Brendan and I were — that we — "

She couldn't say the words, couldn't stand to go on with this another moment. The tears were gathering; she could feel them, heavy in her throat and stinging her eyes. But she wouldn't let him see her cry. She swept past him like a whirlwind and stumbled out onto the porch, attaching herself to the farthest upright post. And she stood there, still and silent, listening to the soughing of the night breeze through the trees, and trying to make sense of her jumbled emotions.

Morgan fought back the urge to run after her. He had to stay calm to handle this right, and as it was now, he was far from that. Lexi hadn't given him any kind of answer. He was no closer to knowing how she felt than he had been all along.

Heaving an exasperated sigh, he tossed the open sketchbook onto the table. As he did so, the pages fluttered wildly, and he noticed that an odd sort of drawing had been made on one of them.

Curious, he retrieved the book and searched for the page. He found it, hidden amongst the clean sheets near the back of the book. Upon the page was an odd set of intersecting lines. Studying the drawing more closely, Morgan recognized that it was, in fact, a map of Stevensville and the surrounding countryside.

The main roads were all laid out, the watercourses, the bridges; even the high ground was marked. He knew at once that this was too complex a project for Jacob to have undertaken. It reminded him of the military maps he'd seen when he'd been with the army.

For the moment, he put aside his problems with Lexi, as the odd bits of information he'd been storing in his brain finally began to fit together, and a terrible realization came to him. Snatching at the page, he tore it from the book, and clutching it in his fist, he charged out of the house.

"O'Neill!" he bellowed as he strode out into the clearing to meet Brendan, who was just returning from his rendezvous with the pasture gate.

With the edges of the map waving like a banner from his upraised fist, Morgan shouted, "What the devil's the meaning of this?"

"Whatever are you goin' on about, man?" Brendan exclaimed.

With his free hand, Morgan reached out, and seizing him by the shirtfront, he glared down at him. He felt a strange satisfaction in the act, especially when he saw the brief flash of alarm in the younger man's eyes.

"This map, you scheming Irish blackguard," he hissed, squaring his jaw. "You made it, didn't you? You didn't come out here after Lexi at all. You're a part of some damned Fenian plot."

Brendan wrenched himself free, his temper flaring. "Aye, an' you'd like to believe that, wouldn't you, Doctor? But you didn't think much on poor Lexi yourself after you'd had a toss with her and spoilt her for the likes of any decent man."

"That's a bloody lie!" Morgan retorted, and then all at once he remembered Lexi. She'd run outside; she must still be somewhere nearby. Turning back to the house, he caught sight of her, standing there on the porch, her face paling in the moonlight, her eyes bright with unshed tears.

Morgan had had more than enough of Brendan O'Neill. At that moment, he could have forgotten all his suspicions and his hatred, for he needed to go to Lexi, to take her in his arms and dry those tears of hers. But before he could get his wits about him, he was blindsided by a ham-fisted blow to the jaw.

A glaring flash of white lit up the night sky and thunder crashed inside his head. Morgan didn't know precisely how he'd lost his balance, but when he regained his senses, he found himself flat on his back.

"I owed you that one, Doctor," Brendan said as

he looked down on him. His anger seemed diffused now and he smiled, pleased by what he'd done. "She never said a word to me about you, in case you're wonderin'. She's too good for that. But we've been friends a long time, and I knew, just the same. Whatever may come, just you remember, there's nothin' I could ever do to hurt her as much as you have. You're the man she's in love with."

Lexi had been afraid of this, ever since Gran offered Morgan the invitation to supper. Just as she'd predicted, they'd come to blows. She wasn't even aware that the cry of Morgan's name broke from her lips as Brendan viciously struck him. She rushed down the steps and out of the yard, but by the time she reached the clearing, Morgan had already gotten to his feet and was brushing the dust from his trousers.

Without even thinking, she threw herself against him and reached up to take his face in her hands. "Morgan? Are you hurt?"

"Only my pride," he replied as she gently swiped at the blood trickling from a cut in his lip with the pad of her thumb,

"But your jaw . . ." she persisted, pressing her fingers to the bruised spot.

"Never mind that." Hooking an arm around her waist as if to prevent her escaping, Morgan took a bold step forward and thrust the piece of paper he had been clutching in his fist into Brendan's hand. "Tell her the truth, O'Neill," he said.

272

Lexi looked from one man to the other in confusion. She hadn't been able to hear the details of what they'd been arguing over before, but it seemed to have something to do with that piece of paper.

"Why, 'tis a map of our fishing spots, Jacob's and mine, nothing more than that," Brendan said, and crumbling the paper into a ball, he tossed it off into the tall grass.

Lexi was feeling none too charitable to her old friend just now. There was no denying that he'd struck Morgan an unfair blow. He'd never have been able to bring him down otherwise.

"I think you've said enough for tonight, Brendan," she said sharply. "And you've no right to fight my battles for me, if that's what you thought you were doing."

"But, Lexi, I —"

"Goodnight, Brendan."

Grudgingly, he obeyed the dismissal, shaking his head as he headed off toward the barn.

When they were alone at last, Lexi turned to Morgan. "I'm sorry for this," she told him. "If you'll come up to the house with me, I'll wash off that cut of yours and put a cool cloth on that bruise before it begins to swell."

Morgan's arm tightened across her back. "I'm the doctor here, young lady, in case you've forgotten, and I say I'll be just fine if you'll stop fussing over me."

Instead of heading back toward the house, he led her out into the shadows of the orchard, where the trees were white with blossoms and fallen petals carpeted the ground like a blanket that shimmered silver in the moonlight. Lexi closed her eyes and breathed in, filling her lungs with the sweet fragrance of apple blossoms. She found herself assailed by the memories of that first night that they'd come here. They'd been little more than strangers then. It seemed so long ago. So much had come between them since. Was it too late to start again?

"Morgan, I—"

"Hush!" he whispered as he turned her into his arms and drew her against him. For a long time they stood there, and neither of them spoke. With her head resting against his chest, Lexi contented herself in listening to the strong, steady rhythm of his heart, in enjoying once more the sheltering comfort of his embrace. When he propped her chin up on his crooked finger so that he might look into her eyes, she welcomed the warmth of his touch, and as he bent to brush his lips over hers, her heart thrilled.

But neither of them could be content for long with only that, and soon the tender kiss had deepened into something more. Familiar desires were rising anew, but Lexi drew back when she tasted the blood from his cut on her lips. Morgan was undaunted, though, and gathered her close again. He plucked the ribbon from her hair, combed his fingers through the unbound mass, then cradled her head in his hands. He kissed her cheek, her throat, her eyes.

274

"How long I've wanted this—wanted you, here in my arms again," he whispered, in a voice half-strangled with emotion.

"It's where I've wanted to be," she admitted to him.

"Then send him away, Lexi."

For a moment, Lexi was puzzled, and then she realized that he was speaking of Brendan. "You needn't be jealous, truly," she told him. "He's a friend, nothing more."

"He's using you," Morgan retorted. "He's come here to spy for the Fenians. His people are planning—I don't know what. But you have to send him away before you're caught up in the middle of it."

As she considered what he'd said, Lexi began to realize just how deep Morgan's hatred of Brendan ran. She did not doubt that Brendan had earned it to some degree, especially with what had happened tonight, but to credit that he was a part of some plot, simply because he was Irish . . .

"No, I can't believe it," she decided. "Brendan has been my friend since we were children. He's emotional and impetuous, perhaps. He might even have sympathy for these Fenians, but he would never betray my trust."

Morgan released her all at once, and Lexi felt as if a chill breeze had swept between them as he turned a chilling gaze on her. "Are you calling me a liar?"

She reached out to lay a hand on his arm, anxious to reestablish contact. "No. No, of course not.

I think you're mistaken, with all that's happened. But I know Brendan O'Neill better than anyone. I know—"

"You don't know how war can change a man, Lexi. Your young friend has spent the last four years watching his fellow soldiers die horrible deaths. He's had to march in the sweltering heat, filling his lungs with smoke and gunpowder, sleeping in rain-filled trenches. . . . You can't know how all that has changed the young boy you used to know."

A chasm had opened between them once more, and Lexi realized with no small measure of regret that she was to blame for it. Morgan squared his jaw and regarded her with a look so grim that it pained her.

"I promise I'll talk to him in the morning," she said, hoping it would be enough to placate him.

"Yes, you do that, since it seems my word is not enough," he replied sharply, and turning from her, he walked away.

Chapter Nineteen

By the time the sun had risen the following morning, Lexi was already busy in the kitchen. She was becoming accustomed to the routine: up at five, start a fire in the stove, put the tea on to brew, and get breakfast started. Jacob rose shortly after that and went out to the barn to do the milking, and by the time the ham was sizzling in the skillet, Gran had dressed and come into the kitchen.

"Good mornin', lass. Can I help with anythin'?"

Lexi kept a close eye on the meal she was preparing, but glowered as she stabbed a fork into the thin slices of ham and turned them over, one by one. She would not let the cheery voice temper her anger. "You'll help me best by sitting yourself down and propping your ankle up on that stool over there."

"Well, now, a wee bit cranky this mornin', aren't we?" Gran remarked.

"I've plenty of reason to be," Lexi replied, and turned on her. She'd been stewing over this, waiting to confront her grandmother ever since she'd gotten out of bed this morning. "I don't know what you thought you'd accomplish last night, stirring up the hornet's nest and then flouncing off to bed like the helpless invalid. But it's all because of you that Morgan and Brendan came to blows last night—"

Gran did not seem at all contrite to hear it. In fact, she grinned. "Blows? They were fightin' o'er ye, were they? An' tae think I missed it."

Lexi forgot herself, glaring as she pointed her fork ominously in her grandmother's direction. "Don't play the innocent with me. I'll wager you saw the whole thing, peeking out from behind the curtains of your bedroom window."

Gran pressed her lips tightly together, trying her best to look inscrutable, but it was a lost effort from the first. "Aye," she admitted at last. "I canna deny it. But I couldna hear a word they were sayin'."

"You still think that this is a game, don't you? It may be tremendous fun for you, but Brendan's been terribly upset and Morgan's sporting a bruised jaw."

Shaking her head, Lexi went back to her cooking and hoped that action would expend some of her restless energy. She transferred the fried ham to a platter, then cracked several eggs into the skillet where they popped and hissed.

"Doctor Glendower canna be feelin' too poorly," Gran said a short while later, "seein' as how he's come away wi' the prize."

Lexi could feel her face flush crimson as she shuttled the eggs onto the platter and put the whole on the table before Gran. "Oh, so you saw that, too, did you?" she said. "Well, if you'd been in a better position to eavesdrop, you'd have known that the reconciliation was short-lived."

"Och, now what've ye done, lass? I've ne'er known a body could make such a tangle o' simple matters."

"I haven't done anything. Morgan asked me to send Brendan back home because he's got the idea that he's part of some Fenian plot, and he got angry when I refused to do it."

Gran's brow furrowed as she digested this new information. "Whose plot, did ye say?"

"The Fenians. You know, they're the Irishmen who are making so much trouble back home in the States. They want a war with England."

Lexi was dismayed to realize that her grandmother was giving the possibility serious consideration. "Don't tell me that you believe it, too," she said.

"Well, lass, now that you come tae mention it . . . I have thought the lad a mite too persistent. I canna deny that I have come tae admire him, if only for his tenacity. But if there's another reason for his bein' here, it would explain a good many things."

"There *is* no other reason," Lexi insisted, with as much calm as she could muster. "He's trying to make amends for treating me badly. That's all there is to it."

But Gran didn't seem to hear her. "We shall simply have tae ask him when he comes in for his breakfast and put an end tae the question."

"No!" Lexi snapped, and slammed the tea kettle

down on the stovetop. "Brendan's been my friend for years. I can't believe he'd do such a thing, and I won't insult him by making such an awful accusation."

When Gran replied, her voice was soft, but the words she spoke struck Lexi with a force that left her speechless. "Aye, lass, but you're not the only one who'll be hurt if ye're wrong."

Silently, Lexi settled into her place at the table. She did not want to think on that; she could not even bear to contemplate—

But she was spared from further thought, for Jacob swept up the porch just then like a whirlwind, with Hawkeye barking furiously at his heel. He shoved open the screen door, and leaving the dog behind on the steps, he rushed to the table, his broad chest heaving, his freckled face pale. "He's . . . g-gone. I canna find him, and I've . . . l-looked everywhere."

"Who's gone, lad?" Gran asked him.

His wide gray eyes were swimming with tears. "Brendan. He's . . . n-nae in the loft, nor anywheres about."

Lexi got to her feet and went to take his hands in hers, but not before she'd cast a long accusing look across the table at her grandmother. "It's all right," she said to soothe him. "I think that Brendan may have decided to go home. He's been away from his family an awfully long time."

Jacob shook his head fiercely, tousling his rusty hair. "He wouldna leave wi'out sayin' good-bye. S-somethin's happened tae him."

"You mustna worry, lad," Gran put in. "Your friend Brendan's a grown man. He can take care of himself."

"Maybe he's only just decided to go into town," Lexi said then, "and in a little while, we'll see him come strolling back up the drive. Sit down and have your breakfast now, and soon you'll see that I'm right."

Jacob did as she bade, but he did not seem convinced. And after breakfast was finished, Lexi herself went out to the hayloft, where Brendan had been lodged. She found that all of his belongings were missing, and there was not so much as a note left behind to explain.

As finally she was forced to accept that he was gone, a peculiar trepidation swept over her. She did her best to ignore it. She went back and busied herself with her chores, determined to put Brendan out of her mind, just as she'd advised Jacob to do. But it wasn't easy; there was a definite sense of foreboding in the air.

When Jacob did not return to the house for the noon meal, Lexi knew that something was amiss. Jacob was a creature of habit, and he never missed dinner. She left Gran to wait for him in the kitchen, while she searched through the barn and the pasture, out in the fields and down by the creek, but he was nowhere to be found. Deep within, she feared she knew where he had gone, or at least what his intentions were. Jacob had been so certain that Brendan had gotten into some kind of trouble; he must have gone off after him.

Lexi felt the uncomfortable prickling of guilt as she realized that this situation was entirely her fault. It was she who had brought Brendan here in the first place, she who had encouraged his friendship with Jacob. She would never have imagined that Brendan would pick up and leave without saying a word. Of course, after last night she could hardly blame him. She had been awfully harsh to him after he'd lost his temper and struck Morgan.

She would have to go after Jacob, of course. But before she headed back to the house to tell her grandmother that she'd been unable to find any trace of him on the property, Lexi wandered by the clearing by the orchard and combed through the tall grass.

It did not take long to find what she was looking for: the crumpled sheet of paper that Brendan had tossed carelessly aside last night. Lexi knelt to retrieve it, then carefully smoothed the page so she might examine it. It was a map, just as Brendan has said, and even if the places marked were, indeed, no more than fishing spots where Jacob and Brendan had spent their time, they might be places where Jacob might go to search for his friend. She folded the paper, tucked it into the waistband of her skirt, and, pulling a long, uneven breath, she marched toward the house to inform Gran of her plans.

For all her pretense at being a crusty old character, Gran had a soft spot where her son was concerned. She was ever worrying after him, troubled by thoughts of what would become of him after she was gone. She'd admitted as much to Lexi on more than one occasion, and Lexi had then assured her that she would look after him. She'd always been close to Jacob, and he was family, after all. How could she do less?

"He's not here," Lexi announced as she swept into the kitchen. "I'm going after him."

Gran looked up from the table, her expression solemn. "Then he has run off. Lord help us, I was afraid of it after that outburst this mornin'. But where will he go, d'ye think?"

"I told him that Brendan had probably gone into Stevensville, so he'll likely try there first. We needn't worry, really," Lexi added then, hoping the words would reassure them both. "He knows the area—hereabouts, at least—and people know him. If he doesn't find Brendan in town, I'm sure he'll head back home."

But Lexi was not so sure of that at all. There was no way to tell what was going on inside of Jacob's head. He'd grown quite fond of Brendan in the few weeks that he'd been here, and he could hardly be expected to understand the complicated situation that existed between Brendan and Lexi and Morgan. All that mattered to him was that his friend had left without saying goodbye.

"Perhaps Dr. Glendower would be willin' to help—" Gran suggested then.

Lexi scowled. "Jacob's probably only gone into Stevensville," she repeated. "There's no need to get anyone else involved just yet."

Of course, Lexi did not tell Gran that she was

not particularly anxious to face Morgan so soon after last night's confrontation. "If I start walking towards town," she continued as she took off her apron, hung it on the kitchen peg, and headed for the door, "I'll probably meet him on the road."

"And if ye don't?" Gran inquired, her voice uncharacteristically tremulous.

"Then I shall ask for help in town, from Mr. Newcomb or Mr. Peterson. In any case, I shall be back home by nightfall."

But Lexi did not meet Jacob on the road, nor did she find any trace of him in Stevensville. The town seemed peculiarly quiet for a warm spring morning. There was no one in the street, but as Lexi neared the general store, she saw Hannah Newcomb on her porch, holding court from her rocking chair. Although the woman seemed to be engrossed in conversation with several of the ladies who were her neighbors, she waved excitedly and called out to Lexi as soon as she spotted her.

"Have you heard what's happened, dear?" she asked as Lexi joined the ladies on the porch. "The Fenians have come. They've crossed over from the States last night, and they're camped somewheres east along the river, just waitin' for the right moment to attack us."

A shiver ran through her, and Lexi felt as if her heart were rising in her throat and swallowed hard in response. Fenians? And they'd come last night? Brendan had disappeared last night. Did she need more proof than that? She realized now, to her shame, that Morgan was probably right; for all his pretty words, Brendan had only been using her.

"Has the militia been called out?" she asked.

Mrs. Newcomb nodded sagely. "I expect so. They've been waitin' for this for months. Our men have gathered at the inn, and they're deciding what ought to be done."

While Mrs. Newcomb was speaking, Lexi reminded herself why she'd come here in the first place. Jacob was missing, and with the Fenians on the march. Suddenly her task took on a more urgent aspect.

"Have any of you seen Jacob today?" she inquired of the ladies.

"He came by just before noon," Clara Miller told her. "He was lookin' for that hired man of yours. Come to think on it, he's an Irishman, ain't he?"

The question had a decidedly pointed ring, and Lexi blanched, sensing that everyone's eyes were fixed on her. She had to say something. She could not have the townsfolk believing that Gran had harbored a Fenian spy—even if it was true.

"He's an American, same as I am," she retorted, "and besides, he's already gone back home to his family. Jacob's having a bit of trouble accepting his friend's departure, that's all. You know Jacob."

That explanation seemed enough to dissuade the ladies, and before long, they'd gone back to worrying aloud about the dangers they might soon be facing. *Had* the militia been alerted? Were the British troops from Hamilton already on the way? What did these Fenians hope to achieve by invading a sleepy farming community? And most important of all, where and when precisely did they plan to attack?

Lexi asked them to send Jacob home at once if they saw him again, then left them to their wondering and crossed over to Peterson's. A babel of voices, raised in argument, carried through the open windows of the dining hall, but she did not tarry long to listen. She'd heard enough to know that the townsmen were far too busy to help her. She'd have to find Jacob on her own, and if the news about an invasion was accurate, there'd be no time to waste. But it would be foolish to chase him across the countryside on foot.

In addition to his inn, Mr. Peterson ran a small livery business, renting out horses to the locals who were in need of transportation, and Lexi decided now to make use of this service. Mr. Peterson was, of course, busy moderating the tumultuous congregation gathered in his dining room, but Lexi found his youngest son busy sweeping out the stalls.

"Samuel?" she called as she advanced into the stable. Her nostrils quivered as she was confronted with the pungent odor of fresh manure. "I've come for a horse."

"A horse, Miss Merritt?"

"Yes. I'll only need him for two hours or so. I've got to go . . . to Ridgeway. By the way, you haven't seen Jacob today, have you?"

"No, miss," the boy replied, as he absently scuffed his toe in the dust. "I been busy with chores all morning."

"Well, anyway, as I was saying, your papa is too

286

busy for me to bother him right now, but I do need a horse. Do you think you can manage?"

" 'Course I can," he said, puffing out his chest. "I'm nearly eleven years old now. Pa lets me groom and curry and saddle an' everythin'. I'm sure he wouldn't mind if I let you take out Cinnamon. She's a sweet-tempered filly."

"Could you saddle her for me?"

Samuel was responding well to his new mantle of authority. "I'll get to it right away, miss," he said, and hurried off to see to the saddling of the horse.

Cinnamon's name was apparently chosen on account of her color, for the bay mare had very little spice in her step. Still, she was surefooted with a steady gait, and Lexi was glad of that. She suspected that she'd have a lot of unfamiliar ground to cover this afternoon.

When she came to the crossroads just south of town, she did not head on in the direction of Ridgeway, in spite of what she'd told young Samuel Peterson. The only clue she had to finding Jacob now was Brendan's map, and the area he'd covered in his drawing lay still further to the east, in the direction of the Fenian troops of whom Hannah Newcomb had spoken. Lexi shuddered and her hands tightened on the reins, but she reminded herself that she did not intend to go so far as the river, where Mrs. Newcomb had said they were camped. If she kept clear of the main road, she ought to be safe. She had to think of poor Jacob. He might be lost or frightened. One way or another, she simply had to find him!

Lexi followed the landmarks on Brendan's map to those places he had marked with an X. Sure enough, each spot was located on one of the various watercourses that ran through the countryside: Black Creek, Beaver Creek, Miller's Creek, and all had several things at least in common—they were places where the ground was even and the waters shallow.

While she told herself that they could well have been favorite fishing spots, just as Brendan had claimed, she had to admit that they could also be places where a large body of troops might easily cross. And to her dismay, Lexi did not find Jacob at any of these places, nor any evidence that he had been there recently.

By four o'clock in the afternoon, Lexi was nearing Fort Erie. Her energy was nearly drained. Her spirits were low, and she was running out of ideas. She'd seen no sign of Fenians anywhere about and had all but decided that Mrs. Newcomb's sources were mistaken. This wouldn't be the first time in the past few months that such a rumor had gotten started and then spread out of control.

Having come this far, she decided to ride on into town. If it turned out that there was nothing to this Fenian business after all, then perhaps she'd been right from the first. Perhaps Brendan had gone home simply because he'd been angered by the way she'd treated him last night.

As she came to think of it, Lexi realized that Jacob knew that Brendan would have to cross the river by the ferry in Fort Erie in order to get home to Buffalo. Maybe he'd come here, hoping to catch Brendan before he left. The possibility buoyed her foundering spirits, and she urged Cinnamon into a canter, convinced that she would find Jacob sitting by the quayside, staring out across the river, like a loyal puppy whose master had gone off and left him.

As soon as she entered the precincts of the town, though, Lexi's hopes began to fade. It was apparent at once that something was amiss. If Stevensville had seemed deserted, Fort Erie was, by contrast, teeming with humanity. Every citizen seemed to be out-of-doors. Some of the townsfolk were busy loading their belongings onto wagons.

Others milled about looking lost and confused. Posted at several key spots throughout the town were soldiers, some of whom wore dark blue uniform jackets faced with green, a combination that was all-too-familiar to Lexi. And flying from the flagpole in the town square was a flag of green, white, and orange: the Irish tricolor.

Chapter Twenty

The color drained from Lexi's face as she looked upon the strange banner. Once she had recovered her wits, she dismounted and led her mare by the reins to the square. Several people were gathered there, reading a proclamation from the Fenian general, Thomas Sweeny, which had been posted on a signboard to serve as an explanation to the residents of what was happening around them:

We come among you as the foes of British rule in Ireland. We have taken up the sword to strike down the oppressor's rod to deliver Ireland from the tyrant, the despoiler, the robber . . . We have no issue with the people of these provinces, and wish to have none but the most friendly relations. Our weapons are for the oppressors of Ireland. Our blows shall be directed only against the power of England; her privileges alone shall we invade, not yours. We do not propose to divest you of a solitary right you now enjoy. . . . We are here neither as murderers, nor robbers for plunder and spoilation. We are here as an Irish army of liberation, the friends of liberty against despotism, of democracy against aristocracy, of the people against the oppressors; in a word, our war is with the armed power of England, not with the people, not with these provinces. Against England, upon land and sea, till Ireland is free . . ."

When she had read the whole of it, Lexi could only shake her head in disbelief. What convoluted logic this was — to glorify the Fenian cause, as if that would be excuse enough to justify to the Canadian people why *their* soil had been invaded, *their* lives and property threatened — all on account of events transpiring an ocean away.

There was no doubt in her mind now: Brendan was a part of this. Her heart twisted painfully as she came to accept that her childhood friend had betrayed her trust. He had lied and deceived her, and all because of his devotion to this misguided cause. Even now she found it hard to credit. But Morgan had warned her that war had likely changed Brendan from the young boy that she used to know. How right he'd been. By now, Sergeant O'Neill had likely joined up with his friends in the invading force. But where was Jacob?

He was not wandering the streets, else she'd have seen him by now. The taverns apparently were off limits to the citizenry — sentries stood barring the doors—so he couldn't have found refuge there, and Lexi doubted that strangers would have taken him in, given his handicap and all that was occurring around them. She watered her horse in the public trough, then walked down to the quays, but there she spotted only a few nervous travelers preparing to depart on the next ferry.

Thus far, Lexi had seen less than a dozen members of the invading force, but she knew there had to be more. "Where are the rest of the Fenian soldiers?" she asked a wizened old man in a sailor's cap, who seemed to be overseeing the arrival of passengers as he stood by the water, calmly smoking a clay pipe.

"They're camped up on Frenchman's Creek," he replied. "There had to be near to a thousand of 'em—and I hear there's five times that many in Buffalo, just waitin' to cross the river. They'll be headin' for Chippewa, I expect, to make their bridgehead along the Welland River. But don't you worry none, missy. Better men than the likes of these have tried and failed to take this land away. When they meet up with our militia, there'll be a swift end to their advance. We turned 'em back in 1812, and we'll do so again, you mark my words."

"I hope you're right," Lexi said with a weary sigh.

All at once, her attention was captured by the young soldier not far away. He seemed to be keeping watch over the quayside activities. Although his back was to her, she could see that he was solidly built, with thick auburn hair, and he was wearing a

Union Army uniform jacket that bore the markings of the Irish Brigade. Brendan?

Fatigue and frustration had frayed her nerves, and soon Lexi was shaking with tremors of barely suppressed rage. Before she knew it, she'd lost control. Balling her fists, she rushed over to him and struck him a solid blow to the shoulder. It felt good, so she did it again and again, and all the while she was shouting at him. "Damn you, Brendan O'Neill! How could you? After all these years of friendship, how could you? You filthy traitor! And now Jacob's gone missing, and it's all your fault! I hate you!"

When the young man whirled around and grasped her roughly by the shoulders, it was hard to say which of them looked the more surprised, for now that they were face-to-face, Lexi could see now that this was not Brendan after all.

A few of the people standing nearby were applauding her pluck. True, they'd only made out a few words of the frenzied outburst, but those were telling enough . . . "damn you" . . . "filthy traitor" . . . "I hate you." Lexi's face paled, and she sputtered a few incoherent syllables before the elderly gentleman she'd been conversing with only a few moments before came along, hooked her arm, and apologized to the soldier as he led her away.

"Forgive my granddaughter, sir," he said. "She's not been quite right since her husband run off. Come along now, girl, and leave this young gentleman to his duties."

When finally they were out of earshot, the old man loosed her arm. " 'Twill do you no good to take on these soldiers all by yourself, miss," he warned. "You just wait till our boys get here, and it will be over soon enough."

"Y-Yes," Lexi stammered, realizing now the danger that she could have been in, but for his intervention. "Thank you for your help. I don't usually behave so foolishly. But it's just that my uncle's disappeared, and I've been searching for him all day long, and I'm worried he may be lost or hurt, and it's all my fault he ran off in the first place."

"Your uncle, did you say?"

Lexi began kneading her temples, endeavoring to calm herself. "Jacob is only a few years older than I am, but he doesn't—that is to say—well, you see, he's . . . simpleminded."

The old man removed his cap and scratched his balding pate. "This uncle of yours. He wouldn't happen to have a freckled face and red hair, would he?"

"Yes."

"And a monstrous black dog following at his heels?"

"Why, yes," Lexi repeated, nearly breathless with amazement. "Do you mean to say that he's been here?"

"Aye. He wandered through town an hour or so ago and tried to strike up a conversation with that same poor guard you just attacked. He seemed so confused that I took him aside, and he explained as

294

how he'd come a long way to find his friend. After I saw what was what—if you know what I mean, miss—I knew he must have someone lookin' for him, and I told him that he ought to get himself back home at once before his family got worried."

"Do you know what happened to him after that?"

The old man nodded vigorously. "I saw him and his dog headin' back down the road from whence they'd come."

Lexi breathed a long, low sigh of relief. It certainly sounded as if Jacob was already heading back home, and if she'd kept to the main road, instead of following Brendan's map and hiding from the Fenians in the shelter of the trees, she'd likely have encountered him before she'd come this far.

She was feeling better already, and leaning forward, she kissed the old man on his leathery cheek. "Thank you, sir, for the help you've been to my family today."

Lexi would have sworn that the weathered face flushed a shade deeper. "My pleasure, miss."

She had to return the little mare to Mr. Peterson's stables, and so it was more than two hours before she'd finally walked the last mile back to Gran's. She fully expected that Jacob would be there to greet her, but a prickling of uneasiness swept through her as she drew near the house and Hawkeye did not come barking up to greet her.

The worst was confirmed when she spotted Gran sitting alone in her chair on the porch. As soon as Gran caught sight of her, she got to her feet and, leaning heavily on her cane, met her with an expectant air. Crossing the yard and preparing to face her grandmother seemed to Lexi the most difficult portion of today's long journey.

"You've not found him, have ye?"

Lexi could only shake her head as she climbed the porch stairs. "I've been all the way to Fort Erie," she explained. "I met an old man there who'd spoken to Jacob earlier this afternoon, though. He said that he thought he'd convinced him to head back home."

"Maybe he's on his way, even now," Gran suggested, with a hopeful air.

Lexi agreed, although she could not believe it herself. He had at least an hour's head start on her, and she'd had to stop in Stevensville to return Mr. Peterson's horse. Surely Jacob would have made it home by now, if he'd been headed home . . . unless something had happened to him.

"Come inside now," Gran bade her, and laid a gentle hand on her shoulder. "I've made a little supper for us. Ye maun be tired."

"I just need to wash up, that's all, and maybe have something cool to drink, and then I'll go to Doctor Glendower's and ask for his help."

"Ye'll do nothin' of the kind," Gran retorted. "It'll be dark soon. Ye canna do any more today. Come have your supper and rest yourself, lass. We'll say a few prayers together, and Jacob may yet come home tae us."

Lexi was indeed exhausted. She was sweaty and

dusty from her journey, and the muscles in her back and legs were stiff and sore. In short, she felt awful, but worse, much worse, than any of this was the guilt that was eating away at her insides.

"You don't understand," she protested. "Those Fenians we were talking about this morning, they've come. Their soldiers have crossed the river—more than a thousand of them—and taken over Fort Erie. There's bound to be a battle when the militia tries to stop them, and Jacob's out there in the middle of it, looking for his friend, Brendan. This is all my fault. I brought Brendan here; I brought a traitor into your house. I'm so sorry, Gran. Morgan was right. I've been blind."

Gran was clearly affected by the news, for her face had paled considerably. But she revealed no other emotions, and her voice was calm and even. "Dinna fash yerself, lass. God will take care o' Jacob. I willna have ye goin' off again. Then there'll be the two of ye I'll have tae worry after."

"But we have to do *something!*"

"In the mornin'," Gran said to her. "Now, inside wi' ye and not another word on it."

Lexi found herself unable to eat much with her stomach as it was, twisting in knots. She did feel somewhat better, though, after she'd bathed and changed and climbed into her bed. Still, sleep was long in coming that night, and when she'd settled down at last, she tossed fitfully, plagued by jarring nightmares—of wandering alone through the blackness of the forest, calling out for Jacob until her throat was raw, and starting in terror as the ground beneath her feet shuddered with the ominous rumbling of a battle that was raging nearby.

Lexi woke the following morning to the whistling of songbirds in the oak tree and the persistent jingle of harnesses that cut through the fog in her brain and told her that a wagon was coming up the drive. Forcing her eyes open, she realized that she had overslept. It must be after eight o'clock already. The sun was high in the sky, for it filled the room with a blinding brilliance. As her thoughts came more clearly into focus, she remembered that Jacob was missing. She threw back the bedclothes, rushed to the window and clung to the sash as she realized that she was reeling like a drunken sailor.

But the wagon coming up the long drive was not bringing Jacob home. It was filled with all their neighbors from Stevensville—the women and children, at least. Clara Miller had the reins, with Mrs. Newcomb at her elbow. Mrs. Peterson had squeezed in beside her, looking pale and tired, and all the Peterson girls and young Samuel as well were crowded into the wagon bed. One of the farmer's wives was there, too, with a pair of sons and a newborn babe who'd begun squalling when the wagon jounced over a deep rut in the road.

Lexi didn't like the looks of this at all. Turning away from the window, she snatched her rose-colored calico from a peg on the wall and tossed it on

298

over her head. She looked into the washstand glass only long enough to smooth back her hair, leaving it in a long plait down her back; and then, gathering up her shoes and stockings, she hurried downstairs to see what Gran was up to.

She found her standing at the screen door, silently watching their neighbors' approach, as if she, too, sensed some impending disaster.

"You didn't wake me!" Lexi accused, as she pulled up a kitchen chair, plopped into it, and bent over to wriggle her toes into her stocking.

"Ye needed your rest," Gran replied simply.

"And Jacob's not come home yet?"

"Nay," she said, her voice drifting off.

As soon as Lexi had put on her shoes, she and Gran went down to the gate to meet the wagon. She was not reassured by the ladies' pale, pinched faces, nor their solemn air.

"Doctor Glendower asked us to fetch you," Hannah Newcomb explained. "The militia's come down by rail, and there's fighting broke out between here and Ridgeway."

"Ridgeway?" Lexi echoed, "but I thought the Fenians were headed north."

"Who can say what they're up to?" she replied. "The men have decided that it's too close for comfort, though, and we're to go out to Humberton Marsh to wait till it's all over."

"And Doctor Glendower's in town, ye say?" Gran inquired.

"He came in this morning, but when he heard the

news he set straight off for Ridgeway. There's sure to be those there who'll need his help."

Lexi pressed her fingertips over her mouth, and only then did she realized how badly her hand was trembling. Of course, Morgan was a trained surgeon, well used to work on the battlefield, but Lexi did not like to think of him out there in the midst of the fighting.

"Come along now," Clara Miller urged them, "and we'll be on our way."

"Take Lexi wi' ye. I canna come," Gran explained matter-of-factly. "My Jacob's gone missing, and I maun wait for him. If he comes home and I'm gone, he'll not know what tae think."

"You can't stay here, Gran," Lexi argued. "If the fighting should move closer, you'll be trapped out here. How far do you think you'll be able to get on that bandaged ankle of yours? I'll stay and wait here for Jacob. You go with the others."

"And what'll *you* do, lass?"

"If the worst comes, I'll hide in the cellar, or hitch Jacob's horse and follow after you in the wagon, or run off into the woods, if I have to," Lexi replied. She was thankful that she sounded more confident than she felt. "I'll get Grandpa's old musket down from the mantelpiece. You don't have to worry about me."

Gran shook her head. "I dunna think this i wise."

She was still arguing as Lexi helped hand her up into the wagon bed, but Lexi wouldn't listen. "Thi is all my fault," she said to Gran as Mrs. Miller snapped the reins and the team stepped up, rocking the wagon into motion. "Let me handle it."

It was a deceptively placid spring day. The sun was bright overhead in a cloudless sky, the air was warm, and there was only a slight breeze stirring. There was no hint at all that somewhere not far away, men were fighting and possibly dying. Lexi was not sure, even now, that she believed it herself.

She tried to go about her work as if nothing was amiss, but her thoughts kept straying to the look that she'd seen in Gran's eyes as the wagon pulled away—the utter confusion of a strong, sensible woman whose entire life had been turned upside down.

And then there was Jacob. If he hadn't continued to tag along after the Fenians troops looking for Brendan, then he must have gotten lost. He could be almost anywhere between here and Fort Erie; he could have wandered into the midst of the fighting.

As helplessness welled in her, Lexi could not prevent herself from thinking of Brendan and the part he'd played in this. Four years of war hadn't been enough for him; he'd had to carry on the bloodshed, bringing it here to this peaceful place. She hated him for that.

But what distressed her most of all were her fears for Morgan's safety. He'd been an army surgeon, well used to the battlefield. If there was a battle being fought, there was no doubt but that he was in the thick of things now, putting his own life at risk to save the lives of others. He was a good man, an honorable man, and should he be hurt by this . . . or worse, God forbid, she'd carry the ache in her heart forever.

She loved Morgan Glendower, and only now was she beginning to understand how much. To her regret, Lexi realized that she'd never said the words, never told him so. Shame flooded through her as she recalled how, scarcely two nights ago, he'd held her in his arms in the orchard and tried to warn her of Brendan's perfidy. And rather than trusting the man she loved, she'd defended the man she'd thought was her friend.

When midday came and went without word of what was going on in the outside world and without any sign of Jacob, Lexi's patience wore out. Maybe it was all over by now; maybe, just as the old man in Fort Erie had told her yesterday, the militia had arrived and routed the invaders. She couldn't concentrate on trivial household chores for one moment longer. She could not simply wait around, hoping that everything would work out for the best. She had to *do* something.

Lexi penned a quick note for Gran, in case she should return before Lexi got back, then gathered a small store of supplies that she thought might be useful: blankets, clean rags, a washbasin, a pail of drinking water, and a pair of battered tin cups. She carried all of these out to the yard and arranged them in the wagon bed.

Although she had helped Jacob hitch the horse to the wagon before, she'd never attempted it alone, and it took her some time and no small amount of patience to manage the huge draft horse. But she did not give up and was proud of herself when she'd succeeded at last. Climbing up on the seat, she took the reins in her hands, eager to be on her way.

With a last backward glance, Lexi considered that if Jacob wandered back home to find everyone gone, he might be upset, but she was far more concerned that he was in trouble somewhere and needed rescuing. Even if she could not find Jacob, surely Morgan would need help tending the wounded. She'd told him once that she'd be willing to work by his side; now was her chance to prove it.

Chapter Twenty-one

Lexi started south toward Ridgeway, keeping an eye out for Jacob all along the road. The air was hot and still, and the countryside seemed far too quiet. She began to question whether there'd been a battle at all. But then when she was still some two miles from the town, she spotted a young man on horseback. Even at a distance, she could see that he was clad in a uniform with a crimson tunic and wore a small pillbox cap. He was riding hard in her direction, but he pulled up as he drew near to address her.

"May I ask where you're headed, miss?"

"Ridgeway," she replied, pleased to see another human being at last.

"Town's deserted. Folk made off when the Fenians come through."

"There's been a battle, then?" she guessed.

He nodded, without elaborating.

Lexi felt her heart thumping hard against her breastbone, and she found it difficult to speak. "And the militia . . . wasn't able to stop them?"

With that, the soldier gathered the reins of his

restless mount tighter and regarded her soberly. "Temporary setback, miss," he said. "The regulars have started down towards Stevensville. We'll soon have those Irishmen where we want them, caught smack between us.

"I'd advise you to go on back home, though, till things cool down. You'll not be safe anywhere near Ridgeway. A battleground's not for the likes of a lady to see, and there's liable to be Fenian stragglers hereabouts."

"But I've come to help Doctor Glendower with the wounded," Lexi protested. "Can you tell me where I might find him?"

The soldier shook his head as he heard her intentions. He pondered for a moment as if he did not recognize Morgan's name, and then he asked her, "Do you know the inn out on the Garrison Road?"

"The Smuggler's Inn?"

"Aye. You might try there. They've been carrying the wounded there, and a few of the farmhouses out on Ridge Road as well."

"Is it bad, then?" she asked cautiously, afraid to hear his reply.

"Not as these things go, miss," he replied, "but bad enough."

Lexi thanked him, and after he'd left her, she drew a deep, calming breath to prepare herself for what lay ahead and turned the wagon eastward.

Once she reached Ridge Road, the atmosphere changed. For the first time, she noticed that the weather had turned uncomfortably warm, and the bodice of her starched calico was damp with perspiration and clinging to her skin. The acrid stench of burnt powder still hung heavy in the air. Split-rail fences had been tumbled over, and the wheatfields on both sides of the road had been trampled into the dust.

A few men, dazed and bleeding, were sitting alongside the road yet with their heads in their hands. Lexi stopped to offer them water and then made a place for them in the wagon, so that she might take them to one of the nearby farmhouses that had been set up as field hospitals.

Further up the road, a small detail of Canadian soldiers were spread out over the fields, searching for the dead and wounded, and Lexi pulled up on the reins and called out to the one of them who was closest.

"Can you tell me, Sergeant, is Doctor Glendower at the Smuggler's Inn?"

"No, miss. You'll find him at the next farmstead ahead on your right," he told her. "Are you takin' in wounded?"

This was the first confirmation Lexi had had that Morgan was alive and well, and she paused for a brief moment to say a silent prayer of thanks before she replied to his question.

"I am, Sergeant."

"Then hold up a minute," he said, and waved to his men. "We've a few more boys who'll need the doctor's attention."

Two of these were bloodied and pale, but able to

walk with the aid of their comrades. One had his arm cradled in an improvised sling, and the other's head had been rudely bandaged with a length of cotton flannel. The third man was borne on a stretcher. He was barely conscious, and after room had been made for him in the wagon bed, and the stretcher was slid in, he moaned piteously.

Lexi could see that his condition was grave. There were powder burns on his jacket at the place where the ball had struck. At the site of the wound, his flesh was torn and discolored, and blood from the oozing hole in his side had spread across the whole of his shirtfront.

She turned away quickly and swallowed hard, gripping the reins so tightly that her knuckles blanched, and then, spurred by the fear that Jacob might have suffered the same fate as this poor soldier, she addressed the soldiers who'd been combing the fields. "Have any of you seen a young man with red hair?"

"Is he one of them Fenians, miss?" one of them asked innocently.

"No, he's Canadian, a farmer, and he's a relative of mine. . . . There's probably a big black dog trailing at his heels," she added, as the thought came to her. "Have you seen anyone like that?"

One after the other, they shook their heads and finally their sergeant replied for them all. "No, miss. Sorry. Can't say that we have."

"If you should happen to come across him, could you please see to it that he gets to the farmhouse?

307

I'll be there helping Doctor Glendower."

They agreed to do what they could, and after she'd thanked them, Lexi hurriedly flicked the reins, urging the horse onward in the direction of that farmhouse, where she'd been told her passengers' injuries could be tended.

As they approached, Lexi could see that the small white frame building was teeming with activity. Several of the men who were not so seriously wounded were sprawled on the grass in the shade of two ancient elms that flanked the walk, each waiting his turn with surprising patience. They were not a pretty sight, these soldiers whose bleeding limbs had been hastily bound with whatever scraps of cloth were handy. To a man, their faces were blackened and streaked with perspiration, many contorted with silent pain.

The doors of the house had been thrown open so that stretchers might be more easily carried in, and harried aides were shuttling in and out. No sooner had Lexi turned the wagon into the drive than one of these aides came running up to assess the new patients, and spotting the man on the stretcher in the wagon bed, he called at once for assistance. Another young aide soon joined him, and they proceeded to carry the badly wounded man on into the house.

Leaving the wagon in the stable yard, in the care of a pair of soldiers who'd been stationed there, she smoothed the creases from her apron and scurried after the stretcher-bearers, following them up the steps and into the farmhouse.

Lexi was not ready for the sharp, strong odor of blood, black powder, and sweat that struck her as she entered, and she felt a rush of dizziness as her body lurched backward in an instinctive response. But she reined in her emotions, and fixing a serious look upon her face, she steeled herself and strode forward.

The pegged wood floor beneath her feet was slippery, and she stepped cautiously, her skirts sweeping past the cots where lay the most seriously wounded of the soldiers. A quick glance downward made her shudder, for it revealed that the boards beneath her feet were slick with blood.

The air was heavy and still inside the house, and the stench was nigh on unbearable. But swallowing the bile that rose in her throat and threatened to choke her, Lexi told herself that she *would* do this. She *had to* to prove herself to Morgan. He needed her help.

The surgery was set up in the kitchen. All the window shutters and the door had been thrown open to provide light, with the long trestle table serving as an operating table. And Morgan was there, just as Lexi had been told.

Relief washed through her as she caught sight of the familiar broad shoulders straining the fabric of his linen shirt and the satin back of his waistcoat, and his dark head bent in concentration upon the patient he was tending.

Lexi came around the table silently, brushing past

the bloodied rags that littered the floor. She forced herself to watch as he methodically removed metal fragments from the torn flesh of a gaping thigh wound. One by one, he tossed them into a metal dish beside him on the table, where they struck with a clear ring.

The sight of him at work both awed and frightened her. Over his clothes, he wore what appeared to be a butcher's apron. His shirtsleeves had been rolled carelessly, and the whole of his forearms were red with blood. It was smeared in a great crimson arc across the front of his apron and was even spattered upward along his jaw.

His face was devoid of expression. He worked with a swift precision, but Lexi could sense the difference in him, even at a distance. He was protecting himself from the human misery that surrounded him with a veneer of cold reserve.

It took her some time to gather the strength and then she called his name softly. When he glanced up, the look he met her with was one of startled surprise, as if at first he had not recognized her. "Lexi? How did you—? What are you doing here?"

"I've come to help," she told him.

"Go home," he replied brusquely, and went back to his work. "You don't want to see any of this."

"I want to help you," she insisted. "I can't just sit at home waiting . . ."

She almost told him about Jacob then and all the worries that plagued her, but she knew it was not the right time. He had enough weighing on his mind. How many men's lives were depending upon him today?

She'd sensed the change in him, but only now, as she noticed the fleeting look of distress in his eyes, did the realization strike. He'd told her once before that after the time he'd spent at Scutari, he'd crossed an ocean trying to escape from the horrors of war. Standing here now, with men suffering all around them, Lexi could well understand why he'd felt as he did. He'd come out here to the country looking for peace, and once more war had invaded his life.

At that moment, Lexi could not help but feel as if she were at least in part to blame, if only because she'd not trusted him when he'd warned her that this was coming. She ought to have trusted his judgment; she ought to have listened when he told her to send Brendan away. A stab of fear pierced her heart. Was that an unforgiving look she saw in his eyes?

As if he sensed that Lexi did not intend to be moved from her purpose, Morgan blew out a harsh breath and regarded her. "There's naught for you to do in here now. Go outside, if you truly want to help, and see to the comfort of those waiting for attention."

Lexi nodded and left him without a word, eager this time, at least, to do what he asked of her. She spent the next several hours offering comforting words and drinks of cool water to those who reposed in the shade of the elm trees.

She filled an enamel basin with water from the pump in the yard, and using the clean rags she'd brought, she wiped the traces of powder from their blackened faces, then carefully bathed each man's wounds, hoping at least to stave off infection in the mangled flesh until they could be tended by more capable hands than hers.

Morgan did not call her inside once all that afternoon, but instead relied upon the aid of the young soldiers who were scurrying about. Lexi knew he wanted to spare her, but she'd have endured the most ghastly of experiences, if only she could have stayed by his side. She wanted to help him somehow. For all that he looked strong and capable, Lexi knew with a terrible certainty that something was amiss.

At first, she'd been relieved to see him standing in his surgery, whole and undamaged. But now she knew that that wasn't how it was at all. He *had* been wounded, and with each soldier who passed beneath his hands, yet another invisible wound would be inflicted upon him, causing him to make stronger the wall he was building around himself. Soon it would be too strong even for her to penetrate. Soon he'd go back to the way he was when she'd found him, hiding out in his cabin, unable to let anyone into his life, and this frightened Lexi more than she dared admit.

By the time the sun had set, she was wearied: heart, mind, and body. Her hair was coming loose

312

from the long plait that hung down her back, and wispy curls were plastered against her temples. Her skirt and petticoats were damp with perspiration and the water she'd spilt on them in the course of her work, and they clung to her legs with each step she took. Her arms and back and legs ached, and as she carried yet another sloshing basin out behind the house and tossed the bloodied water into the bushes, she wondered how much longer she could keep on. But she could not complain. What were her petty inconveniences when compared with the sufferings of these brave men, who'd risked their lives today to protect their homeland?

From time to time when she'd come back here, Lexi had snuck a peek at Morgan through the open kitchen door. He labored with the seemingly effortless precision of a machine, but a toll was being taken. She knew that it was.

All at once, there was a rustling just beyond the place where she stood, and in the twilight, she saw a bedraggled man emerge from the bushes. He was wearing the remnants of a dark blue uniform faced in green. Startled, Lexi let the empty basin drop from her hand. There was a dull clang as it struck, then rolled unevenly across the grass.

He was struggling with a heavy bundle, and before she could arrange her thoughts to speak, he stepped forward to place it carefully on the ground before her feet. It was difficult to see for the shadows of the trees and the scant light, but as she knelt down, Lexi noticed that the bundle was, in

313

fact, the crumpled body of a wounded man.

She reached to wipe away the thick shock of hair that had fallen across his face, but only when she heard the pitiful whining of the great beast of a dog who'd been as good as invisible in the darkness until now, and felt Hawkeye's cold nose nudging her hand, did she recognize that the stark white face was Jacob's—and that the man who'd brought him here was Brendan O'Neill.

Chapter Twenty-two

The breath left Lexi's body all at once, as though she'd been struck a painful blow, and the scream that caught in her throat emerged as no more than a strangled whimper.

"He followed me," Brendan explained, and his words, choked with emotion, came out in tangled rush, "for all the day yesterday. I told him to go home. I thought he'd listened, but then in the midst of the battle, I turned and saw him standin' there behind me. He thought it was a game. He didn't understand. He couldn't understand. He kept sayin' that I was his friend. Sweet Jesus, what have I done?"

But Lexi was not listening to Brendan at all as she gathered Jacob onto her lap, whispering his name over and over in his ear, and trying to reassure him with soothing words, even as she stared in horror at the bloodied tangle of bandages that covered his left shoulder. And when she'd recovered her wits, she cried out for Morgan to come at once.

He appeared in the kitchen doorway almost im-

mediately, and spotting Jacob, he called for the
stretcher-bearers. As they carried him into the
house, Lexi remembered Brendan. But when she
turned back to look, she saw no sign of him at all.
He'd run off—like the coward that he was—and se-
cretly, she felt glad of it, for the violence of the
rage welling within her at that moment was fright-
ening.

Morgan was working on Jacob, who lay upon the
surgery table, when Lexi came into the room. He
was attempting to cut away the pieces of his shirt
and the strips of rag that someone had used to im-
provise a bandage. The whole of it was stiff with
dried blood, though, and he daren't tear it away
from the wound lest the bleeding should begin
anew.

A brief glimpse of Lexi in the lamplight revealed
to him just how frail and fragile she looked tonight
. . . and frightened. Of course, she would be that,
too, with Jacob lying here, so gravely wounded.
Morgan wondered how the young man had ever
gotten caught up in this. But there wasn't time now
for such questions.

His thoughts returned to Lexi. He knew that she
had been working tirelessly, for he'd heard her voice
as she'd comforted the wounded soldiers; the sweet
sound of it had drifted in to him even while he
worked. It surprised him to realize just how much
comfort he himself had drawn from the familiar

316

timbre of her voice and from the knowledge that she was nearby. If he hadn't lost his heart to her long ago, he'd have lost it that day.

Regarding her now, he felt the warmth of emotion well in him. Threads of red-gold hair that had slipped from her braid floated around her head like a radiant nimbus. Her apron was stained with soot and blood, and the simple calico dress, dampened by perspiration, clung to her trim figure. Her whole body quivered as she pulled a deep breath. She must be exhausted. How much more of this could she take?

"It might be best if you waited outside," he told her. "Go out on the porch, sit down, and have one of the orderlies fetch you a cup of coffee. You deserve a rest."

Lexi stood her ground. "Jacob won't be so frightened if I'm here," she protested.

Morgan wanted to tell her that Jacob was barely conscious and probably unaware of what was going on around him, but he sensed that she already knew that. It was only that she could not bear to stand by helplessly.

"Take that basin of clean water and a sponge and bathe the shoulder area, then, will you?" he instructed. "We need to soften up this dried blood so that I can remove the cloth and examine the wound."

She did precisely as he bade her, her hands scarcely trembling at all while she worked, bathing the bandages in the warm water in order to loosen them. Morgan noticed that every now and then she would speak to Jacob, sometimes merely repeating his name, sometimes reassuring him that she was there and that everything would be all right.

They worked together, and as Lexi softened then removed the final layer of makeshift bandages, Morgan cut away the torn shirt, exposing a blackened, jagged hole.

" 'Tis not a clean wound," he noted solemnly as he carefully probed the area with his fingers. "There's been some tearing of the tissue. He's lost a great deal of blood. It's weakened him, no doubt of that, but I can't leave things as they are. I've got to try and get that ball out."

Once more he turned to Lexi, intending to send her away, but the resolve in her expression left him silent. It amazed him that this mere slip of a woman, already wearied from hours of nursing, still stood by her young uncle's side, with her back straight and her ashen face mirroring only calm. Without hesitation, she helped to prepare Jacob for what was to come and then held his hand tightly as Morgan readied his instruments and took the scalpel in hand.

But in spite of the years he'd given to his calling and this whole day spent patching up mangled bodies, when Morgan looked down to see that blood had begun to seep ominously anew from Jacob's gaping wound, he was aware of a sick feeling in the pit of his stomach. There was an inexplicable anxiety stirring inside him, and it came full to the fore as he stole a glance at the young man's still profile.

At once, he was overwhelmed by a flood of memories: of Jacob penciling drawings on Gran's best tablecloth, and sheltering a wounded bird in his jacket, and watching Lexi through the windows of the inn while she danced. In his head, Morgan heard the young man's laughter and the friendly stammer of his voice. He saw his broad smile — and all at once, his hand was paralyzed, his knuckles whitening as he clutched the scalpel.

The weight of responsibility fell full upon him. Perspiration beaded across his brow as other, more painful memories seized him. Dear God, not now! He thought he'd put it all behind him, but in an instant, the years melted away and Morgan found himself standing in another surgery, the smell of death thick around him, with another person who'd been important to him lying pale and bloodied on the table. This was what he'd feared all along; this was why he'd given up. He strove to stem the tide, but he was too exhausted to fight.

"Morgan?" Lexi cried out, when she noticed that something was amiss. "What's happened? What's wrong?"

The cold chill of fear swept through her as she saw that her words had no effect on him. He only stood there, staring with eyes that did not seem to see. His body stiffened, the scalpel in his hand still poised in midair.

319

"Do something," she entreated, panic rising in her. "Please, Morgan."

But Morgan's face had drained of color, and his breathing was shallow and uneven. And all the while he hesitated, more blood was oozing from Jacob's wound. Frantically, Lexi daubed at it with the sponge, then pressed down to stem the flow.

"I can't," he told her, the voice pained and breathless. "I can't. He'll die . . ."

Lexi had been afraid of this. All day she'd wondered how long Morgan could go on performing like a heartless machine before his mind and body rebelled. But he could not break now, not now. There was no one else to help Jacob. She found herself torn between the dangers facing her relative and her concern for the man that she loved.

"He'll die if you don't do something," she persisted. Rushing around the table, she reached up to grasp his face between her hands, forcing him to meet her eyes, which were brimming over now with hot tears. "I'll help. I'll stay by your side and do whatever I can, but you are the only one here with skills enough to save him. You can do it. You *have to* do it. Please, Morgan."

Lexi had begun to despair of ever getting through to him when, all at once, he reached out his free hand, and with his thumb, he smudged a tear that had rolled down her cheek. With that, the spell was broken. Morgan drew a deep, resonant breath, set his jaw firmly, and turned back to the table. The scalpel wavered for only a moment before he swiftly made the incision and went to work.

Just as she'd promised, Lexi stood close by his side, watching as he probed for the ball beneath the torn skin. She might have appeared calm, but within she was quaking. It hurt to breathe, as if she'd laced her stays too tight, and then she remembered that she wasn't wearing any today. Wave after wave of lightheadedness assaulted her; still, she managed to endure until finally Morgan had located and drawn the ball from the wound, stitched it closed, and then covered the whole with a fresh bandage.

"Will he be all right?" she asked in a voice that was soft and hesitant.

"We shall have to watch carefully for infection," Morgan replied, wholly in charge now, "and he'll need to rest. But he's young and strong. He has that in his favor at least."

For now, though, there was nothing more to do but wait.

Only after Jacob had been removed to a cot in the parlor so that the next patient might be brought in did Lexi leave her post and go out back to dispose of the basin of bloodied water. Morgan looked after her longingly and realized, with more than a hint of regret, that he would have to face the next patient all on his own.

After what had just happened to him, he was still badly shaken. He was ashamed, too, that Lexi had been witness to his weakness, but he consoled himself with the knowledge that the worst had passed. In the end, he'd faced the fear; he'd done what needed doing. And then a voice inside of him uttered the simple truth that he'd been fighting against for so long. He could face anything—if only Lexi was at his side.

It was a dangerous admission to make. To need someone that much was to put yourself at their mercy. With all they'd been through, hadn't he learned that much already? But he had learned, too, that Lexi was like one of those wild creatures of whom Jacob was so fond. The moment she felt herself ensnared, she'd thrash her wings and fight to be free. Perhaps the only way to capture her was with a cage of her own making.

For what seemed like the hundredth time that day, Lexi tossed a basin of dirty water into the bushes and turned back to the house. A voice that she recognized at once drifted out of the darkness, stopping her in her tracks. "Is he goin' to be all right?"

Lexi turned back, glaring. "We don't know that yet, and if he is, it'll be no thanks to you," she spat.

Brendan took a step toward her, but stopped when he saw the unfriendly glint in her eye. "You needn't worry about the fightin'," he told her. "It's over. The British regulars will be here by mornin', and we've not the men to stand against them. We've been ordered to fall back."

Although she was glad to hear it, Lexi did not give him the satisfaction of a reply.

"I swear to you by all that's holy," Brendan persisted. "I never meant to hurt you, not any of you."

Lexi's jaw dropped in disbelief. She tossed away the empty basin, ignoring the sound as it clattered to the ground, and twisted her two hands tightly in the fabric of her apron to keep from striking out at him. She did not want to lose control, not just yet. She wanted somehow to make him face up to what he'd done.

"You . . . let me think . . . that you'd come here to help me," she began haltingly. "You abused Gran's hospitality and traded on our friendship. You made me take a stand against the man I love. You nearly caused Jacob to be killed, and yet you can stand there and say that you never meant to hurt us?"

Lexi could feel the warmth of color rising in her face. Her body began to shake with violent tremors and she crossed her arms tightly over her breast to quell them. "Damn you, Brendan O'Neill. Damn you to hell!"

He turned his hands up to her, a pleading look in those wide, amber eyes. "Ah, but you don't understand, Lexi. How could ye? The Irish people have been for too many years crushed into the dirt, with England's boot in our back."

An odd fire had begun to gleam in his eyes now, and Lexi watched as a change came over him. "Each time we try and pick ourselves up, they knock us down again. They've stolen our land, taken the food from the mouths of our babes, denied us our religion, our freedom . . ."

She stared at him, bewildered. It struck her that she hardly knew this man spouting political dogma with such vehemence. Morgan had been right. He was not the same boy she used to know. These Fenians had changed him.

"You've lived most all of your life in the United States," she reminded him. "Your family has thrived and prospered there. You've been a free man—with no one's boot in your back. What gives you the right to come here, to this country, and turn everything upside down?"

"We mean no harm to these people," he insisted, fairly brimming with self-righteousness. " 'Tis the English must be made to pay, and we'll strike at them wherever we can, until they set Ireland free."

Lexi kept a firm rein on her temper. "Jacob was born here. Is he English?" she shot back. "Is Gran? Am I? Those soldiers you faced on the ridge today weren't Englishmen, no matter what you might like to think. They were members of the Canadian militia. The wounded men inside this farmhouse, and those who died—Canadians, all of them. What lesson did you hope to teach the English by murdering Canadians who were only protecting their homeland?"

But regardless of her calm and rational reasoning, Brendan did not seem at all repentant. "They ought to have joined with us then and turned their arms

324

against the British tyrants. I regret that men had to die here today, Lexi, but I'd do it all again, if I thought we had a chance to right the wrongs done to the Irish people."

Lexi balled her fists, wanting nothing more than to knock some sense into that thick Irish skull of his. But he'd never change, she saw that now, and her two small fists were incapable of inflicting the same depth of pain he'd caused here today. Weary now, she shook her head. I might forgive you your politics, however misguided," she said. "But you've betrayed our friendship and that's something I can never forgive. I ought to call for the soldiers right now and have you arrested."

Brendan met her eyes without flinching, as if accepting that his fate lay in her hands. But even with all the trouble he'd caused her, when the moment came, Lexi could not do it. She turned away, disgusted by her own weakness.

"Go on, then," she told him. "Go back home to your family, keep your twisted ideals, and forget all the grief that you've caused here today. But I won't forget. I can't forget. I never want to see you again."

Without waiting for a reply, she left him, strode briskly around the house, and lifting her skirts, she climbed the front porch stairs, all without once looking back. And with that final action, she sought to erase Brendan O'Neill from her life. The cheerful young man who'd once been her friend was dead, she realized finally, a victim of the bloody

War Between the States, just as surely as if he'd been stricken on the battlefield.

Once inside the house, she peeked into the parlor to check on Jacob, and when she'd assured herself that he was resting quietly, she strode back into the kitchen to take up her place at Morgan's side. She knew now that this was where she belonged.

Morgan accepted her presence and her help without comment. They worked, side by side, late into the night, but all the while, Lexi was aware of the distance he'd put between them. She could hardly blame him if he'd decided that he could not forgive her for all that she'd done. Even if she could not be held to account for anything more, it was wholly her fault that poor Jacob was lying in the next room, fighting for his life.

If only she had taken Morgan at his word, trusted him instead of Brendan. But it was too late now for regrets. There was no going back. Today, Lexi had seen firsthand how Morgan had had to adapt himself to deal with the horrors of the battlefield and how deeply he'd been hurt by it all. And with the tragedies that this day had wrought, Lexi feared that if she should put it to the test, she'd find that the wall Morgan had built around himself would be impenetrable, even to her.

Chapter Twenty-three

Lexi woke, with startled surprise, to find herself lying curled upon a cot in the parlor of the farmhouse. Sunlight streamed in between the curtains, and nearby she could hear the reassuring cadence of Jacob's even breathing. As she raised herself up, she recalled how last night, when she'd finally grown unsteady on her feet, Morgan had chased her off, exhorting her to rest for a while.

She hadn't intended to sleep through the night, though. She stood up, and a coat that had been spread over her like a blanket slipped to the floor. It was Morgan's dark blue frock coat, she noticed as soon as she bent to pick it up. She folded it neatly over her arm. He must have covered her last night when he came to check on Jacob. That simple gesture gave her hope; maybe he'd not closed his heart to her. Maybe there was a chance for them yet.

As she soon discovered when she'd searched all the rooms, though, Morgan was not in the house. Outside on the front porch, Hawkeye kept a silent vigil, his head resting on his paws. His ears pricked up and he lifted his snout as Lexi came out and stooped to pat him reassuringly, then he settled back down to his waiting.

The yard was filled with men in crimson uniforms—the British regulars come down from Hamilton—but there was no sign of Morgan.

"Excuse me, Captain," Lexi said, smoothing back her sleep-tousled hair as she stepped down from the porch to address the officer who seemed to be in charge. "Can you tell me where I might find Doctor Glendower this morning?"

"You're his nurse, aren't you, miss?"

"I . . . well, yes, I suppose you could say—"

"I'm afraid he's gone," the officer replied then. "If there's a question about a patient, you'll have to speak to Doctor Barlowe. He's taken over things here."

"Gone?" Lexi repeated, barely hearing what he'd said afterward. "But where did he go?"

"Up to Hamilton, I expect," he said. "When Doctor Barlowe—he's our company surgeon—arrived early this morning, he brought news about the health of one of Doctor Glendower's relatives."

"It's his godfather," Lexi heard herself reply. "He's been ill."

"I'm sorry to tell you that the news is not good. As I understand it, the gentleman is not expected to live out the week."

"I see," she said dully, and found herself clutching at Morgan's jacket, which still hung over her arm, as if it were a lifeline that bound them together.

328

Of course Morgan would go to his dying godfather—she would expect nothing less of him—but a part of her could not help but think that this provided him with the perfect opportunity to draw back, to hide himself away from the world once more.

Lexi remembered now how frightened she'd been by the odd paralysis that had gripped him last night as he prepared to operate on Jacob and the pitiful desperation that had been written on his face. For Morgan, the events of the past twenty-four hours must have been a terrible reminder of what he'd been through at Scutari.

She worried now that this, coupled with the strain of his godfather's impending death, might be too much for him to endure. Last night, she'd feared he was withdrawing into himself, but it could be worse, far worse, than just that. What if his nerves were unable to bear the stress? What would become of the man she loved then? And what could she possibly do to help him?

"The doctor did leave word, miss," the officer told her, intruding on her thoughts and drawing her sharply back to present concerns, "that we should arrange to transport you and your uncle back home as soon as you're ready."

"Yes. Yes, thank you, Captain. I'd like to leave at once."

To Lexi it seemed much longer, but, in fact, it

was no more than an hour later when the wagon, driven by a young lieutenant who'd been assigned to the task, arrived at Gran's. With Jacob still resting peacefully—aided by the morphine Dr. Barlowe had prescribed—Lexi jumped down from the wagon bed and ran across the yard to her grandmother, who was leaning on her cane as she waited by the gate.

Gran opened her arms and Lexi rushed into them. Her grip was so tight it was painful, but to Lexi it was a comfort nonetheless. She tried to speak. There was so much to explain, but she could only whisper, "I'm sorry," before a sob choked off her words.

"It's all right, lass," Gran soothed. "It'll be all right. Your father's been worried sick about ye. He's sent two telegrams already this mornin' from Hamilton."

"Hamilton?" Lexi echoed.

"Aye, he'd gone up there with his new wife to see about the sale of her house when the trouble started down here."

Gran paused a moment as if to catch her breath, and then began anew. "Doctor Glendower sent word tae us about Jacob. He said how much help ye'd been tae the lad when he needed it, and how you'd helped them all. I want ye tae know I'm proud o' ye, Lexi."

Lexi dropped her gaze. "But, Gran, it's my fault. Don't you see? Jacob went out after Brendan—if I hadn't brought him here in the first place—if I hadn't been so trusting—"

"Och, ye give yerself far too much credit, lass. You canna be held tae blame for what's been done by Irish zealots, nor for Jacob's mistaken intentions either. Now, let's go and see to it that my puir wanderin' lad is tucked safe in his bed."

And so, with Lexi and the lieutenant each managing an end of the stretcher, they carried Jacob into the house and settled him in his room. Hannah Newcomb was waiting in the kitchen. A good neighbor as always, she'd stayed to keep Gran company after Morgan had sent word about Jacob, and it was she who insisted now that Lexi sit down and have something to eat — while she related to them all that she'd witnessed.

Lexi obliged, managing a few bites of breakfast between the telling of the tale, but she was still sorely distracted by the worries weighing on her mind. She did not realize how much so, however, until Gran innocently inquired if Doctor Glendower would be stopping by later to check on Jacob.

Bolting from the table, Lexi shoved open the screen door and swept to the farthest edge of the porch, where she wrapped her arms around the upright post, clinging to it as if she might collapse without the support. Gran followed at a more-patient gait, her cane thumping on the wooden boards, and a moment later, Lexi felt a strong hand on her shoulder.

Gran did not need to ask what was wrong. "You've got to make your peace with him," she said, "one way or the other."

"I've made so many mistakes," Lexi explained, her eyes filling with tears. "And now he's hurting and I don't know what to do. I don't even know if I can make a difference."

"D'ye love him, lass?"

Tears were making warm, wet trails down her cheeks now, blurring her view of the orchard just across the road—the trees under whose boughs she'd walked and talked with Morgan, and where he'd kissed her for the first time. The scent of apple blossoms was sweet and strong in the air, and Lexi filled her lungs with it and let the memories rush through her. "Yes," she replied breathlessly, "oh, yes."

With that the old woman sighed. "Well, then, that'll make all the difference in the world."

Lexi had to believe that Gran was right. She'd go to Morgan at once. She'd pledge her heart, offer him the comfort of her arms, and somehow . . . somehow she'd make a difference.

It was early evening, certainly not the proper time for visiting, when the cab let Lexi off in front of Arthur Sinclair's home in Hamilton. But she had no choice, for she was determined to see Morgan, to make certain that he did not shut himself off from the world again.

She'd been traveling for all of the afternoon. Her pretty cherry-colored silk dress was wrinkled, and the feathers on her bonnet were sadly wilted, but she drew herself up, brushed off the worst of the dust, grasped the iron knocker, and rapped sharply.

A sturdy white-haired woman soon appeared. Reaching into her drawstring purse, Lexi drew out her card and handed it to her. "I'm sorry to call upon you unannounced," she began, "especially with Doctor Sinclair so ill, but I'm a friend of Doctor Glendower's. I've come all the way from Stevensville, and I really must speak with him."

The woman perused the card in her hand and then her faded brows arched high. "Miss Merritt? Well, why didn't you say so. You're the young lady who's to marry our young doctor, aren't you? He told us all about you the last time he was up. Come in, dearie, you must be tired after your journey."

Lexi found herself ushered into the front parlor, where she was soon settled on the sofa with a cup of tea in her hand and a tray of cakes on the table before her.

"I'm Mrs. Edmunds," the housekeeper explained. "Doctor Glendower has gone out, but he'll likely be returning soon. You just make yourself comfortable until then and ring if you need anything."

With that, another bell — presumably from the sickroom — began jangling and Mrs. Edmunds hurried out. When she found herself alone, Lexi felt more than a little guilty. Perhaps she ought to have explained that Morgan was not expecting her, and that a marriage between them was no longer in the offing, but Mrs. Edmunds moved with all the force of a whirlwind, and Lexi had found herself with almost no chance to speak. And she'd scarcely considered how she might phrase her explanation before the whirlwind swept back into the room again.

"If you please, miss. Doctor Sinclair has asked me to bring you to him."

Lexi got to her feet hesitantly. "But do you think that's wise, Mrs. Edmunds? He's ill, he's—"

"Dying? Aye, he may be that. But if you knew him, you'd know that as long as there's a breath in his body, he'll not be denied, and he says he wants to meet the bride."

"Bride?" Lexi repeated slowly, realizing that the situation was getting out of hand. "Oh, please, you must listen to me."

But Mrs. Edmunds was already conducting her across the room and through the hall and up the stairs. "Come along, miss. You needn't worry about upsetting him. It'll make the old man happy to meet you at last. He's been worrying over his godson for more years than I can count, and I've never seen him looking quite so pleased as the day young Doctor Glendower told him of your plans to wed."

That would have been on Morgan's last visit here, Lexi told herself, before she'd found out about Celeste, before she'd gone home to Buffalo. So much had happened in just a few short months. But how could she tell that to a dying man?

She wished that Morgan would arrive in time to spare her this interview, but it was not to be, and she soon found herself standing shyly in the doorway of a richly decorated, masculine bedchamber,

334

its walls covered in heavy, dark paneling, damask hangings in a regal blue draped across the windows. Mrs. Edmunds shut the door firmly behind her as she went out.

A voice, surprisingly strong, called out from the bed. "Do come in, Miss Merritt, and let me have a look at the woman who managed to succeed where I could not."

"How is that, sir?" Lexi inquired, curious at his remark.

Advancing further into the shadowy room, she found herself being studied intently by a pair of sharp brown eyes. Arthur Sinclair was propped up in his bed by several well-stuffed pillows. A circle of light from the lamp on the table nearby illuminated his features. He must have been a robust man once, but his form was clearly wasted and his skin was tinged with sickly pallor. His smile, however, was bright, and those eyes of his were still brimming with life.

"Sit down beside me, Miss Merritt, if you please."

He pointed to a tapestry-covered chair that stood near the bed, and when Lexi obliged him, he began to speak.

"For the past two years I've tried everything in my power to convince Morgan he ought to start practicing medicine again," he explained, "instead of hiding out from the world in his cabin in the woods. I wanted him to take up practice here with me, but he wouldn't listen. And then you come along. Of course, you're a pretty little thing, it's no wonder he'd listen to you."

A smile tugged at the corners of Lexi's mouth. She could not help herself. It was apparent that he meant to put her at ease. "I prefer to think it's that I convinced him of how much he was needed."

"Yes. Yes, I'm sure that's what it was," he replied, sounding serious, although there was a mischievous glint in his eye that said otherwise. Lexi decided that she liked this man.

"I understand that you've a flair for Latin, Miss Merritt," he continued. "I've a rather extensive library. Perhaps later I might impose upon you to read to me? You will be staying for dinner, of course."

Was everyone in this household of the whirlwind sort? she wondered, as she stammered out a reply. "Well, I—I don't know, that is, I—"

"I'm sorry that I won't be able to join you, but I'm sure Morgan will keep you sufficiently entertained, and then afterward, you can come up and read to me."

Mrs. Edmunds had warned her that gravely ill or not, Arthur Sinclair was a man who would not be denied, and Lexi saw for herself that she'd been right. "If you like," she agreed, as if she had a choice in the matter.

There was a long moment of silence, and Lexi suspected he was marshaling his strength before he spoke again. When he did, the voice sounded different, solemn and thoughtful. "I'd like to thank you, Miss Merritt, for what you've done for my godson."

She did not mean for the breath to catch in her throat, but once it had, it was too late to pretend that there was nothing wrong. Sinclair was a sharp hand; she'd known that from the first. He would not fail to notice.

"What is it, my dear?"

Lexi ought to have used this opportunity to clear up the misunderstandings about her and Morgan. But when she looked into the old man's eyes, she saw someone who cared for Morgan as much as she did, and before she knew it, she was confiding in him. "I'm afraid I've not been so successful as you think. I'm worried about him, sir."

"It's on account of that Fenian raid down at Ridgeway," he guessed, nodding to himself as he saw by her expression that he was right. "I saw the change in him myself when he arrived this morning. He was helping with the wounded there, no doubt. We haven't had much reliable word yet . . . but you were there, weren't you? How bad was it?"

Lexi could no longer meet his eyes. She focused instead on her own hands, which were clasped tightly in her lap. "It wasn't much as battles go, or so I understand. Still, there were more wounded men than I care to see again. Morgan did a fine job; you'd have been proud of him. But—"

"But afterward, he seemed strange—cold and withdrawn," he finished for her.

Morgan had always seemed such a solitary sort

337

that somehow Lexi had not expected Dr. Sinclair would understand him so well. "How could you know that?" she asked him.

He closed his eyes, settling back into the pillows as if all at once the strength had drained out of him. "It's happened before."

Much as she wanted to question him further, Lexi saw that he was fading. It was surprising he'd gone on for as long as he had. She got to her feet. "I should leave you now. You're tired —"

At this, the old man pulled himself upright, startling her, and even as his chest heaved from the exertion, he put out a hand and lightly touched her arm. "I'll be fine, Miss Merritt. I've all eternity for resting. Just now we need to talk. Now, if you'd truly like to help, you may pour me a brandy from the decanter over there. My throat is parched."

Lexi wasn't sure she ought to, but then she asked herself what harm it would do to indulge him. And so she did as he bade her and then took up her place once more beside the bed. Sinclair took a swallow of the liquor and, closing his eyes, savored the taste of it. She had to admit it did seem to fortify him.

"I'm going to tell you something now," he said, beginning anew, "something that I hope will help you understand. I've kept it to myself for all these years, never discussed it, not even with Morgan himself, although I've begun to see that that may have been a mistake. At any rate, I'll soon be gone, and I feel that this is something you'll need to know about him if the two of you are ever to find happiness."

He sounded so serious, how could she refuse to hear him out?

"You may have heard that Morgan's father and I were friends. On the whole, Thomas Glendower was a good man: honest, well-disciplined, an ideal leader, and the perfect soldier, even if not always the perfect father. Morgan was cut from wholly different cloth—thoughtful, compassionate, more dreamer than soldier. I suppose you can see why there'd be trouble between them, and it came to a head when Morgan decided to study medicine rather than follow his father into the army."

Lexi had been keeping a close eye on him and feared that his breathing seemed more labored now, and the fingers that clutched the brandy glass were whitening. Why was he so insistent upon relating family history to her, even as the life was draining from him? "Much as I appreciate your telling me this, sir," she said, "I think perhaps the story should wait until after you've rested."

But Sinclair ignored her plea. He downed another generous swallow of brandy and pressed on:

"You know that Morgan went to the Crimea. It was to please his father more than anything. He became an army surgeon, trying as best he could to fit into his father's world. But Scutari was a hellish place. Supplies were scarce, and the doctors were forced to work and to house their patients under deplorably filthy conditions. They lost five times more men to disease than from battle wounds.

And after Balaclava, through a horrible twist of fate, Morgan found himself in the surgery with his own father lying wounded on the table before him."

"My God," Lexi whispered. She saw now why the old man had been so insistent, and she understood with an awful clarity all that she'd witnessed last night in the farmhouse. Exhausted, mentally and physically, Morgan had been reliving his nightmare, and as he'd looked down at Jacob on the surgery table, it was his father he'd seen instead.

"My godson is a gifted surgeon," Dr. Sinclair continued, "you may take my word on that. But there was nothing he could have done to save Thomas; the wounds were too severe. He carried the blame nonetheless, and it nearly destroyed him."

"And how did you find out about this?" she wanted to know.

"A fellow surgeon apprised me of what had happened, and I wrote to Morgan at once and suggested that he come out here. The change helped him some, I think, but I'd despaired of ever seeing him wholly recovered—until the night he came into this room and told me that the two of you were to wed.

"I say again, Miss Merritt, you have my gratitude, for you've accomplished what I could not."

Still stunned, Lexi shook her head. "I've loved him, believed in him, but nothing more than that, and now I don't know what to do."

"Perhaps you've already done enough," Dr. Sinclair replied, ending on a hopeful note.

Lexi gave a start at the sound of a door being thrown open somewhere below. "That'll be Morgan returning," he advised her. "He'll come up directly."

But Lexi was not ready to see Morgan just yet. After she'd had time to sort through all that Dr. Sinclair had told her, after she'd had time to think on what she'd say, then she'd be ready to face him.

"If you don't mind," she said, quickly getting to her feet, "I think I'd like to freshen up. I fear that I'm dusty and windswept from traveling. That will give you two some time alone together."

"Of course. Go down the back stairs into the kitchen and have Mrs. Edmunds show you to the guest room," he said in a conspirator's tone. "I won't tell Morgan you've arrived. It'll be our little secret. Then later when you're feeling up to it, you can surprise him."

"Thank you, sir," Lexi said, and bent to kiss his cheek before she headed for the door, "for everything."

Chapter Twenty-four

Morgan's blood was racing as he hastened up the stairs and across the hall to his godfather's room. He hadn't meant to stay away so long, and he hoped that Sinclair's condition hadn't worsened since this morning. There was so much more he wanted to say to him yet. But then wasn't that always the way?

When he entered the room, though, he was surprised and perhaps just a bit piqued to find the supposedly dying man, about whom he'd been so concerned, sitting up in his bed, his face ruddy with color, a glass of brandy in his hand.

"You do plan on enjoying yourself to the very last, don't you?" he accused good-naturedly as he took up the stethoscope from the bureau and came to stand beside the bed.

"And just where have you been all afternoon?" the old man retorted. "And wearing your finest suit of clothes?"

Morgan took away Sinclair's brandy glass and sternly and silently finished his examination before replying. "If you must know, I had an important business appointment."

"I trust all went well."

Morgan met the comment with a smile, for he was quite pleased with himself in that regard. "Yes, indeed it did, sir."

From the first, he'd suspected that his godfather was hiding something, and now as he regarded him more closely, and noticed the devilish glimmer in those dark eyes of his, he was sure of it. "And what have you been up to while I've been gone to get your poor, weak heart to racing like this?"

"If you must know, I've been entertaining a most charming young lady."

Morgan rolled his eyes. "I know you've always professed to be the most devout of hedonists, sir, but I don't believe Mrs. Edmunds would allow that sort of thing to go on under her roof."

"It's my roof, I'll remind you, and I'll wager if you closed your eyes, you could still smell her perfume. . . ."

As a matter of fact, Morgan did catch a whiff of perfume: the sweet scent of violets. But that was Lexi's scent, he realized, conjured out of his mind. And his godfather was only playing games with him.

"Have I told you that it's good to have you home, my boy?"

"No," Morgan retorted, "and don't try and smooth things over. I'm still vexed with you, you know. You ought to have sent for me after that last attack. If old Barlowe hadn't told me how bad off you were, I'd not have known to come at all."

Sinclair frowned at the censure. I didn't want you to remember me this way," he said. "But now that you've come, I'm glad you're here. I've had a lot of time for thinking lately, and it's crossed my mind we haven't talked about your father—"

The muscles in Morgan's jaw went taut. It was the last subject he wished to discuss. In his mind, Arthur Sinclair had been more of a father to him than Thomas Glendower ever had.

"You need to rest," he snapped. "All this talking will do you no good—"

But Sinclair was not about to be outmaneuvered. "You will hear me out this time. Your father and I were good friends. I knew the man was stubborn, how much he wanted the army for you, but I never imagined he would let you go for all those years without telling you . . ."

"Sir?"

The old man waved his hand at something across the room. "Bring me that box—the cigar box, over there on the bureau."

"You're not thinking of smoking now, are you?"

"Just bring it here."

Morgan fetched the box and handed it over. Lifting the lid, Sinclair slowly drew out one of the packets of folded pages and waved them at him. "These are all the letters I received from your father over the years, while he was off fighting his glorious campaigns. Mrs. Edmunds saved them for me

344

You know what a sentimental old fool she is.

"I want you to take them with you and read them," he continued, "so that you'll see how things were. You must know, my boy, that even if he never said the words, he loved you—and he was proud of you, as proud as any father could be. Maybe then you'll stop blaming yourself for his death. It's all there, in the letters. Read them and you'll see."

Lexi did feel better after she'd splashed her face with cool water and combed and repinned her hair. But she was sure she must have worn a hole in the patterned carpet that covered the guest-room floor as she paced back and forth from the window to the door and considered what to say to Morgan, how to break down the wall he'd rebuilt around himself. She still had not come up with the words, but there was no use in putting it off any longer.

She found him in the study, sitting in a chair by the windows, his dark form silhouetted against a gleaming orange sunset, his head bent at a thoughtful angle as he read through what appeared to be a packet of letters he held clutched in his hand.

Lexi stood there watching him for a long while, touched by the emotion she saw mirrored in his face. There were strong memories attached to those words he read, of that much she was certain. She noticed a fleeting smile before the melancholy overtook him and the pages began to tremble in his hand.

Seeing him this way, with cracks in the facade, reminded her of why she'd come, of why she'd fallen in love with him in the first place, and it gave her the strength to face him.

"Morgan?"

As he got to his feet, the letters slipped from his fingers, drifting down upon the carpet like a flurry of autumn leaves. Lexi had been all but convinced, in that first instant when their eyes met, that he was pleased to see her, but her hopes vanished as his features quickly settled into an unreadable mask.

"Ah," he began slowly, cautiously, "so you're the young lady my godfather's been entertaining."

"Yes. We've had a long talk."

"Discussing my deep, dark secrets, no doubt."

"I won't deny that he's worried about you," she said, "especially now. You can't blame him for wanting to see that you're happy."

"And what brings you here?"

The words took her by surprise, even though she had been preparing for this moment all day long. She pulled a long breath to sustain herself and then began. "I'm here to ask you to come back. Jacob will need you, now more than ever. Gran still isn't well herself yet, and she's awfully worried about him, even if she won't admit it. And you know that Mrs. Peterson's rheumatism is sure to flare up when the summer rains start, and Mr. Miller's wife is expecting a baby—"

"And what about you, Lexi Merritt?"

He'd advanced on her now; there was no more than an arm's length between them, and his eyes were searching her face. Lexi felt the heat as color flooded her cheeks, and she avoided his gaze, training her eyes on the carpet.

"I don't blame you for being angry with me, Morgan. I've been the worst kind of fool. I ought to have seen what Brendan's intentions were. If only I'd realized, we might have seen what these Fenians were up to . . . before anyone had to die—"

"You can't take on all the responsibility for yourself," he said. "No one could have predicted what happened. But some good will come of it, I think. I've spoken with friends in town who say that what's happened will only strengthen the argument for confederation. Maybe the people will see now that we need one Canada, united and strong."

Lexi hoped it was true. It would mean that the men who'd died had not given their lives for nothing. But she hadn't forgotten the reason she'd come here. There was still Morgan to worry about. "Now that I've met Doctor Sinclair and Mrs. Edmunds and seen this house," she said, beginning anew, "I can see why you might be tempted to stay here. But you can't, don't you see that? You would only be running away again."

She tilted her chin upward warily to gauge his reaction and saw him arch one brow and then cross his arms over his chest. "You think you know me so well, do you? You and my godfather have put your two heads together and decided that poor, battle-scarred Morgan has all but lost his reason, that he needs to be protected, but it's not true."

With lightning swiftness, his arm flashed out, caught her waist, and he drew her to him. "Do you feel these arms around you, Lexi? They're strong enough to build a life for us, whatever comes."

She caught her breath as he gathered up her hand and pressed it against his chest. "And this heart beating beneath your fingers? It's not one easily broken; you've put it to the test yourself.

"God knows I bear the blame for nearly letting Jacob down, but it isn't fair to use last night to judge my mental state. I was exhausted. Under any sort of normal circumstances, I wouldn't have been pushed to such a limit."

"I know," she told him, resting her head against his broad chest. "I'm sorry that I couldn't understand."

"For so many years I argued with my father that the life I'd chosen was better than what he wanted for me because I had the power to save lives, but then when it was him lying there on the surgery table, depending upon me, I could do nothing, *nothing,* to save him."

"But you've done so much," she argued, "helped so many others. You've proven yourself a thousand times over. Surely your father would have realized that."

"He did," he replied thoughtfully. "I know that now."

Catching his face in her hands, the stubble of his beard rough against her palms, Lexi drew him down to her and gently pressed her lips on his. Morgan responded by pulling her nearer, and he returned her kiss with one that was far more potent, one that heated the blood in her veins and left her trembling.

"Please come home, Morgan," she whispered against his ear.

He drew back just far enough for her to see the question in his eyes. "And what shall I come home to?" he asked. "An empty cabin and endless suppers of beans and dried-up biscuits? Lonely days and nights spent longing for a woman who cannot decide if loving me is worth the risk?"

Lexi stiffened at the accusation. "That's not true," she protested. "I do love you. I've never stopped loving you."

"Then marry me, Lexi. Right away. There's nothing to prevent it. Your father's given his permission."

Her eyes went wide. "You've already spoken to my father?"

"Mrs. Edmunds told me that he and Celeste were in town; she'd come by to visit before I arrived. So I went off to ask him while I had the chance. Where'd you think I'd been all afternoon?"

"Then, you'd planned all along to come back for me?"

"You didn't think I'd let you escape me a second time?" he replied with a devilish grin. "And now— after I've gone through all this trouble, Lexi Merritt—you are going to marry me, aren't you?"

A smile curved on her lips as she saw, in the depths of those blue eyes of his, the love that she'd been missing for so long. And she wondered if it was right for one human being to be so happy.

"Yes," she said. "That is, if *you're* willing to take the risk."

But total happiness was a fleeting thing. All at once, a thought occurred to her, and Lexi pulled back, wearing a concerned frown. "We haven't discussed yet where we shall live, Morgan. I know that Doctor Sinclair would like you to take over for him here. . . ."

"There'll be no discussion on the matter," he replied so firmly that it startled her, and then one corner of his mouth crooked upward, ever so slightly. "We're going back to the cabin. We couldn't possibly live in Hamilton. There'd be far too much trouble for you to get into up here. Just think how it would scandalize the neighbors if my fairy wife were to decide one day to hitch up her skirts and go wading in the local pond.

"No, I think I'd rather keep you out in the woods where I can keep an eye on you," he said, bending to steal another kiss, "and where I'll be sure that no one else can."

Author's Note

On the night of May 31, 1866, one thousand of the nearly six thousand Irish-American troops (all members of the Fenian Brotherhood), who had massed at Buffalo, New York, crossed the river to establish a bridgehead on the Niagara Peninsula of Canada.

Their actions, in concert with those of Fenians set to cross the border at points further west, were meant to draw attention—and a good number of British troops—away from the Fenians' main invasion force, which would then cross into Canada from St. Albans, Vermont, with the objective of attacking Quebec and setting up that city as the capital of an Irish Republic-in-exile.

It was a bold scheme and more carefully thought out than might be imagined, but it was doomed to failure from the start. After the Fenians engaged the Canadian militia at the Battle of Ridgeway on the morning of June 2 and successfully drove them back, the Fenian general became aware of several factors that made him decide in the end to abandon his plans and withdraw his troops.

Not only had the Fenians' western forces failed to cross the border, but the American government (which had turned a blind eye upon their actions thus far) had decided to intervene and refused to allow the remainder of the Fenian forces at Buffalo to cross into Canada. Facing the arrival of some five thousand enemy reinforcements (British regulars and additional units of Canadian militia), the Fenians decided wisely to withdraw.

The Battle of Ridgeway was a minor engagement as these things go. The Canadian militia lost ten of its men and suffered thirty-seven wounded. As for the Fenians, eight of their soldiers were killed and sixteen wounded. But in terms of historical importance, it can be said that the battle helped to convince the British North American colonies of the benefits of confederation, for it was less than one year later, in 1867, that the Dominion of Canada was formed.

Catherine Wyatt
P.O. Box 88082
Carol Stream, IL 60188-0082